CHERUB

THE FALL

CHERUB

MISSION 7
THE FALL

ROBERT MUCHAMORE

Simon Pulse

New York   London   Toronto   Sydney   New Delhi

SIMON PULSE
An imprint of Simon & Schuster Children's Publishing Division
1230 Avenue of the Americas, New York, NY 10020
First Simon Pulse paperback edition April 2014
Text copyright © 2007 by Robert Muchamore
Cover design and illustration by Sammy Yuen Jr.
Originally published in Great Britain in 2007 by Hodder Children's Books
All rights reserved, including the right of reproduction
in whole or in part in any form.
SIMON PULSE and colophon are registered trademarks of Simon & Schuster, Inc.
For information about special discounts for bulk purchases, please contact
Simon & Schuster Special Sales at 1-866-506-1949 or business@simonandschuster.com.
The Simon & Schuster Speakers Bureau can bring authors to your live event.
For more information or to book an event contact the Simon & Schuster Speakers
Bureau at 1-866-248-3049 or visit our website at www.simonspeakers.com.
Interior designed by Mike Rosamilia
The text of this book was set in Apollo MT.
Manufactured in the United States of America
6 8 10 9 7
Library of Congress Control Number 2013944226
ISBN 978-1-4424-9947-8 (pbk)
ISBN 978-1-4424-9945-4 (hc)
ISBN 978-1-4424-9948-5 (eBook)

CHERUB

THE FALL

WHAT IS CHERUB?

CHERUB is a branch of British Intelligence. Its agents are aged between ten and seventeen years. Cherubs are all orphans who have been taken out of care homes and trained to work undercover. They live on CHERUB campus, a secret facility hidden in the English countryside.

WHAT USE ARE KIDS?

Quite a lot. Nobody realizes kids do undercover missions, which means they can get away with all kinds of stuff that adults can't.

WHO ARE THEY?

About three hundred children live on CHERUB campus. JAMES ADAMS is our fifteen-year-old hero. He's a well-respected CHERUB agent with several successful missions under his belt. KERRY CHANG is a Hong Kong–born karate champion and James's girlfriend. His other close friends include BRUCE NORRIS, SHAKEEL DAJANI, and KYLE BLUEMAN.

James's sister, LAUREN ADAMS, is twelve and already regarded as an outstanding CHERUB agent. Her best friends are BETHANY PARKER and GREG "RAT" RATHBONE.

STAFF

With its large grounds, specialist training facilities, and combined role as a boarding school and intelligence operation, CHERUB actually has more staff than pupils. They range from cooks and gardeners to teachers, training instructors, nurses, psychiatrists, and mission specialists. CHERUB is run by its newly appointed chairwoman, Zara Asker.

AND THE T-SHIRTS?

Cherubs are ranked according to the color of the T-shirts they wear on campus. ORANGE is for visitors. RED is for kids who live on CHERUB campus but are too young to qualify as agents (the minimum age is ten). BLUE is for kids undergoing CHERUB's tough one-hundred-day basic training regime. A GRAY T-shirt means you're qualified for missions. NAVY—the T-shirt James wears—is a reward for outstanding performance on a single mission. Lauren wears a BLACK T-shirt, the ultimate recognition for outstanding achievement over a number of missions. When you retire, you get the WHITE T-shirt, which is also worn by some staff.

SEPTEMBER 2006

A Ford Focus pulled up amid a line of deserted parking bays as a powerful wave crashed against the adjacent sea wall. The spray turned into an ankle-deep wash that swirled across the wooden promenade, while a line of partially submerged huts fought for survival on the pebble beach below.

The man behind the wheel was fifty years old, with a beer gut and a bloodshot face that gave him a look of permanent sunburn. His name was George Savage.

"Some storm," George said, raising his voice to make himself heard above the rain pelting the metal roof. "Haven't seen one go off like this in donkey's years."

The young woman in the passenger seat wore the same

uniform as her driver: black pants and a white shirt with epaulettes bearing the words *HM Customs & Excise*. She pulled a hefty flashlight out of the glove compartment before reaching between the seats and grabbing a waterproof jacket out of the back.

"Are you coming with?" she asked, though she already knew the answer.

"No point both of us getting drenched, is there, Vet?" George grinned.

Yvette Clark hated her partner. George was old, lazy, smelled like a night in the pub, and took particular delight in never using her proper name. She was Vet, Vetty, Vetto, Vetster, sweetheart, and even occasionally cupcake, but if the word Yvette had ever passed George Savage's lips, she hadn't been there to hear it. She could have happily kneed George in the balls, if it wasn't for the dent it would put in her three-month career as a customs officer.

The wind practically tore the waterproof coat from Yvette's hands as she stepped out of the passenger door into the darkness. By the time it was zipped up, her shirt was soaked through and she had a horrible vision of George leering at the black bra that would show through when she got back in the car.

Yvette felt sorry for herself as she stepped up to the sea wall. She'd joined customs straight from university, expecting to spend her days uncovering serious fraud and hunting down drug dealers. The recruitment brochure hadn't mentioned ten-hour shifts patrolling the coastline with an obnoxious pig for company.

And just as it seemed life could get no worse, the wave hit. Bigger than its predecessors, its tip crashed over the wall and kept on coming. Yvette turned to run, but was outmatched and quickly found herself wading in icy water. She lost her footing on the slippery promenade, and grazed the hand she put out to save herself as the receding tide swelled over her shoulders and all but covered her head.

As Yvette gasped from the cold and staggered back to her feet, George triumphantly blasted the horn. It was 1 a.m., but the promenade was illuminated with strings of bulbs and Yvette got a good view of her colleague roaring with laughter from his cocoon behind the flapping windshield wipers. She wanted to steam over and tell George exactly what she thought of him, but knew that a tantrum would only enrich the story he'd tell everyone back at the office the minute he got the chance.

Close to tears and with salt water burning her eyes, Yvette stumbled back to the wall and slid the powerful flashlight from her pocket. Anticipating another blast of water, she gripped the railing atop the wall before pointing the beam of light out to sea.

Much to Yvette's surprise, she spotted the very thing she'd come looking for.

The narrow strip of water between Britain and France is the busiest waterway in the world. At any given moment there are over a thousand ships in the English Channel, ranging from 100,000-ton supertankers down to one-man sailing boats. With so much traffic, accidents are frequent—and when one of the big boats hits one of the little ones, the little boat always comes off worst.

Three hours before George and Yvette pulled up on

the seafront near Brighton, a 15,000-ton catamaran with two hundred and thirty passengers on board radioed the coast guard after colliding with a small motor launch. The launch appeared to be damaged and a lifeboat and a French naval helicopter were sent on a rescue mission. Despite the fact that the launch was listing badly and taking on water, the captain refused help and tried making a run for it. He clearly had something to hide.

The helicopter tracked the crippled boat for ninety minutes as it headed for the safety of international waters, but eventually had to fly back to base for fuel. Under normal circumstances, a naval patrol would have intercepted the launch by this time, stopping it by force if necessary. But the awful conditions had left other boats in distress and resources were stretched to the limit.

As a last resort, the coast guard was asked to track the stricken launch on radar. But tracking a small boat through a stormy sea is close to impossible and the coast guard put out a radio request asking other ships to report sightings of a crippled white launch.

Just after midnight, the captain of a container ship radioed in to say that she'd passed a vessel matching the description. It appeared dangerously close to sinking and was making a desperate attempt to reach the English coast.

With nobody available to intercept the boat at sea, police, customs, and coast guard units along a ten-mile stretch of coast were told to head for the seafront and search for the stricken motor launch.

George Savage sounded put out as his dripping colleague leaned inside the car. "Bloody hell, are you sure?"

Typical George, Yvette thought. He was clearly annoyed that his peaceful night had been spoiled.

"There's a boat tied up at the end of the jetty. It fits the descriptions and it's listing badly."

"Could just be moored there," George said thoughtfully, as he dragged a finger over his stubble.

"There are lights on inside, George. I think it's the one.... I mean, you'd *have* to be desperate to moor a boat outside of a harbor in this weather."

"We'd better wait here. I'll call for backup."

This pushed Yvette over the edge. "For all we know they've only just tied up," she screamed. "The bad guys could be out there *right now*."

"Smugglers carry guns, sugar plum. We don't know what we're up against."

Sugar plum . . .

"I'm sick of you!" Yvette yelled, as she banged her hand on the top of the car. "I tell you what, George; you sit on that giant arse of yours and wait for backup. I'm going to walk up there and try doing my job."

"Temper, temper." George grinned, as he reached for the radio mic. "I've been at this game a lot longer than you...."

Yvette knew she'd only get madder if she stood around listening to another lecture on the benefits of thirty years' experience. She flicked the flashlight on and set off briskly down the promenade toward the steel jetty.

The rusting structure went fifty meters out to sea and was less than three paces wide, except at the head where it widened out to enable a ship to come alongside. The jetty had been built decades earlier to accommodate pleasure cruisers, but nowadays it only served anglers and a few brave swimmers who used it as a diving platform.

Despite the foul weather and the sheets of water crashing over the jetty, the lampposts that ran its length were working and Yvette had a decent view of the boat. It appeared to have been hurriedly lashed to a single mooring point.

The crew had fled without even turning off the lights, leaving the raging water free to slowly wreck the launch. The windows along one side were shattered and the rear jutted out of the water, as if the bow was flooded. Only the length of rope lashing it to the jetty kept it above the water.

Part of Yvette wanted to encounter the crew and make her first arrest, but her sensible side was relieved to find the baddies long gone.

And then she heard a scream.

Yvette thought she was imagining it, but the noise had coincided with a particularly fierce wave engulfing the head of the jetty. She heard the high-pitched noise again when the water cleared away.

"Hello," she yelled. "Is anybody out there?"

A gust of wind ruined her chance of hearing any response, but her shout had apparently reached an audience. Yvette sighted a skinny figure with her arms wrapped around a lamppost. It looked like a child, no more than twelve years old.

"Holy Father," Yvette said to herself, panicking as she fumbled for her radio. "George, are you out there? There's a young girl at the end of the jetty. She's holding on to the railings for dear life, too scared to move."

"I'm coming down," George shouted. Even he couldn't ignore a stricken child.

But Yvette couldn't imagine her partner being of much help. "What about our backup?" she asked.

"Negative," George said. "At least, don't hold your breath. There's tiles coming off houses, trees down in the road, and the nearest cop car is dealing with a major accident on the A27: articulated lorry turned over by the gale. Serious injuries."

"Roger that," Yvette said. "I'll have to go get the kid myself."

"Keep your head on your shoulders and wait till I get there," George said. "That's a direct order."

But despite thirty years in the service of Her Majesty, George had never been promoted and had no authority over his partner.

Yvette was drenched and knew she ought to be shivering, but the tension made her face burn. She wrung her hands as she watched the raging tide, trying to pick a moment to run on to the jetty. She imagined that it might be like the video games she played with her young nephew, hoping for some magical pattern that would allow her to run along the jetty, grab the child, and escape unscathed.

But there were no breaks. All Yvette could do was set off quickly and grab the handrail when the waves tried to knock her off. Figuring that bare feet were better than her flat-soled shoes, she slipped them off along with her socks and raincoat. She was already soaked and the waterproof fabric would drag as it billowed in the wind.

"Hold on there, sweetheart," Yvette shouted, as the

wind caught the abandoned coat and whipped it into the air. "I'm coming to get you."

She took a deep breath and considered a prayer, but George was coming toward her in the Focus. She didn't want him to stop her, so she settled for a quick kiss of the gold cross around her neck.

When the swirling tide dipped, Yvette vaulted the three steps at the front of the jetty, grasped the metal railing and began to run. The first wave to hit barely broke over the wooden decking, but the fierce wind gave it impressive force and Yvette had to curl her toes into the gap between planks to stop her legs being washed away.

The next wave was huge and swept across the jetty from the opposite direction, pressing her back against the metal railings as the surging water forced its way up her nostrils. She hacked and spat as a break in the wave allowed her to dash another thirty meters, almost making it to the head of the jetty before the next blast.

When the water cleared, the stricken boat was less than five meters away and the child was in clear view. It was a girl, with long blond hair. She wore leather boots, leggings, and a soggy polo neck. Although the girl had been too petrified to let go of the post and make a dash toward the shore, she'd managed to protect herself by wedging her leg into a gap between the post and a garbage bin.

"Are you okay?" Yvette shouted.

The girl shook her head and said something in a language Yvette couldn't understand. The girl's pale skin and cheap but warm clothing suggested that she hailed from Eastern Europe.

Yvette realized that the runaway boat had been smuggling illegal immigrants. The terrified girl must have become separated from her companions as they escaped along the jetty, and they'd either thought she'd been washed out to sea or not cared enough to go back and rescue her.

Yvette's next move was the hardest: The head of the jetty was designed for boats to dock and had no handrail. She'd have to wait for a break in the waves and then dash to the girl, grab her, and run back. If she timed it wrong, she'd be swept away to certain death: either drowned or brutally smashed against the legs of the jetty or the sea wall.

The sea looked black and the erratic gusts made it hard to time the waves. Yvette tried giving the youngster a reassuring smile, but as she crouched down holding on to the last section of railing, her heart banged like it was trying to hack its way through her chest wall.

She dipped her head as a massive wave reared up. The metal structure made a groan like whale song, then shuddered as the launch strained at its mooring post. Its plastic hull thudded into the side of the jetty.

"Here I come," Yvette shouted.

It took less than three seconds to reach the girl and wrap an arm around her waist. The youngster's teeth chattered and her skinny body felt eerily cold. Yvette realized that the girl was in the early stages of hypothermia and would be unable to support her own weight.

As Yvette twisted the girl's leg out of the gap, she saw a colossal wave break over the end of the jetty, almost at head height. The water knocked her onto her back, but she managed to keep one arm around the girl.

Yvette felt pure terror as the water lifted her body off the wooden decking and shoved it toward the edge. She heard the hull of the boat slam again, then something heavy hit the decking directly in front of her.

"Grab hold," George shouted.

Yvette reached out for the object, which she now realized was a tethered life preserver. George had one leg wrapped around the railings and the nylon rope coiled around his chunky wrists. He struggled to hold on as the wave tried to push the two females over the edge.

Yvette and the girl both screamed, coming up for air as the last of the wave drained between the wooden planks. Still clutching the girl, Yvette rolled onto her chest and was horrified to see how close she'd come to going over the side.

She rushed toward George and the relative safety of the railings.

"I told you to wait," George shouted furiously, before they all ducked down, grabbing the railing as a modest wave washed over the deck.

"I didn't want you to stop me," Yvette said, close to tears and coming to the awkward realization that she now owed her life to a man she detested. Maybe she'd never like George, with his sexist jabs and nicotine-stained fingernails, but he'd proved himself to be a better man than she'd realized.

As more water rushed over them, Yvette huddled herself around the girl and felt oddly reassured by the fat hand pressing against her shoulder. The nylon cord had sliced George's wrists and blood streamed along his fingers.

When the last of the water had drained away, Yvette looked through the railings and saw that the sea around the jetty had taken on an eerie calm.

"Lull before the storm," George said hurriedly. "Spot of high pressure, but the big buggers will come back in a minute."

The wind howled against the structure of the jetty as the break in the waves gave them a clear run back to shore.

CHAPTER 1

RUSSIA

Aero City is located in a rural area three hundred kilometers northwest of Moscow. Built in the Soviet era, the town was a major center for aviation research and many of Russia's civil airliners, military transport aircraft, and guided missiles were built within its giant factories.

In 1994 the government announced plans to sell the whole of Russian industry under a scheme known as "mass privatization." The process was riddled with corruption and many of Russia's most valuable assets fell into the hands of a small group of men and women who became known as "the oligarchs."

One such man was Denis Obidin, who used his position as a junior bank official to fraudulently lend large sums of money to his own wife and parents. Obidin then used the cash to buy up shares that the government had given to factory workers who had no idea of their true worth. By 1996, he owned a slice of the Russian aerospace industry that was thought to be worth more than $800 million.

Today, Obidin not only controls all of the factories and most of the land and property in Aero City, but has had himself appointed mayor in a rigged election. When a local police chief announced plans to investigate corruption within Obidin's administration, the officer was found dead in his apartment and Obidin put his brother Vladimir in charge of law enforcement.

Obidin initially laid out grand plans to design and build a modern Russian airliner that could compete with Boeing and Airbus, but his reputation for corruption scared off foreign investors and no airline will purchase aircraft from a company with a shady past and an uncertain future.

After a series of layoffs, the unemployment rate in Aero City exceeds 80 percent. Obidin's one remaining factory produces a small number of missiles for the Russian military and upgrades elderly Russian

airliners by fitting efficient
British jet engines. But with the
Russian military slashing its budgets
and airlines steadily replacing their
fleets with Western aircraft, this
work is drying up.

Obidin has given up hope of
raising the billions needed for his
airliner project and put out word
to international weapons dealers
that everything is for sale. For
the right price, a visitor to Aero
City can purchase anything from a
batch of rocket fuel or blueprints
for a missile guidance system, all
the way up to a truckload of anti-
ship missiles capable of sinking an
American aircraft carrier.

(Excerpt from a classified mission
briefing for James Adams, August
2006)

Denis Obidin's luxury home had featured in glossy magazines both in Russia and across northern Europe. The rambling wooden structure was three stories high, with eight bedrooms, a ballroom where Obidin's wife hosted parties, and an eighty-meter spire at one end. The spire was topped off with a rotating platform and a retractable dome that would occasionally be opened to reveal a large telescope.

Denis claimed to love astronomy, but everyone knew that the tower was really a sniper post. Wealthy Russians were often targeted by kidnappers, and the sniper was a last line of defense against anyone who managed to breach the electrified perimeter, avoid the guard dogs, and make it past the machine-gun-toting guards who patrolled the compound.

The huge double-glazed windows in Denis Obidin's library looked out over an expanse of forest. The leaves were autumnal and the ground was dusted with snow. A romantic might have found it beautiful, but James Adams could only see cold.

It was warm inside the Obidins' house, with its under-floor heating and a gas generator buried beneath the garage, but the rest of Aero City got its electricity from a decrepit nuclear power station five hundred kilometers away and suffered regular outages. After a month living in Aero City, James had concluded that the only thing in the world worse than school was a school where you spent the entire day wearing fingerless gloves and watching your classmates' breath curling up toward the ceiling.

"It's snowing," James said, in Russian, as he looked across a long desk at Denis Obidin's six-year-old son, Mark.

James had been learning Russian intensively for three years and was fluent, though his accent was nowhere near good enough for him to pass as a native. James asked Mark to repeat the phrase in English.

"Zisss nowing," Mark said.

"Not bad," James said cheerfully. "Now let's try English numbers again."

The little boy shook his head and screwed up his face before breaking into a giant yawn. "I'm too tired."

"Come *on*, Mark," James said sternly. "I'm your tutor and if you don't concentrate you're not going to pass your entrance exam."

Mark broke into an evil smile. "I'll tell my daddy it was your fault and he'll punish *you*."

"Oh, you reckon, do you?" James scoffed.

Mark folded his arms. "My uncle Vladimir is the chief of police. He's got his own police station and his own cells. He can do whatever he likes."

"Maybe he'll put you in a cell if you don't pass your exam."

"Nah, he loves me." Mark grinned. "He buys me all the biggest Lego sets. I don't ever want to go to a stupid English boarding school. I like it here."

"At least the classrooms are nice and warm in England," James said, giving a shrug. "And the lights never go out in the middle of the day. Besides, we all have to do things we don't like, kiddo. My aunt and uncle make me come here after school every day and teach English to a horrible *smelly* little boy. And all because they're trying to be nice to your daddy."

Mark got out of his chair, ran around the desk, and tried looking mean as he bunched his fist under James's nose. "I'm not smelly. You're smelly."

"You wouldn't dare."

Mark smiled as he gently nudged his fist against James's nose.

"GRRRRR," James bellowed. "You're dead, you chicken nugget."

The little boy cracked up laughing as James scooped him off the floor and flipped him upside down so that his hair hung down in strands.

"Now I'll use you as a broom," James said, as he lowered Mark's head toward the floor and swung him gently from side to side, before setting the youngster down on the edge of the desk.

"Do that again," Mark squealed, giggling so much that he had spit bubbling out the corner of his mouth.

"I'll do it again, but only if you say *I want to be a broom* in English."

"Never in *stupid* English," Mark said indignantly, as he jumped off the table and crashed face-first onto a beanbag by the window.

Both boys turned toward the door as it clicked open. Vladimir Obidin stood in the doorway. The powerfully built man wore the crisply tailored uniform of a senior police officer.

"James, you're leaving now," he said.

James looked at his watch as Mark sighed with disappointment.

"It's only twenty past," James said.

"There's a meeting here tonight," Vladimir said. He abruptly changed his tone to one of anger. "I don't justify myself to children. When I say go, you go."

Vladimir sent a shiver down James's back. The man had worked for Russian military intelligence and had a reputation for extracting confessions from Aero City's criminals with a set of dentist's tools and a blow lamp. James tried not to feel intimidated as he said good-bye to Mark, grabbed his backpack, and stepped out of the library.

"I've got a long trek home," James said nervously. "Can I use the bathroom?"

Vladimir huffed as though James had just imposed some great burden upon him. "Quickly then."

James stepped into a plush washroom, with a huge spa bath and beech-panelled walls. He slid off his backpack and—all too aware that Vladimir was on the other side of the door—quietly pulled a Nokia communicator out of the side pocket.

As James flipped it open, he noticed that the communicator had picked up some e-mails. Cell phone coverage in Aero City was flaky and his phone tended to receive a whole bunch of messages and missed calls whenever he passed through an area with good reception. But this wasn't a good moment to read them. He switched to a wireless messaging application and tapped in a four-digit number to access a hidden menu.

James had dropped a dozen pinhead-sized listening devices around the Obidins' house over the three weeks in which he'd been tutoring Mark after school. Rows of bright green signal bars on the communicator screen showed that they were all powered up and transmitting perfectly.

"Shift it," Vladimir shouted, pounding his fist on the door. "I'm a busy man."

"Just shaking off," James said, as he shoved the communicator inside his pack and raced for the door. At the last minute he remembered to flush the toilet.

Mark gave James a friendly wave from one of the first-floor windows as Vladimir escorted him down the wood-chip driveway toward the solid steel gate at the front of the Obidin compound.

"All right, Slava," James nodded, as he passed a guard and stepped through a reinforced steel door cut into a half-meter-thick wall.

The bored and half-frozen guard usually exchanged a few sentences with him, but he clammed up under Vladimir's gaze and didn't even acknowledge James's nod.

Once James was out of the compound, he zipped his jacket and pulled up the collar to ward off the cold. For the purposes of this mission, James lived in an apartment block six kilometers away with a fake aunt and uncle. They were posing as weapons dealers who wanted to buy missiles from Denis Obidin. In reality they both worked for MI5.

A bus ran into town from a stop half a kilometer from Obidin's house, but Aero City's transportation was erratic. The wait for a bus in subzero temperatures was unbearable, and on the odd occasion when a bus actually turned up, it was filled with cigarette smoke and mean-tempered pensioners with vile coughs. Running home was the healthier option and it meant James would still be in decent physical shape when he returned to CHERUB campus.

The first part of James's run took him along a gloomy road, with little traffic and trees packed along each side. He loved this section of his daily run home, with the crisp air and the smell of pine needles. The trees ended when he reached factory seven. A kilometer and a half long, the massive hangar had once employed thirty-five thousand workers who turned out a three-hundred-seat airliner every ten days.

It had been graffitied and vandalized in the years after closing, but most young families had left Aero City in search of work and taken the city's delinquent teens with them. The only life James had ever seen around the plant were a few homeless boys who lived rough in an abandoned apartment block. They sniffed glue inside the dilapidated remains of a cargo plane and occasionally kicked a half-inflated soccer ball around inside the hangar.

Once he was sure nobody was about, James stopped running and sat on a concrete step with his back against a fire door that had been taken off its hinges, probably to be burned as firewood. He slid the communicator out of his pocket and checked his messages.

The first was from his girlfriend back at CHERUB campus:

> HAPPY 15TH BIRTHDAY.
> MISS U
> LOVE U
> COME BACK SOON!
> HOPE IT'S NOT 2 COLD.
> KERRY.

James had heaps of other birthday messages from friends on campus and even a message from his handler, Meryl Spencer. The oldest unread message was from his sister, Lauren. It had been sent the evening before:

> HAPPY BDAY 4 2MORO SCUMBAG!
> SORRY THIS IS EARLY. MR LARGE IS
> DRAGGING US OFF ON SOME BLOODY
> HIKING EXPEDITION.
> UR PREZZIE WILL BE WAITING
> WHEN U GET HOME!
> P.S. KEEP UR HANDS OFF THE
> RUSSIAN GIRLS U PERV!

CHAPTER 2

SNEAK

Lauren Adams's life had been ruined when a pair of recently qualified CHERUB agents returned from a mission in the USA. The lads had spent much of their time tucking down hamburgers, ice cream, and bucket-sized containers of soft drinks, and none of it following the strict exercise regime designed to keep them in shape. Every cherub has to undergo a medical and fitness test after a long mission and both boys failed spectacularly.

CHERUB's handlers and training instructors put their heads together and decided that all of the younger agents needed a sharp reminder about the importance of keeping fit. The reminder would take the form of a three-day hike across the Yorkshire Dales, led by the notorious Norman

Large. All CHERUB instructors are tough, but Large was the worst because he got a huge kick out of making kids suffer.

Twenty-six CHERUB agents, all aged twelve or under, were dumped off the back of a truck just after sun-up, and Large gleefully announced that they each had to carry a ten-kilogram metal weight, on top of the tents, utensils, drinking water, and clothing already crammed inside their packs. Hot drinks and porridge were to be served ninety minutes later at a meeting point fifteen kilometers away, and those who didn't make it would go hungry until the evening.

Lauren made it in time for breakfast, but that had been the high point of her day. It was dark now, and she lay inside a two-person tent with swollen ankles and red welts where her pack had chafed her shoulders. She watched the sleeping bag of her best friend, Bethany Parker, swelling and dipping as she breathed.

"Bethany?" Lauren whispered, as she reached across and gave her companion a gentle nudge.

Bethany didn't stir, so Lauren decided that it was safe to wriggle out of her sleeping bag. She'd kept her jeans on, so she only had to slip her unlaced boots over her socks before she crawled up to the zipper holding the tent flaps together and opened it slowly to keep down the noise.

The full moon gave Lauren enough light to see by as she crept between two rows of tents and into a cluster of trees at the edge of the field.

"Rat," Lauren whispered. "Are you out there?"

The heavily built twelve-year-old called softly back in his Australian accent. "Over here."

Lauren smiled as she sighted Rat, sitting with his back against a tree trunk. "How's it going?"

"Been better," Rat said, as he ran a grubby hand through his tangled hair. "Twisted my ankle when we crossed that lake and my back is *killing* me. You?"

"About the same," Lauren said, giving a resigned shrug as she sat in the grass and snuggled up beside Rat.

"How come you're so late?"

"Bethany. I thought she was *never* gonna fall asleep."

The pair turned to face each other and exchanged a quick kiss.

"Is that all I get?" Rat asked indignantly.

"You smell like BO and you've got dried-up baked-bean sauce around your mouth."

Rat tutted. "Well, Large had us walking and running for like, twelve hours. You're no potpourri yourself."

Lauren gave some thought to this before leaning in again and giving Rat a much longer kiss.

"You know," Rat said when they broke off, "I've been thinking."

"Riiiiight." Lauren grinned. "That explains the clanking noise I could hear when you and Andy were walking in front of me earlier."

"Seriously," Rat said, a touch irritated. "We've been sneaking around behind everyone's backs ever since I finished basic training. I reckon it's time we went public."

Lauren scowled at the grass between her legs and let out a deep groan. "If I'd known you were gonna start on that again I would have stayed in my tent."

"I want a *normal* girlfriend. This is driving me nuts."

Lauren grabbed hold of a branch and hauled herself off the ground. "Good night, Rathbone."

"Don't be like that," Rat said, as he reached out and grabbed Lauren's pant leg.

"Let off or I'll boot you one."

"You're doing my head in, Lauren."

"I like it the way it is. I don't want the pressure of everyone talking about us, and making snide remarks and asking what's going on all the time."

"You're so full of crap," Rat snorted. "You're just scared that James will take the mickey. It's totally immature."

"Hey," Lauren snarled, raising her voice above a whisper for the first time. "I'm not immature. Now let go of my *bloody* pants."

"You'll have to tell James that you've got a boyfriend sooner or later," Rat said, as he defiantly tightened his grip and tugged Lauren toward him. "I mean, he'll get upset if you don't invite him to your wedding, and he's bound to suspect something when you start knocking out kids. . . ."

"What makes you think I'll ever be getting married?"

"I spent all day looking forward to meeting up with you," Rat said, as he gave up the struggle and let Lauren go. "But you know what? I'm sick of this. It's pathetic."

Rat letting go coincided with an almighty tug from Lauren and the sudden lack of resistance caught her by surprise. She took an awkward stumble, tripped over a tree root, and ended up clattering into the low-slung branches of a neighboring tree.

"Moron," Lauren growled.

"This was *totally* worth losing an hour's sleep over," Rat said caustically.

As he stood up, he grabbed a golden object from the pocket of his fleece and threw it at Lauren.

"What's that?" Lauren asked, as she picked it off the ground between her boots.

"Mint Twix bar, limited edition. The one you're totally addicted to."

Mr. Large had given the cherubs strict instructions not to bring extra food or items that weren't on the equipment list.

"Large would have made you exercise till you puked if he'd caught you with this," Lauren said. She tried to keep up her grouchy tone, but couldn't help letting a rush of warm emotion into her voice.

"I know," Rat said, trying to make out that he couldn't care less.

Lauren was totally flattered that Rat had taken a huge risk, just so that he could give her a gift. Rat cared about her and why the hell *was* she ashamed of that?

She stepped back toward Rat and gave him a big hug followed by a theatrical smooch on the cheek.

"Sometimes . . ." Lauren smirked, but was unable to finish her thought. "Sod it, we'll tell everyone. We can go to the cinema together and hang out in each other's rooms and . . ."

Lauren's excitement was contagious and Rat tightened his arms around her back and pulled her feet off the ground. He might have made more of it, if it hadn't been for a blast of pain from the ankle he'd twisted earlier in the day.

"I don't care what James says," Lauren said happily. "But there is one condition."

"What?"

"You've got to get a decent haircut."

Rat sounded shocked. "What's wrong with my hair?"

"Nothing," Lauren said. "I mean, if I was the sort of girl who went for guys who looked like they had a bird's nest mounted on their head . . ."

Rat self-consciously inspected a strand of his tangled hair. "Do you really think it's that bad?"

Lauren slowly nodded, but her smirk disappeared when she heard the clatter of a diesel engine coming up the dirt path toward the camp.

Rat poked his head out between the branches. "It's Mr. Large and Arif in the truck."

Arif was a nineteen-year-old ex-cherub who was being paid to help out around campus until he returned to university.

"Dammit," Lauren said. "They're right between us and the tents. If Large does an inspection and finds us missing, we're gonna be *so* dead."

The pair crouched down low and watched as the army-green truck came to a halt. Arif sat at the wheel as Mr. Large opened the passenger door and stumbled out of the cab.

"Are you sure you're okay, Norman?" Arif asked.

"I'm a happy man," Large boomed, as his giant body rippled with drunken laughter. "I can't wait for the looks on those kids' faces when they see those granite blocks and the size of the hill they've got to drag them up."

Arif had been through many of Mr. Large's training exercises himself and clearly didn't share the joke.

"Okay, misery guts," Large slurred. "You'd better get moving, 'cos the supermarket closes at half past twelve. Stick to the cheap sausages and don't go buying any extra stuff; I want to keep those brats lean and hungry."

Large slammed the door of the truck and a thick blue plume shot out of the exhaust as Arif pulled away. Back in the trees, Lauren and Rat exchanged looks of dread as they contemplated spending a day dragging granite blocks up a hill.

"At least he's in no state to inspect tents," Rat whispered.

"Yeah, but think of the mood he'll be in tomorrow if he's got a hangover."

Mr. Large clearly had no idea that he was being watched as he unself-consciously scratched between his legs and broke into song:

"*I've been a wild rover for many a year, and I've spent all me money on whiskey and beer. . . .*"

"Total saddo," Lauren whispered, stifling a giggle. "My dad always sang that when he was off his face."

"*But now I'm returning with gold in great store. . . .*"

Rat smiled briefly, until he saw Mr. Large turn and start walking toward them. The cluster of trees was isolated, which meant they'd be spotted if they tried to run off. All they could do was crouch down low and hope Mr. Large didn't come too close.

"*And it's no nay never . . . ,*" Large sang, as he unzipped his fly and began liberally peeing against a trunk less than a meter and a half from Lauren and Rat. "*No nay never, no more. Will I plaaaaaay the wild rover . . .*"

Lauren covered her mouth and gagged slightly as the smell of alcohol-tinged urine caught on the breeze. But Rat couldn't help seeing the funny side of Mr. Large's singing and the extraordinary capacity of his bladder as the hot liquid steamed in the moonlight.

"That is *sooooooo* much better," Large told himself happily, as he zipped up and turned back toward the tents.

Rat cracked up as soon as Mr. Large was out of earshot. "I thought he was never gonna stop."

Lauren screwed up her face. "I don't know why you're laughing. It's all soaked into the knee of your pants."

"Eww!" Rat gasped, as he sprang out of the grass.

"Gotcha," Lauren giggled, as she tore the wrapping off her Twix.

She put one chocolate-covered end in her mouth and closed up to Rat, who bit on the other. The idea was to munch toward each other and end with a kiss, but after the first bite they heard a choking noise.

Lauren looked up in time to see Large's silhouette doubling over, then crashing onto the grass near the tents.

"Holy *shit*," Rat said as he jumped up, intending to run over and find out what was wrong.

But Lauren pulled him back. "Maybe he spotted us. It might be one of his tricks."

Rat looked at her uncertainly. "Even he wouldn't stoop that low."

"It's Mr. Large," Lauren muttered. "He'll do anything, especially to me. He hates my guts."

Large now lay at the side of the dirt road, his legs twitching as he fought for breath.

"You stay here if you want," Rat said. "It looks serious."

As soon as Rat ran out of the trees, Large gave a desperate scream for help, which finally convinced Lauren that he wasn't playacting.

"Are you okay?" Rat said nervously, as he leaned over Mr. Large.

Large's face was white and cold sweat bristled all over his forehead. "Do I damn well look okay?"

Lauren arrived a few paces behind Rat and did a better job of remembering her first-aid training. "Have you got pains down your arms or in your chest?"

"Both," Large slurred as Lauren undid his belt and loosened his collar.

"He's clammy all over," Rat said. "Is it a heart attack?"

"He's got all the symptoms," Lauren nodded.

The kids hadn't been allowed to bring their mobiles on the training exercise.

"Sir, I need your phone," Lauren said.

Large managed to briefly point at his pant pocket before retching violently and erupting into another spasm.

Lauren flipped the mobile open, staring briefly at the wallpaper image of Large's beloved Rottweilers before dialing the CHERUB campus emergency number. She held the phone up to her ear waiting for a connection, but all she heard was a metallic bing-bong sound.

No service. Please try later.

Lauren gave Rat a spooked look. "There's no signal out here," she said anxiously. "Arif's gone off with the truck. We'll have to figure out some way of getting him to the hospital ourselves."

CHAPTER 3

NUMB

The six-kilometer run and the birthday messages boosted James's mood, but it sank as soon as he sighted the apartment complex that counted for home.

The Brezhnev Apartments were a three-story block that had been built for Aero City's elite during the communist era. It was now owned by an elderly relative of Denis Obidin, who collected the rent but spent little of it on keeping the building in shape.

The interior walls were decorated with dangling wallpaper and clumps of mildew, the boiler room in the basement only provided warmth and hot water when it fancied, and the prefabricated sections from which the apartments were constructed were badly cracked and didn't seem up to a strong sneeze, let alone a Russian winter.

Despite this, the small community of foreigners who worked in Aero City all resided here and stumped up the extortionate rent because it was protected by Vladimir Obidin's best police officers.

Any foreigner brave enough to set up home elsewhere could expect to find their valuables stolen if they were lucky, while the unlucky found themselves brutally mugged or escorted to one of the city's two cash machines to make a withdrawal at knifepoint. When the victims complained to the police, they were greeted with indifference and advised to move back into Mr. Obidin's apartment block.

Damp hung in the air as James stepped through the entrance. Most of the lighting tubes were either burned out or flickering. After squelching up four flights on damp carpet, James cut down a short corridor and put his key in the door of apartment 2-17.

The interior was slightly more accommodating than the public spaces. There was a modern kitchen and bathroom fitted by a previous tenant and some half-decent furniture. But no amount of airing quelled the damp that penetrated every fiber of the building.

"Honey, I'm home," James yelled, as he slammed the front door and dumped his backpack on the hallway carpet.

He put his head around a bedroom door, where his fake aunt and uncle stood in their underwear. Cheap body spray hung in the air and the smart clothes laid out over the double bed showed that they were getting ready for an evening out.

"Oops," James gasped, embarrassed as he sighted the giant knickers stretched over Auntie Isla's cellulite-pitted bum.

Uncle Boris stood buttoning up his shirt. He was in his forties, a birdlike figure who stank of small brown cigars. He wore a pair of aviator-style glasses with a dark orange tint, even on the gloomiest Russian days.

"Come on in, James," Isla smiled. "Don't be shy. How did it go at the compound?"

"I didn't get the two bugs in," James said, as he tried not to see too much of the decrepit bodies standing in front of him. "Vladimir came in and chucked me out before I had the chance to go in the kitchen. But all the others are working fine."

"Don't worry yourself," Isla shrugged. "They weren't important."

"Do you think tonight's meeting will be enough to secure the missiles?" James asked.

Boris broke into a slightly girlish laugh. "Anxious to get back to that girlfriend of yours at CHERUB?"

"Don't be daft," James said, shaking his head in mock protest. "I love it here: the cold musty air, the half-starved pensioners, the corrupt cops sitting at the front gate stroking their machine guns, the fact that there's nothing to do except go to school and freeze my butt off all day, then come home in the evening and sit in front of the TV—provided the power stays on. I mean, why would I *ever* want to leave?"

"Obidin will either sell us the missiles, or tell us to take a walk," Isla said, as she zipped up her skirt. "Either way, we'll be out of here soon, ten days at the most."

"Thank god for that," James groaned. "Have you done me any dinner?"

Boris nodded. "Macaroni and cheese in the fridge. It'll take two minutes in the microwave, just make sure you give it a stir halfway through. Oh, and I checked the Internet. It looks like that TV show downloaded okay. I burned it onto a DVD so you can watch it on the big screen."

"Sweet." James nodded. "That should kill half the evening. What's the hot water been like?"

"I'd stick to the bowl and sponge if I were you," Isla said. "The water pressure is down to nothing and the shower is running close to boiling."

The taps in the bathroom only provided water with a yellow tinge, so James stepped through to the kitchen and ran scalding hot water into a plastic bowl, before adding some cold and carrying it through to his bedroom. He caught a blast of cold air as he put the bowl on his bedside table, then splashed a crusty flannel and bar of soap into the water before shutting the window. James faced a daily choice between opening his window to clear the smell of damp and keeping it closed for warmth.

After washing as well as a washcloth and bowl allows and putting on clean underwear, James wandered out into the hallway and was surprised to see Isla, smartly dressed and carrying a large suitcase out of the bedroom.

"What's all that in aid of?" James asked. "Looks like you're moving out."

"Documents, recording equipment," Isla explained. "It was either this or that little attaché case, and it won't fit in there."

Boris came out of the bedroom in a shabby suit and bow tie.

"Snazzy." James grinned.

"Do you like it?" Boris said proudly, totally missing the irony in James's voice.

"Boris, baby, I could see you on a Paris catwalk in that getup."

Boris now realized that James was teasing him and looked slightly cross. "It's an appropriate outfit," he said, twitching his nose. "We're leaving now. I wouldn't wait up, we might not be back until two or three in the morning."

"No worries," James said. "I've got my DVD and my macaroni and cheese."

James sauntered into the kitchen and put his plate in the microwave. While the little oven buzzed, he dashed through to the living room to set up his DVD. It clattered into the tray and he was relieved to see that the download had worked as the title screen popped up: *When Movie Stunts Go Wrong Volume II.*

"Nice one," James told himself, as he grabbed the now steaming hot macaroni from the microwave and hoped that the DVD had something as cool as the spurt of blood when the stuntwoman got her arm chopped off in volume one (James had laughed, Kerry had screamed and said he was a heartless pig, but they'd made up and had a great snog afterward).

The meal wasn't gourmet, but it was the kind of grub that felt satisfying after being out in the cold all day. James put his feet up on a coffee table as a man with his arm in a sling earnestly told him that the stunts he was about to see were performed by professionals and should not be attempted at home. Then the screen cut to a scene of two fat men running toward each other with chainsaws buzzing in their hands.

"*Even with the very best preparation, the art of the stuntman is a dangerous one,*" the commentator said solemnly, as the fatter of the two men tripped over and let out a piercing scream.

"*Sick!*" James grinned as the stuntman rolled onto his side revealing a huge wound in his chest.

Then the screen went blank and the lights went out. Electrical appliances shut down as James found himself plunged into complete darkness.

Sometimes a power surge caused a fuse to blow and the caretaker would restore power within a few minutes, but James walked to the window and saw that the streetlamps and all the lights in the surrounding apartment blocks were off too. This meant there was a full-scale power cut, and once the electricity went down, it never came back on before morning.

All he could do was sit in the dark and try to stay warm.

CHAPTER 4

STRETCHER

After helping Lauren to lay Mr. Large out in the recovery position, Rat dived into his tent and woke his training partner, Andy Lagan. Lauren woke Bethany, who in turn woke up a bunch of other kids including her ten-year-old brother, Jake. Within minutes of collapsing, Mr. Large was illuminated by the flashlights of twenty-six partially dressed cherubs.

"He's drifting in and out of consciousness," Lauren explained anxiously, as she crouched over Mr. Large. "If his heart's weak and he's not getting enough oxygen, he could end up brain-damaged."

"Has anyone started making a stretcher?" Bethany asked.

"How?" a boy asked sleepily.

"Use your initiative," Lauren tutted. "Tent fabric, tent poles, branches, whatever. You're supposed to be trained CHERUB agents. I'm asking you to rustle up a stretcher, not build a time machine."

Jake interrupted. "We all hate his guts; do we even *want* to save him?"

"Don't be a tit all your life," Bethany said, flicking her brother's ear. "He may be a scumbag, but we're not gonna stand here and watch a man die."

"Shouldn't we be giving him the kiss of life?" Rat asked.

Lauren shook her head. "His breathing is okay and his heart is beating. I think he's just gone into shock."

"Maybe he's had a stroke," a boy said.

"Maybe, maybe, maybe," Lauren yelled, irritated by the gawpers surrounding her as she stood up and backed away from the patient. "We only know basic first aid and all we have is like, bandages and stuff. We need to get him to a hospital and fast."

"Where's Arif and the truck?" Jake asked.

"He just left to drive to the supermarket," Rat said. "I tell you what, how about we send messengers off in different directions? There's gotta be a farmhouse or something around here."

"Good idea," Lauren nodded. "Sort it out and someone else can take Large's phone up to the top of the hill. You might get a signal from there."

Rat picked Andy and three other fast runners and sent them off in different directions. A fifth was told to run up the adjacent hill.

"Are you *completely* sure it isn't one of his tricks?" Jake asked suspiciously. "I wouldn't put it past him."

Bethany tutted. "Look at the state of him, moron. You can't fake all that sweat."

"What if he took a special pill that made him go queasy, or something?"

"Jake, you're *not* helping," Bethany shouted. "And you're starting to wind me up, so why don't you get out of my face before I deck you?"

"Try it," Jake sneered. "I might be little, but I'm harder than you."

"Oh, you reckon?" Bethany sneered back, giving her brother an almighty shove.

The crowd moved aside as Jake lashed out at his sister. His boot connected with her thigh but his fist swished past her nose, missing by millimeters. Bethany grabbed her brother's flying arm and twisted it up behind his back. She took the elastic waistband of his tracksuit bottoms with her other hand, hitched him off the ground, and slammed him down on his belly. While Jake was still winded, Bethany straddled him and sat across his back.

"Yeah, Jake, you're *so* hard," she yelled jubilantly.

Lauren was furious. She couldn't believe that her best mate was having a pointless fight with her brother in the middle of a major crisis.

"Leave it out," she screamed. "We all need to think straight. A few minutes could save his life."

"Coming through," a couple of girls shouted.

The pair had made a stretcher by breaking two wooden stakes from a nearby fence and running them through a couple of sleeping bags.

Jake was humiliated and tried to hide it as Bethany let him up. Meanwhile, the girls laid the stretcher on the grass beside Mr. Large.

"He's really heavy; we'd best roll him on," Rat said.

Not only was Large extremely tall, he also carried a great mound of fat around his midriff.

It took five kids to roll him onto the sleeping-bag fabric. Once he was in position, Lauren and Rat took up the poles at the front, with the pair who'd made the stretcher at the back.

"Heave," Lauren shouted, as the foursome bent at the knees and raised Mr. Large off the ground.

Some of the other kids realized that they were struggling and took part of the weight by grabbing the poles along the side.

"He stinks of booze," someone complained.

"Which way?" Rat groaned.

"GRAHHHHHHHHH," Large shouted groggily.

"He's awake," said one of the boys standing along the side.

"Forward," Lauren ordered. "Head toward the track, we're about a mile from the main road. We can jog it in ten minutes and hitch a ride from there."

But as Lauren and Rat stepped forward, Large insisted on sitting up.

"Stay *still*," Bethany shouted desperately. "You've just had a heart attack."

"Poppycock," Large bellowed. "Let me off of this contraption."

Large swung his legs around, upsetting the balance of the stretcher. The two girls at the back couldn't hold on and the wooden beams slipped through their hands, splintering their fingers as the stretcher crashed to the ground. As the girls moaned in pain, Large made a brief attempt to stand up before clutching his chest and collapsing into another spasm.

"I'm dying," he gasped.

Rat tried to calm him down. "You need to sit still, Norman. We've sent messengers in all directions to get help."

"*Norman?*" Large growled. "How *dare* you call me Norman. You address me as sir."

"He's drunk on top of everything else," Lauren said, shaking her head with contempt.

"Shall we try getting him back on the stretcher?" Bethany asked.

"What's the point? He's too heavy for us to carry if he won't stay still."

"I want my Hayley," Mr. Large moaned as he sat in the grass. "I want to live to see my beautiful girl get married."

"You're *not* going to die," Rat insisted, making a brave second stab at calming Large down. "You're in shock. You're very weak. You've got to lie flat on the ground and try to stay calm."

Lauren felt massively relieved as she saw a set of car headlights crawling along the dirt track toward the lines of tents. It was a small Hyundai with an elderly lady behind the wheel and Rat's mate Andy Lagan in the passenger seat. The woman looked appalled when she stepped out of the car and saw the giant man thrashing about on the ground.

41

"He's dead drunk," the woman said. "Are you *sure* he's had a heart attack?"

Andy ran around from the passenger seat and tried to reassure the heavily perfumed woman that Mr. Large wasn't just roaring drunk.

"I'm not having *that* in my car," she said indignantly. "I can smell the drink on him from here. It's only done four thousand miles. What if he vomits inside?"

As she said this, Large twisted over on his side and made a deep groaning sound.

"Now listen, lady," Lauren said desperately, "we're out of options here. He could die. You've got to help us get him to the hospital."

"No, no, no. I'll drive back to my house and call an ambulance from there. It's less than ten minutes' drive."

Lauren couldn't believe what she was hearing.

"An ambulance might take a half hour or more to get here, you stupid old bat!" Bethany squealed.

Lauren looked at Rat and pointed toward Mr. Large. "Get him into that car."

"Hold on, young miss," the old lady yelled. "I'm not taking orders from you. I'm not driving that man anywhere."

"I'll drive him then," Lauren shouted back. "Isn't a man's life *slightly* more important than your precious upholstery?"

Rat, Andy, and several others began dragging Mr. Large toward the car. The woman turned to go after them, but Lauren grabbed her willowy arm and pulled her back sharply.

"I'm truly sorry," Lauren said, as she saw that the

elderly lady was frightened and close to crying. It was odd that she'd been kindly enough to stop her car for Andy and drive to their aid but now seemed more concerned about her car than Mr. Large's life. Lauren guessed it was just that she was old, eccentric, and not up to handling stress.

"Come on," Lauren said, trying a gentler tack as the lady struggled to free her arm. "We need your help. Can you tell us the way to the nearest hospital?"

But the old woman screamed and made a desperate sobbing noise, which made Lauren feel absolutely awful. The two girls who'd built the stretcher grabbed her flailing arms and tried getting her to calm down.

With all the madness going on, Lauren hadn't noticed another messenger arriving inside a BMW. The wax-jacketed driver emerged, holding a leather bag of the type usually carried by doctors.

"What is this, *Lord of the Flies*?" the man said, shaking his head as he surveyed the scene.

"Are you a doctor?" Rat asked.

"A vet, I'm afraid," the man explained. He knelt over Mr. Large and grabbed his wrist to take a pulse. "His heartbeat is extremely weak."

"Will he live?" Rat asked.

"Depends upon a lot of things," the vet said, as he reached into his pocket for his car keys and dangled them in front of Andy. "Two of you lads go around to the trunk of my car. You'll see a black oxygen cylinder and a box of disposable masks. It's heavy, so lift it together. Pure oxygen will make his breathing easier and take some of the strain off his heart. Then we'll lay him out over the backseat of my car and I'll take him to Accident and Emergency."

The presence of the vet was a great relief to the cherubs. Unfortunately, Lauren and Bethany still had the old woman on their hands.

"I'm telling the police," the woman shouted, as she pointed accusingly at Lauren. "You're car thieves, you . . . You tried to kidnap me."

Lauren grasped the woman's shoulder and spoke as gently as her adrenalin rush would let her. "Why don't you take some deep breaths? We'll make you a nice cup of tea and then you can drive home after you've calmed down."

"Criminals," the woman screamed again. She turned her head with surprising speed and bit on Lauren's middle finger.

Lauren instinctively ripped her finger out of the woman's mouth. Unfortunately, a denture came flying out with it, and Lauren squealed in horror as the warm plastic teeth hit her in the face.

Meanwhile, Rat, Andy, and the vet had settled Mr. Large in the rear of the BMW, and the vet had fitted him with an oxygen mask.

"Have you got no other adults here?" the vet asked the girls.

"There's one," Lauren nodded, as she clamped her bloody finger beneath her armpit. "But he's gone into town to buy groceries. I expect he'll be back pretty soon."

"Right," the vet nodded. "I'll call the police and tell them you're out here. I don't like the thought of leaving you lot unsupervised for too long." Then he turned and looked at the old lady. "You look like you've had a bit of a turn, my dear. How about you take a ride to the hospital with me?"

"Yes," the woman sobbed. "Get me away from these *animals*. This one attacked me, now she's stolen my teeth."

"That's *not* what happened," Lauren said defensively.

The vet gave Lauren a reassuring look. "Okay, my dear," he said to the old woman as he put an arm around her back. "No hanging around; I've got a very sick man in the backseat."

Bethany chased after the two adults and caught up just as they were getting in the BMW.

"That's her teeth," Bethany explained, as she handed them to the vet. "They've been in the grass, so you'd better rinse them off before they go back in her mouth."

CHAPTER 5

RAID

The electricity had gone off before James's room had warmed up, so he'd carried his duvet and pillows through to the living room and spent the evening snuggled up on the sofa, reading an out-of-date motorbike magazine by the dim glow of a portable gas lamp.

He'd been asleep for several hours when he woke with a jolt and an eerie sense that something was up.

"The boy's not in bed," a man shouted angrily.

The men were in the hallway just a few meters away—hard to say how many. James realized that the sound of them kicking the front door in had woken him up.

"Check the living room," Vladimir Obidin shouted fiercely.

James shuddered when he recognized the voice. This wasn't a burglary. Something had gone *seriously* wrong at the meeting.

He threw off his duvet and spun toward the door that he knew would crash open at any second. The only light was a tiny glimmer through the curtains and James felt blindly along the sideboard, desperate for some kind of weapon. He stopped when his hand touched the base of Boris's marble and glass cigar lighter.

"Got him, boss," one of Obidin's henchmen shouted, as he burst through the door and blasted a powerful xenon flashlight in James's face.

Boris and Isla were only supposed to be having a business meeting with Denis Obidin. Maybe their cover got blown, or . . . But James had to shut out the whys and wherefores and concentrate on not ending up in a cell facing an angry Vladimir Obidin and his blow lamp.

James charged into the light, clattering into his assailant as he swung the heavy cigar lighter and smashed it into the side of the man's skull. It was too dark to see if the first blow had knocked him cold, but the second left no room for doubt. James spotted a holster under the man's jacket and reached toward it, but found two men plucking him off the ground before he got hold of the gun.

Each man tucked a hand under one of James's armpits and made the room shudder as they slammed his back against the wall. The larger man punched him in the stomach.

"Keep him conscious," Vladimir shouted from the kitchen. "He's our only link to those bastards."

The punch would have crumpled most grown men, but

James had taken worse in combat training and surprised his attacker by kicking him in the balls. As his assailant doubled over and stumbled backward into the coffee table, James reached out for the other man and grabbed his long hair. He quickly looped some hair around his wrist. The man threw a soft punch as James snapped his arm backward. The hair pulled tight and the dude's neck crunched. He went down so fast that James barely managed to let go before going down on top of him.

After a panicked breath, James ran forward to finish off the man who was trying to untangle himself from the coffee table. There was enough light from the abandoned flashlight for James to see him reach for his gun. James grabbed his wrist, twisted the pistol out of his grasp, and pulped the man's face by repeatedly smashing the barrel against the bridge of his nose.

Three down, one to go, James thought, backing up to the wall as he inspected the automatic pistol in his bloody left hand. He wasn't familiar with the type, but it looked like it was ready to shoot.

Vladimir Obidin shouted from the kitchen. "Mikhail, what's going on? Cuff the boy and start searching."

James only had seconds before the lack of a reply made Vladimir suspicious. He used them to shut off the flashlight and creep out into the hallway.

"Mikhail?" Vladimir repeated, sounding a touch uneasy now. "Did he get away?"

James crouched down low. A flickering light came through the kitchen doorway, suggesting that Vladimir was nosing around with a flashlight.

"Have you got the boy or not?"

James was tempted to throw a smartass line back at Vladimir. But he thought he'd leave the comebacks to Hollywood and let Vladimir stay confused.

"Guys?" Obidin said, with something in his voice that James had never heard before: fear.

Buoyed by Obidin's discomfort, James crept right up to the kitchen door as Obidin turned off his flashlight. James would have happily made a run for the front door, but he'd have to pass the kitchen to get there and that would give Vladimir an easy shot at him.

James considered backing up and jumping off the living room balcony, but they were two stories up and even if he landed without injuring himself, he'd probably be spotted by the rentacops who stood guard at the front of the building.

As James crept closer to the kitchen door, he heard Vladimir whispering into his police radio. "This is VO1. Requesting *urgent* assistance. All nearby units come to Brezhnev Apartments, flat two stroke seventeen. Searching for a boy aged fourteen or fifteen. Blond hair, stocky build. Looks like he's taken out three officers already."

James realized that he had to deal with Obidin and get out of the building before he had half of Aero City's police force on his back. Judging by Obidin's voice, James reckoned he was near the washing machine at the back of the room.

He poked his arm through the doorway and fired three shots into the darkness. If Obidin had kept still, James would have shot him in the chest, but Obidin had also decided to take the offensive and was walking toward the door. As James's bullets ripped through the metal shell of the washing machine, he sensed Obidin standing less than a meter away from him.

James practically swallowed his tongue with fright, but he had his finger on the trigger and realized that whoever got the first shot in would win the duel. While Obidin took aim, James fired, shooting Obidin in the thigh from point-blank range.

The force of the bullet knocked Obidin backward. James bundled on top and snatched Obidin's gun, before racing back to the living room.

After checking that the other three men were still unconscious, James grabbed his sneakers from in front of the couch and slipped them on. With the gun poised, he walked back into the hallway, trying to ignore Vladimir's moans as he put on his jacket and stepped through what remained of the front door.

The corridor was pitch black, but as James reached the stairwell he spotted flashlight beams and heard men with equipment jangling up the stairs: backup. Returning to the apartment seemed like a bad idea and James couldn't go down, so he took an instant decision and raced up the musty staircase to the top floor. The unlit third-floor corridor bought him time, but if Obidin was still conscious and told the cops that he'd only just run out, they'd be on to him in seconds.

James considered his options, none of which looked good: He could stay where he was and get caught; going up on the roof would only buy an extra half minute; and if he knocked on any of the apartment doors, it was unlikely that anyone would let him in. His only realistic option was to run down the metal fire escape at the back of the building, but wouldn't the cops have it covered?

However improbable escape seemed, James wasn't giving up. He'd just shot the chief of police and the cops around here weren't big on human rights. If they got him in a cell, they'd torture him until they got answers.

A blast of cold air hit James as he broke open the fire door. His haste almost cost him as his sneaker glided across icy metal. There was a flurry of snow and a touch of light coming from the headlights of the police cars parked at the front of the building. James looked down and couldn't see anyone about, but it was impossible to be sure: The night was as black as the cops' uniforms.

The steps were in a tight spiral and James moved as fast as he could, trying to keep his footsteps silent, with one freezing hand on the snowy railing and the other clutching his gun. He took another look when he got near the bottom, but there was still no sign of life and he made it safely to the pavement.

James was in a parking lot, surrounded by cheap cars owned by the residents. While little money had been spent on the upkeep of the Brezhnev Apartments, the perimeter was well defended, and James realized that he'd have as much difficulty climbing out over the four-meter-high spiked railings as kidnappers and thieves were supposed to have climbing in.

But at least it was safer than being trapped in a corridor: There was plenty of space and plenty of cars to dive between if someone came after him. James felt nauseous as he crouched between a Nissan and a Volkswagen, trying to gather his thoughts. He glanced at his wrist and realized that his watch was still on the table back in the flat.

There was one thought that he couldn't get out of his head: *What could possibly have gone wrong at the meeting?* Maybe Boris and Isla had blown their cover, or maybe Denis Obidin had known they were MI5 all along. Maybe they'd unearthed one of the bugs he'd placed inside the house. . . .

But none of this quite rang true. Denis was a smart man: He was used to the attentions of the world's intelligence agencies and would have dealt with the situation clinically. Vladimir turning up and kicking down doors in the middle of the night suggested that the Obidins were angry about something that had taken them by surprise.

James could mull over theories all night long and he'd still be trapped inside this parking lot. He needed to escape first and think later.

Although the adrenalin made it feel as if an age had passed since he'd woken up, James knew it couldn't have been more than ten minutes; and it was less than half that time since Vladimir had called for backup. The cops who guarded the gate had run up the stairs and nobody had been covering the fire escape because there were no other cops in the area.

At least, not *yet*.

In a few minutes there would be cops all over the joint, but James reckoned he had a decent chance of making it through the front gates if he didn't hang about. As he sprang up, he heard a cop emerge at the top of the third-floor fire exit. He slipped over like James had almost done and yelled as he clonked down seven steps.

James ducked behind the parked cars as he raced toward the entrance gates. As usual there were two ancient Russian-built cop cars parked outside the entrance, but Vladimir Obidin's bulletproof Mercedes had been parked across the road to stop any vehicles from escaping.

He emerged close to the headlights of one police car and was relieved to find it empty, but a thuggish-looking driver was propped on the hood of the Merc, with a compact machine gun around his neck and a cigarette between his lips.

It wasn't ideal, but James figured that one against one with surprise on his side was about as good as the odds were likely to get. Aware that the cop who'd slipped down the steps would soon be on his tail, he crept around to the back of the police car and poked his head up over the trunk.

The driver looked spaced out and James considered shooting him, grabbing his machine gun, and making off in the limo. But it would take time; his gun wasn't silenced and with more police on the way, it could turn into a full-blown chase. Besides, there's a big difference between shooting your way out of a corner and going on the offensive, and James wasn't sure he had the heart to sneak up and shoot a man in the back.

So while the driver dropped his cigarette and ground it under a highly polished shoe, James ducked behind his car, crossed the deserted street and jogged stealthily into the blackness with only a trace of moonlight giving his position away.

He crossed a stretch of pavement that ran between two

high-rise housing blocks. By the time he'd reached a stairwell at the rear, three police cars and an ambulance had parked outside the Brezhnev Apartments, their flashing blue lights making quite a show in the powerless town.

James decided to run toward the derelict area near the edge of Aero City. He could hide in one of the thousands of abandoned apartments that had once housed the city's factory workers. But first he had to get in touch with the CHERUB emergency desk and tell them what had happened.

He reached inside his jacket, then padded down his jeans and came to a horrible realization.

His phone was still inside his school backpack and his backpack was still inside flat 2-17.

CHAPTER 6

POOL

The boys' gymnasium was one of the oldest buildings on CHERUB campus. It had recently been refurbished with the latest exercise machines and weight-training equipment. A small extension had been built to provide changing rooms and showers for girls and the derelict basement cinema where cherubs had watched newsreels and movies in the fifties and sixties had been stripped out and turned into a lounge, complete with pool, snooker, and air hockey tables. Big-screen TVs showed sports channels, there were oversized sofas, and the glass-fronted fridges and cupboards along one side of the room were stocked with snacks and soft drinks.

The lounge had been completed less than a month

earlier and the novelty had yet to wear off. It was packed with cherubs whenever it was open and a rotation restricted access to certain age groups to prevent overcrowding.

Cherubs usually had lessons on Saturday morning, but the lounge had been specially opened for the twenty-six kids who'd returned from the aborted training exercise in the Yorkshire Dales. After making grave threats to a bunch of younger kids who'd been hogging one of the full-sized snooker tables for more than an hour, Lauren, Rat, Bethany, and Andy managed to get a game.

None of them was very good. Rat was the most naturally gifted player, but he'd spent the first eleven years of his life inside a religious cult and was struggling to master the rules.

"So I've knocked in the red. Now what color do I have to pot first?"

Lauren tutted. "Whatever color you nominate, for the *third* time."

"But I thought you had to do yellow, green, brown, or whatever," Rat said.

"That's only after all the reds have been potted at the end."

"Right," Rat said. "Blue ball, corner pocket."

Lauren, Andy, and Bethany all went quiet as Rat lined up his shot.

"AWWWOOOOOOOOOOO," Andy howled, trying to sound like a wolf as he made Rat totally miscue his shot.

"No *way*," Rat said, as he grabbed the white ball off the table. "I'm retaking that."

"Cheater." Bethany grinned.

"Well it *was* out of order," Lauren said.

"Oh, there's a shock," Bethany said, before making a smoochy sound. "Lauren defends her secret love."

"Bite me," Lauren said, as she flicked Bethany off.

Rat took the shot for the second time, and the blue rattled in the jaws of the pocket but didn't drop.

"Righty ho," Andy said, as he grabbed his cue. "One-four-seven break, here I come."

Rat sucked a mouthful of orange juice from his carton before moving to stand alongside Lauren. "I'm glad we told everyone," he smiled.

Bethany huffed, "Oh yeah, it was such a *big* secret. We all knew what was going on anyway."

Bethany was starting to wind Lauren up. Lauren had put up with several of Bethany's stupid crushes, but now that *she* had a boyfriend, Bethany was acting all jealous.

Bethany's brother Jake and some of his mates were sitting on a sofa waiting for the next game. Jake started singing: "Rat and Lauren sitting in a tree, B-O-N-K-I-N-G."

Lauren turned her head sharply and glowered at him. "Unless you want this cue rammed up your arse, I'd suggest that you *shut* it."

"Ooooh, tetchy," Jake giggled.

"Do you want me to make you cry again, baby brother?" Bethany threatened, suddenly on Lauren's side again.

Andy missed an easy red. "Your shot, Lauren."

Lauren knew she was hopeless and decided on a radical strategy. There was an unbroken cluster of red balls in the middle of the table and she clattered them as hard as she could.

"Skill," Lauren howled, punching the air as a red ball dropped into a pocket.

"You are *soooo* jammy," Andy tutted.

Even better, one of the flying reds had knocked the pink ball into the jaws of a corner pocket.

"Come on, baby." Rat grinned as Lauren lined up her next shot. "That's six easy points."

She smiled as the pink rolled in, but the white ball followed it.

"Stupid girl," Jake yelled gleefully. "You should have put some backspin on it."

Lauren gave a *couldn't care less* shrug. "I've only played snooker three times. I don't understand how to do all that stuff."

Lauren was sharing a cue with Bethany and as she handed it across, the room went oddly quiet. A bunch of lads who were fighting with Peperamis, throwing chips, and making lightsaber noises all settled back into their seats and tried looking innocent.

Lauren had to look over her shoulder to find the reason: Zara Asker, CHERUB's newly appointed chairwoman, was walking down the spiral staircase that led into the lounge. Zara spotted Lauren and headed straight toward her.

"Can we have a private word in my office?" Zara asked.

Jake burst out laughing and made a sound like a whip cracking. "You're in trouble," he sang, to the delight of his mates.

Zara turned sharply and jammed her finger under Jake's nose. "You're walking on *very* thin ice, Mr. Parker. I've had several reports about your cheek in lessons and I can see punishment laps and a few months of washing-up duty on your schedule if you don't sharpen up."

Jake liked acting cocky in front of his little crew of ten-year-olds, but Zara's glare made him wilt as Bethany poked her tongue at him.

"Is it about Mr. Large?" Lauren asked, once they were out of the noisy lounge and heading up the stairs.

"No it isn't," Zara said, as they reached the top and walked out into the fresh air, heading for the main building. "I think it's best if I explain when we get to my office. Although I did have a phone call from Mr. Large's partner earlier. His condition is improving, but it's still serious and there's a possibility that he'll need a bypass operation. And even if Mr. Large recovers fully, he faces a disciplinary hearing when he comes back to work."

"Why's that?" Lauren asked.

"I've read all the reports on the Dales incident and it sounds like Mr. Large had a skinful before his heart attack. The odd pint or two is fine, but he was in charge of twenty-six children and drunkenness is unacceptable."

"Will he get the boot this time?" Lauren asked, trying to hide a grin.

"Probably not," Zara shrugged. "For all his faults, Norman Large is a hard man to replace. It's unbelievably tough to find good training instructors. I mean, would *you* want to spend your working life running around a muddy assault course and making kids' lives a misery?"

Lauren shook her head. "I suppose it takes a certain type of person."

"You came out well in Arif's incident report," Zara said brightly. "He says that you had the situation under control when he got back to the camp."

"I got the others to pack up the tents and everything." Lauren nodded. "Fortunately, Arif got back from the supermarket just after the vet left, and we managed to clear out before we had police and social services on our backs."

"I reckon you're a natural leader." Zara smiled. "I can see you in politics or running a big company some day."

"Politics is boring," Lauren said, smiling back uneasily. "I certainly didn't feel like a leader. The whole thing was pretty chaotic, to be honest. Especially when that old granny started freaking out on me."

Zara smiled a little. "Oh, I forgot to tell you, we had to take Meatball to the vet."

"Is he okay?" Lauren asked anxiously.

"He wasn't eating properly, which is hardly surprising because the vet found four of Joshua's Lego bricks lodged in his throat. He's recovering, but I have to keep telling Joshua not to leave toys all over the carpet."

"That dog will eat *anything*." Lauren giggled.

"You know, you're still welcome to come over and take him for walks any time you like."

Lauren nodded. "I will, but I've had masses of homework and I've been spending quite a bit of time with Rat."

"I see," Zara said, and grinned knowingly.

They passed the fountain and went up the steps and into the main building. It was a short walk through reception to Zara's office. The previous chairman, Dr. McAfferty, had lined the room with his collection of books, but Zara had yet to settle in. She'd only found time to put up a few family photos and the room looked bare.

Lauren felt a chill as she spotted James's girlfriend,

Kerry Chang, sitting on a chair in front of the desk. She had tears streaking down her cheeks.

"James is missing," Kerry sobbed. "He might . . . He might even be dead."

Lauren felt like a bomb had gone off inside her skull as her limbs went numb and a great ball welled up in her throat. She grabbed on to a chair to keep herself steady.

"Sit down and I'll explain as best I can," Zara said, as she guided Lauren into one of the leather chairs. "James's mission was in a northern Russian town known as Aero City. The local oligarch is a man called Denis Obidin. He owns all of the production facilities, and most of the land and housing, and he's even the city mayor.

"MI5 suspects that Obidin is selling missiles and other sensitive technology to rogue governments and terrorist groups, but he has powerful friends in Moscow and the Russian government has consistently turned a blind eye.

"James was working alongside two MI5 operatives. They aimed to set up a deal to buy some missiles and record evidence of every step in the transaction. Faced with such damning evidence, we were hoping to force the Russian government into taking criminal action against Obidin.

"James's role in the mission was regarded as low to medium risk," Zara continued. "Our biggest problem was infiltrating Obidin's compound and planting listening devices inside. Our MI5 team found out that Denis Obidin was planning to send his only child to a posh English prep school. The boy was having English lessons with a local teacher, but he was struggling. So we flew James out to act as the MI5 agents' nephew, using some kind of background story about James staying with his

61

aunt after his mother had a nervous breakdown.

"Not long after James arrived, the aunt and uncle casually suggested to Denis Obidin that James give his son some informal English lessons. Obidin took the bait and James spent a few weeks giving the boy extra English practice after school. At the same time, he learned the layout of the house and began dropping some of our new pinhead-sized listening devices around the place."

"So what went wrong?" Lauren sniffed, as Kerry reached across the desk and gave her a tissue.

Zara shrugged. "We're not sure. All we know is that James's aunt and uncle were scheduled to go to Obidin's house for an important meeting late last night. According to other sources MI5 has within Aero City, a violent row erupted inside the meeting and Denis Obidin was killed.

"Obidin's brother Vladimir—who is also the local chief of police—set off from the compound with four other men to capture James and search the apartment where he was sleeping. According to some other Brits who live in the same building, there was a struggle. Several of Obidin's goons were knocked out and Vladimir Obidin was shot in the thigh."

"So did James get away?" Lauren asked.

"We have absolutely no idea. With Denis dead and Vladimir helicoptered to a private hospital in Moscow, other members of the Obidin family are jockeying for power and nobody really knows who's in charge or what's going on. There are rumors that James has been captured, but we've also heard that the police are still running a giant manhunt."

"But he hasn't communicated," Kerry said, stifling a

sob for Lauren's sake. "If he was okay, he surely would have contacted the emergency desk by now."

"Did he have a mobile?" Lauren asked.

Zara nodded. "He did, and even if he'd lost it, I'm sure there are call boxes and other facilities in the city. We can't be certain, but he's probably been captured by Obidin's henchmen."

"They could be hurting him," Lauren gasped. "They . . . He might even be dead already."

"I'm sorry, sweetheart," Zara said, as she grabbed Lauren out of her chair and pulled her into a hug. "Until we know for sure, you've got to stay calm and try not to think the worst."

"Oh, God," Lauren bawled, as she squeezed Zara tight. "Please don't let him be dead."

Zara was crying too as she rubbed Lauren's back. "James didn't have a mission controller in Aero City because he was being looked after by the MI5 agents, but Ewart helped to set the mission up. He's already on a flight to Moscow and should be in Aero City by this evening. There are other MI5 officers based in the area and they're going to liaise with Ewart and try to locate James."

But Lauren wasn't taking anything in. She was sobbing so hard and breathing so fast that she was starting to feel light-headed. She remembered feeling the same way on the night her mum had died, three years earlier.

"It might be okay, Lauren." Kerry sniffed. "You know James, he's got a habit of wrangling his way out of things."

"But he would have called by now," Lauren screamed desperately. "Why wouldn't he have called?"

CHAPTER 7

COMMUNICATION

After escaping from the Brezhnev Apartments, James made a stop at one of the city's twenty-four-hour grog shops. These illegal enterprises were mostly run out of shacks or ground-floor apartments and catered to the cravings of the Aero City's addicts, selling cigarettes, alcohol, and glue.

He spent the few roubles in his jacket on a stack of chocolate bars—easy to carry and packed with energy to fight off the cold—as well as a box of matches, four cans of Coke, and a small bottle of vodka.

After that, James set off for the edge of town, with the gun tucked in his jeans, keeping an eye out for a telephone booth as he jogged. But he knew he was unlikely to find one outside of the heavily policed city center.

The lack of telephones was due to a quirk of history. Aero City had been built during the Cold War as a closed city, with all forms of access tightly controlled by the Russian air force. Until the nineties, nonresidents had to apply for a permit to visit and foreign citizens were banned. Private telephones were not allowed and anyone wishing to make a personal call had to spend half a day in line inside City Hall.

Although these restrictions on telephones had been lifted years ago, the city government was desperately short of money and only a few streets near the center of Aero City had ever been wired up for telephones. If James wanted to make a call, he'd have to get hold of a mobile.

The eastern edge of town had once housed the tens of thousands who worked in the giant production plants. But the young and healthy had long since abandoned Aero City in search of work, while the vulnerable citizens they'd left behind had been moved into blocks nearer the city center.

The result was a ghost town: dozens of empty blocks, stripped of anything valuable and slowly crumbling back into the earth. James picked one at random and spent the night in a second-floor apartment. Without heat and with most of the doors and window frames stripped out for firewood, he found refuge in a bathtub, with a plastic shower curtain trapping the heat around his body and making a surprisingly effective blanket.

He could have started a fire to keep warm, or run back into town and broken into an apartment in the hope of stealing a mobile, but CHERUB taught its agents to be patient: The cops would be on high alert and James didn't understand his surroundings. He decided to hide in the bathtub until he had a clearer head and some daylight to nose around in.

James suffered through the night, unable to sleep and wondering what had gone wrong at the meeting. As the wind howled through the missing doors and windows, he sipped the vodka to keep the shivers at bay and clutched his stomach, nursing a dull ache from where he'd been punched in the guts.

James was restless and began exploring his bitterly cold surroundings as soon as day broke. He checked out the apartment, stepping gingerly over missing floorboards, then along the balcony where he was relieved to see nothing but more stripped-out apartments.

After checking his own floor, James surveyed the rest of the building and concluded that his only companions were the hundreds of pigeons roosting on the top balcony. But when he scanned the neighborhood from up high, the clothes hanging out to dry and odd wisps of smoke indicated that he wasn't completely alone on the eastern side of Aero City.

James had already decided that it would be too risky to try leaving via the only road out of town: There was sure to be a police blockade. He considered escaping through the forest to a neighboring town and either hitching a lift to Moscow or making a phone call when he got there. The trouble was, the nearest settlements were more than thirty kilometers away. James had no idea where they were and there was every chance that the Obidins would have goons on the lookout when he arrived.

This left James with one realistic option: sneak back into the city center, get hold of a mobile phone, and call for help. But with only one set of clothes, he'd be easily identified if he went out in daylight. He'd have to stay inside until it got dark and then sneak into one of the city's more affluent areas and either mug someone or break into an apartment.

James didn't have a watch, but he knew it got light at around eight in the morning and was dark when he came out of school at four, which left him with seven and a half hours to kill. It was important to stay warm, and now that he felt more confident about his surroundings, he decided to make a fire.

Although most of the doors and many window frames had been removed from the block, there was still plenty to burn. James collected rags and a few sheets of newspaper and used his penknife to strip splinters of wood from a floorboard. He laid them all in the bathroom sink and used a match to light the kindling.

He kept the fire small, because he didn't want to burn the building down or leave a trail of smoke big enough to be spotted from the ground. But the flames were enough to warm his hands and raise the temperature inside the small bathroom up to a couple of degrees above freezing.

Once he'd warmed up, James's thoughts turned to his stomach. The sugar in the chocolate bars and Coke he'd bought the night before would provide him with enough calories to see the day through, but he craved something hot and his mind turned toward the pigeons roosting on the top floor.

He'd trapped and eaten pigeons during basic training.

The meat was tasty and perfectly safe if you gutted the bird and cooked it properly, but he'd also need clean water for making a hot drink and cleaning up.

More important, James figured that keeping himself busy by boiling water and cooking food would be better for his mental state than spending all day shivering and worrying about whether his future involved an unpleasant reunion with the Aero City police.

There were a couple of centimeters of clean snow on the balcony, but he'd need a pot in which to boil and sterilize the water. Fortunately for James, few of Aero City's former residents owned cars and many had been forced to leave their heaviest and least valuable possessions behind. A tour of a few apartments was all he needed to find a couple of battered pots, an enamel beaker that would serve as a makeshift cup, the wire mesh from a grill tray, and even a plastic office chair to sit on.

James built up the fire in the sink and rested the mesh over the top before stepping out onto the balcony. After checking that there was nobody down below, he began scooping fresh snow into the pot until it was almost full. Back inside, he set it down over the flames.

His next task was to capture the birds. His mind flashed back to basic training and Mr. Large telling him that pigeons are basically stupid and much easier to catch than fish or mammals. They only have two states of mind. The first is *oh my god something's coming let's fly away* and the second is *everything's fine*. If you want to catch a pigeon, all you have to do is make it believe that everything's fine and it will practically walk into the cooking pot.

While his pot of snow melted, James raced upstairs to the pigeon-infested sixth floor, clutching his penknife and the large pot. The balcony was encrusted with bird lime and feathers. Naturally, the pigeons flew away when James came near them, but he crouched down with his back to the wall and stayed deadly still.

Within seconds, the birds forgot that James existed and began strolling around him as if he weren't there. When the first one came within a few centimeters of his hand, James reached out and grabbed it, before snapping its neck and dumping it in the pot. The sudden movement caused the birds to flutter, but within another minute they were all pecking away at James's feet and within ten he had five pigeons in his pot.

Back downstairs, he found the bathroom smoky but warm and the snow melting over the flames. He began preparing the pigeons by slitting their throats and letting the blood drain into the bath tub.

The first animal James had ever cleaned and cooked had been a freshly shot squirrel during basic training. Pushing his hands inside to pull out the guts and the warm blood sticking to his fingers as he stripped away the pelt had made him feel sick. He'd wondered when such a skill would be useful to an undercover agent in the twenty-first century, but he appreciated the knowledge now as he expertly skinned and gutted each bird with his penknife, before snapping its ribcage to turn each one into a flattened slice that would cook evenly on the small fire.

James fed the fire as he worked and by the time the pigeons were prepared he had a saucepan of boiling water. Placing the pigeons on the grill, he headed out to the balcony and washed his bloody hands with snow, before coming back inside and rubbing them with vodka to sterilize them.

After flipping the meat with a stick, James sat on the plastic chair, poured water into the beaker and took three gulps, before cupping it under his chin and enjoying the steam rising toward his face.

This was his first moment of reasonable comfort since he'd been rudely awakened eight hours earlier. But it only served to remind James of his precarious situation: He was a long way from home and had never felt more alone in his life.

CHAPTER 8

DIDDLEYBOMBBOMB

Lauren and Kerry felt weird as they faced each other across a table in the campus dining room. Kerry had a lesson but couldn't face it. They didn't want to be alone, but at the same time they both felt awkward, sitting together and wondering what to say.

Rumors were the only things that spread around CHERUB campus faster than germs. By lunchtime, everyone seemed to know that James was missing. The two girls felt radioactive, as friends offered their sympathy in gentle voices, before sitting as far away from them as they could.

Lauren was supposed to play basketball and Kerry was scheduled to go into town with her friends, but neither girl felt like it. They went back to Kerry's room and somehow ended up spending their Saturday afternoon playing Scrabble with Rat and Kerry's mate Gabrielle to pass the time.

Reasonably warmed and fed, James moved out of the apartment as soon as the sky darkened. The electricity was back on and he knew that his orange jacket and gloves made him conspicuous in the city center.

He'd spent much of the day wondering about the best way to get a mobile phone. He'd considered breaking into an empty apartment in one of the city's wealthier areas, but these tended to be well policed. Besides, there were few landlines around and people generally took mobiles with them when they went out.

He thought about simply walking up to someone and asking to borrow their phone, but it would mean showing his face in a public area, and in an impoverished and crime-ridden city the chances of anyone willingly handing their mobile to a well-built teenager who looked like he'd spent a night sleeping rough weren't good.

James realized that he was going to have to mug someone. It wasn't going to be nice for his victim, but it would be a tea party compared with what might happen if Obidin's men got hold of him.

The gray streets of Aero City were about as far from thriving as you can get, but there were a couple of lively streets in the center of town where the kind of people who could afford mobile phones shopped, ate, and danced the night away inside the city's only nightclub. But these businesses were mostly owned by Denis Obidin's family and the area always crawled with cops.

James decided to pick his victim at the city discount store instead. The large metal shed was one of the few things to have been built in Aero City within the last ten years. He'd been there a few times with Boris and Isla and found it stuffed with everything from Chinese-made tracksuits through to canned food and cheap power tools.

There was a large parking lot, but few people owned cars and most shoppers walked their purchases a few kilometers through the snow in bags or shopping carts. James sat on a low wall at the edge of the lot and staked out the entrance. He needed a customer who was alone and looked wealthy enough to own a mobile. At the same time, he tried not to attract the attention of a gang of tough-looking teenagers who were using a desolate area of the lot as a skate park.

James wasn't exactly God's gift to skateboarding. He'd made an arse of himself on the few occasions when he'd mounted a board, and he was impressed by their display—especially when you considered that they were performing on snow and ice, with nothing but hoodies for protection.

After watching endless pensioners and harassed, impoverished stroller-pushers, James noticed a young woman coming through the automatic doors holding a giant carrier bag with a set of pillows crammed inside. She looked about nineteen and wore tight jeans, black leather boots, and a fur hat. But it wasn't the kind of cheapo fur hat that all the old grannies wore and her brown leather bag had clearly come from some fancy Moscow boutique. It was definitely the kind of bag that had a mobile inside it.

Relieved that she didn't head toward a car, James waited until the woman was on the unlit street alongside the giant store before standing up to go after her.

"Careful, arsehole," one of the skateboarders yelled, as James almost knocked him flying. He'd been concentrating on the woman and hadn't noticed the board clattering toward him.

As the first boarder struggled to keep his balance after swerving, another lad jumped off his board, pulled a flick-knife out of his jeans, and flashed it under James's nose.

"You want trouble?" the lad grinned.

He was smaller than James, but felt confident with a knife in his hand and his mates covering his back.

James backed away and raised his hands. "Sorry."

He stuck to a single word, because the kids might have heard that the cops were looking for an English boy and his accent was a giveaway.

The kid who'd swerved was seventeen or eighteen and he'd circled back toward James, kicked his board up into his hands, and was swaggering toward him.

"This is our space, *idiot*," the big lad spat, puffing up his chest and bunching up his fists.

"Sorry," James said again, as he backed up farther and turned his head quickly to see if his target was still in sight.

The skateboarders all laughed as he backed away.

"He's pissing his pants."

"If we see you around here again, we'll cut you up."

But James didn't give a damn about their attempts to bruise his ego. He wanted the girl, or at least the phone he hoped to find inside her expensive leather bag.

After leaving the parking lot, James took a couple of quick double steps to catch up with his target. She turned left behind the discount store into a wide street with a building site on one side. A faded sign said that 55,000 square meters of shops and office space would be ready by the end of 1998, but the grand scheme had only risen half a story.

The young woman stuck her arm out to hail a passing taxi, but the driver was on his way to another call and didn't pull over. After recovering from the shock of almost seeing his target escape, James realized that it was another good sign: Poor people didn't take taxis.

But there would be another cab along in a minute and the chances were it would stop. James had to act fast. There was no one up ahead or across the street, and he checked over his shoulder to make sure nobody was behind. An elderly man was crossing the road, but he wasn't going to be any kind of problem.

The woman heard James run at her, but only managed two steps before he bundled her into the back wall of the store. She swung out harmlessly with the pillows and kicked him with the point of her leather boot, but James was too strong.

He pinned her to the cinderblock wall and grabbed the bag from her shoulder as she twisted and spat. He'd hoped to be able to snatch the bag easily and run off without doing the woman any harm, but she screamed and clutched at the handle as James tried to take it.

"Let go or I'll hurt you."

"My boyfriend will *kill* you," she snarled. "Do you know who he is?"

James didn't know who he was, but the people who counted in Aero City were drug dealers, money lenders, or cronies of Denis Obidin. Whoever he was, James didn't have time to mess about. Finally losing his patience, he grabbed the woman's neck, slapped her in the mouth, and gave her a shove. She ended up sprawled in the snow with a split lip.

James guiltily snatched the bag and was relieved to see a purse and girly pink phone inside. It was an odd-looking device, branded with the name of the local cellular company.

He stuffed the purse inside his jacket and couldn't resist glancing at the phone's status: two thirds battery, four out of five signal bars. He felt like a six-year-old looking at a big stack of presents on Christmas morning.

He was tempted to dial straightaway, but it didn't seem like a good idea with a fair bit of traffic around and a woman bleeding on the ground in front of him. After running for a few hundred meters, James cut down to a brisk walk to avoid suspicion.

Once in a while he checked the phone and noticed that the reception was getting weaker as he moved farther from the city center. After a kilometer and a half, he cut into an unlit alleyway that ran between two abandoned office buildings.

The phone lit his face with an amber glow as he dialed the 0044 for the UK, but all he got was a KEYPAD LOCKED message on the display. Frustrated, he tried different combinations to unlock it: star followed by hash, like you did on a Nokia; holding down the number nine; holding down the zero; but he got the same message every time.

After two minutes' fumbling, James took a calming breath and studied each key in turn.

"Stupid *poxy* phone," he growled.

He considered taking the battery out and restarting the phone, but he'd be completely stuffed if the phone asked for a pin number when he switched it back on. Then he noticed that his thumb had been covering a little button on the side with a picture of a padlock on it.

After holding it in for three seconds, the phone chimed and KEYPAD ACTIVE appeared on the screen. James felt triumphant as he started dialing—but then he noticed shadows at the end of the alleyway.

They were on top of James before he had turned his head. The first thing he felt was a skateboard smashing him full in the face with enough force to knock the back of his head against the wall behind him. As he raised his arms to shield the next blow, a sneaker plunged into his guts and was followed by a wall of bodies shoving him backward onto the concrete and stomping him.

"English boy," one of them chanted.

James reached for his gun, but before he knew what was happening, his arms were pinned to his side and a big dude straddled him and punched him repeatedly in the face. It was the guy he'd almost knocked off the skateboard.

"English boy," he repeated, before spitting a massive loogie in James's eye.

James thought he'd have half a chance of getting to his gun when the dude stood up, but the skateboarder had felt it pressing into his thigh while he was pounding

James. He ripped it from James's waistband as he stood up, then aimed the gun down at him before savagely kicking him in the balls.

The five skateboarders laughed as James doubled over in pain and spat out a mouthful of blood.

The youngest kid there looked about twelve and he'd picked up the mobile phone. "Let's call the cops." He grinned. "How much is twenty-five thousand split five ways?"

"Math not your strong point?" an older skateboarder giggled.

But the big guy with the gun pointing at James snatched the phone from the little kid and didn't sound so happy. "Don't be thick all your life. If we call the cops, they'll rip us off."

Another skateboarder nodded. "They'll beat the shit out of us and keep the reward themselves."

James looked around for a way out, but the alley was a dead end and the big dude had the gun pointing right at him. He hurt all over and felt stupid for letting himself get jumped by a bunch of teenagers.

"So what *do* we do, Joe?" the little skateboarder asked anxiously.

"Shut up and let me think," Joe said, as he looked down the barrel of the gun at James.

"Let me use the phone," James said pathetically. "I know people. They'll double your reward, I swear."

Joe shook his head with contempt. "Yeah," he tutted. "You look so rich."

He started dialing.

"Who are you calling, Joe?"

"The hotline number they put out on the radio this morning."

"Can you remember it?"

"Triple eight, triple eight," Joe said. "What's to remember?"

The freezing snow was melting into James's clothes and his face was covered in blood. His stomach churned with pure terror. This might really be the end of the line. He'd never get back to campus, he'd never see Lauren or Kerry, he'd never see Arsenal score another goal, or do homework, or take a shit, or any of a million other mundane things that flashed through his mind. Within an hour he'd be locked in some basement cell with a couple of Obidin's goons torturing him until he told them whatever they wanted to hear. . . .

"Hello," Joe shouted into the phone. "Are you the dude from the mayor's office that was on the radio . . . ? Cool . . . Listen, I've got the English kid. Before I tell you where we're at, I want to be sure that we'll get the reward straightaway. Cash on delivery . . . Okay, cool . . . We're over on the east side, street sixteen, near where the cinema used to be . . . Yeah he's alive. I had to beat the shit out of him, but he's just about conscious. . . . So how long roughly . . . ? Right, we'll be waiting."

CHAPTER 9

UNCLE

Barely ten minutes later, a man stepped out of a blinged-up 4×4, with fancy alloys and blacked-out windows.

"Twenty-five thousand," the man smiled as he waved five hundred pounds' worth of Russian currency in the air. James recognized the voice. It was Slava, the dude he used to chat to on the gate of the Obidin compound.

Joe looked happy; his four younger companions like it was too good to be true.

"I want you boys to do me a favor," Slava said seriously. "Divide the money evenly, take it home and keep your mouths *shut*. You go showing that much cash around, you'll get robbed."

"Wise words, boss," Joe nodded.

James had managed to sit up against the wall of the alleyway. He hurt in twenty different places, his jeans were soaked in melted snow, and he was shivering badly.

"What did you hit him with, a steamroller?" Slava grinned, as he stepped up to James and pulled a set of handcuffs out of his jacket. "On your feet, boy."

Not wanting another beating, James tried standing up. But he only managed to prop himself on one knee before he felt faint and slumped back against the wall. As James made a second attempt, Joe grabbed his arm and yanked him up. Slava jerked James around to face the wall and locked the cuffs behind his back.

"You boys help me walk him to the car," Slava said. "Then you'd better clear out of here."

Joe nodded eagerly. "My name's Josef Novosi, sir. Do you think you could put in a word for me? Maybe get me some work with Mr. Obidin? I'm real strong. I did wrestling and gymnastics when I was younger; won medals and everything."

Slava shrugged. "Things are mental after last night, but I'm sure the Obidin family will appreciate what you've done, so I'll see what I can do."

"Thank you," Joe gushed.

One of the younger skateboarders opened up the 4×4, enabling Joe and Slava to bundle James across the backseat. He got a face full of leather smell and warm air, but pain erupted across his face as his nose hit the seat cushion. James reckoned the first whack with the skateboard had broken it.

Seconds later, he heard Slava getting in the front, clicking on his seat belt, and starting the engine. The potholed roads made James's aching head bounce. Slava spoke as James struggled to sit himself up.

"So why did MI5 decide to kill Denis Obidin?"

"What are you talking about?" James mumbled, as it occurred to him that Slava had spoken in English, with an American accent.

"They killed him, James old boy."

James was covered in blood, his head was thumping, and he had a splitting pain in the bridge of his nose. It was hard to think straight, and he decided it would be best to keep his trap shut.

"How's your sister Lauren doing these days?" Slava continued. "Is John Jones your mission controller on this one, or someone else?"

James was stunned. Slava knew about CHERUB, which was *impossible*.

"My handle's Eric Partridge," Slava continued cockily, as he took a sharp turn. "I'm with the CIA weapons proliferation unit. Spent most of the last four years infiltrating Obidin's organization. I've gotta admire the balls of you Brits though: No messing about, you just send a couple of dudes in, set up a meeting, and kill the top dog."

James suddenly wanted to say a few things, but all he could manage was a shake of the head and a few mumbled words. "How come . . . You . . . My sister?"

Slava—or rather Eric Partridge—cracked into a big smile. "I've been on Obidin's security team these past eighteen months. Been all around that big house planting bugs. Obidin had his own video surveillance system installed and we've tapped into that too.

"A couple of weeks back, my colleagues in Washington

DC started picking up interference when they were transcribing the recordings from our bugs. The boffins told us it was crosstalk: two coded listening devices of a similar type interfering with each other.

"So I checked the security cameras to see if there were any new faces inside the compound. Would you believe that the interference started the first day that you turned up to give little Mark Obidin an English lesson?

"I had one of my field operatives follow you back to your apartment. He poked around inside the next day when you were at school. Picked a few hairs off pillows and took swabs from your toothbrushes. We sent them back to our DNA lab and the damnedest thing happened: Uncle Boris and Auntie Isla drew blanks, but your DNA brought up a match to a highly classified file. Took us more than a week to get access. The request had to be approved by the heads of the CIA and the FBI."

"What file?" James muttered as his fuzzy head struggled to grasp what he was hearing.

"You're quite a kid, James. When they finally gave me clearance, your file had all the details of your mission in Arizona two years back: busting out of Arizona Maximum Security Prison, driving across three states with the cops on your tail, and catching Jane Oxford. File said that you're part of some limey child spy unit known as CHERUB. I tell you, when I heard about that it pretty much blew my mind."

James realized that he'd got lucky. The Yanks might not be too happy that his mission had trodden on their toes, but they were unlikely to set upon him with a blow lamp.

"How'd you get to me first?"

"Took a bit of quick thinking, but it wasn't too hard," Eric smiled. "Vladimir Obidin is a tyrant. His men are terrified of him. I suggested we offer a reward and set up a radio broadcast, then started organizing the search. Everyone was happy for me to stick my neck out and get it chopped if things went wrong."

"Where now?" James mumbled.

"I've got a safe house on the edge of the city. We'll head back there. You can wash up, put on a set of clean clothes; you look pretty messed up, so I'll take a proper look at your injuries."

"Won't you be compromised?" James asked.

"Sure," Eric nodded. "Those kids will splash their roubles around and shout off their mouths. People will find out that they put you into my hands and I'll be in as much trouble as you. But I'm not working alone. We have other agents in place who'll keep going after the Obidins, at least the ones you Brits didn't decide to assassinate. My job was to get hold of you before the Obidins and find out what the *hell* you lot were playing at."

James shook his head. "Wasn't assassination," he said wearily. "They were setting up a deal to buy missiles."

Eric turned away from the road and shot James an angry glance. "I saved your butt, kid. If you ain't straight with me, I might just turn back and dump you in the snow."

"They can't have," James mumbled.

"James, I *know* that part of the story. I've got the whole freaking incident in glorious black and white."

CHAPTER 10

BLOOD

The safe house was a ground-floor apartment in one of Aero City's better housing blocks. TV shows and cooking smells drifted in from the neighboring homes, but the plumbing worked well enough for James to take a shower.

Eric told James not to lock the bathroom door in case he collapsed. Once James had washed the worst of the blood off, Eric helped him into a bathrobe and led him toward a double bed. There was an desk lamp on the bedside table and Eric swung it over James and began attending to his cuts and bruises.

The shower had cleared James's head and washed away a lot of blood, but he was still in serious pain, particularly his face, stomach, and balls.

"Do you reckon my nose is busted?" he asked.

Eric was cleaning out a deep cut on his shoulder. "Look for yourself," he said, and he slid a hand mirror across the bedclothes.

James gasped as he saw his crumpled nose and swollen eyes. "If I see that Joe again, I'll kill him."

"You'll have to stay awake for at least twenty-four hours. If you fall asleep, there's a chance you could drift into a coma. I'm also concerned about the cut above your left eye. I'll have to put a stitch in it."

"Are you a doctor?"

Eric shook his head. "I was an army medic. I've got local anaesthetic here, but I'm reluctant to give you anything that makes you drowsy after the knock you took to the head."

"So how can you stitch me?"

"I'll give you something to bite down on."

James gawped. "Maybe if it was my leg or something, but you can't stitch my *face* without anaesthetic."

"I can give you a couple of paracetamol if you like."

"What's that gonna do?"

"Not much," Eric shrugged. "Sorry, kid, but your T-shirt and jeans were drenched in blood. You've lost a pint, maybe two. If you were in a hospital you'd get a transfusion, but all I can do here is get those cuts sealed up before you lose more blood and pass out."

James felt sick as he saw Eric tear a pre-threaded needle out of sterile packaging.

"Put this in your mouth," he said, as he handed James a rubber bit.

James put the rubber in his mouth, clenched his hands, and screwed up his eyes.

"Keep 'em open. I can't sew the cut if the skin is pulled apart."

James thought he was going to be sick as he opened his eyes. His vision was blurry, but he could see the needle as it pierced the swollen flesh above his eye.

"AAAAAAGGHHHHHHHHH," he moaned.

"Keep the noise down and your head still," Eric said firmly. "This is *nothing*: An old buddy of mine was out in the Gulf, got trapped under a tank track, and we had to take his arm off with a fire axe."

James bit down hard and bunched the sheets up in his fists as the needle pierced his eyebrow for the second time. Maybe having your arm hacked off was worse, but he found it hard to imagine how anything could be more painful.

"Good man," Eric smiled as he tied the fourth stitch off and snipped the thread.

James groaned with relief, but then Eric started untying his dressing gown. "What the *hell*?"

"You said you got kicked in the balls. So spread your legs, I need to take a proper look."

"They're fine," James spluttered.

"If your testicle has ruptured, I need to drain the fluid. And believe me, James, I don't wanna be poking about down there any more than you want me to."

An hour later, James sat in an armchair. His cuts were all patched, his balls were only bruised, and he'd managed to drink a couple of glasses of orange juice and eat some canned spaghetti. His vision was less blurry, but his body ached all over from the beating, and his headache and the pain around his eyes and nose had got worse as the swelling increased.

Eric kept asking James questions and it was getting on his nerves. He just wanted to sleep.

"Here you go," Eric said, as he placed a nifty little computer on James's lap. "Try looking me in the eye and saying they weren't out to kill Denis after you've watched this."

James stared at a grainy image of Denis Obidin's study. He used the finger pad to scroll up to the screen and clicked on the mouse button to play the video clip.

The timecode in the corner of the screen indicated that the recording had been made at one o'clock that morning. Denis Obidin sat behind his desk, puffing a cigar while partaking in a jovial conversation with Boris and Isla, who had their backs to the camera.

After a round of laughs, Boris stood up to shake Denis's outstretched hand. James's mouth dropped open as he watched Boris grasp the hand and jerk Denis forward. Isla leapt out of her seat with a length of wire stretched between her hands. As Boris placed his hand over Denis Obidin's mouth, Isla stepped around the desk and wrapped the wire around his throat.

"I-I . . . ," James stuttered. "*Jesus.*"

Within half a minute, Denis was slumped across his desk, unconscious. While Isla kept the wire tight to make sure he was dead, Boris ran to the back of the room and unhitched a large picture frame. He then produced a penknife and used the blade to lever open a metal door built into the wall behind it.

"What's going on?" James asked.

Eric explained. "We have no idea how Boris and Isla found this, but it looks as if Obidin had an emergency escape system built into his house."

"Did you CIA guys know it existed?"

Eric shook his head. "But we suspected. Kidnappings and hostage situations go down all the time in these parts. Wealthy Russians commonly build panic rooms and escape systems into their homes."

James was in a state of shock. "I didn't know squat about this," he said, shaking his head. "I swear on my life."

He watched as Isla and Boris clambered through the escape hatch, leaving behind a static image of Denis Obidin slumped dead across his desk.

"So Boris and Isla got away?" James asked.

"They might have if not for some bad luck. Fast forward about a minute and you'll see."

James clicked on the double fast-forward arrow and watched the timecode in the bottom of the picture advance rapidly, until he saw the door of the study come open. He had to roll back slightly to catch it from the start.

"Your little pal had a bad dream," Eric explained.

James watched as six-year-old Mark Obidin strolled into the room, dressed in Batman pajamas and fur-lined slippers. He walked up to his father and tapped him on the arm, then looked a little confused as he noticed a small pool of blood on the desk where the wire had cut into his skin. The little lad spun around and screamed his head off as he raced out of the room.

Within seconds, Vladimir and two other men burst

in. As Vladimir grabbed the phone off his brother's desk, the other men clambered into the escape hatch after Boris and Isla.

"So MI5's little plan went wrong," Eric smiled. "Boris and Isla knew they'd be searched and hadn't been able to take guns into Obidin's house. They were dead duckies when the guards caught up with them."

James was stunned. So stunned that he almost forgot how much pain he was in.

"This . . . I was told that they were going to the meeting to negotiate a weapons deal."

"Why should I believe that?" Eric shot back.

"CHERUB *doesn't* go around assassinating people. And . . . And besides, do you think I would have sat in the apartment and fallen asleep knowing that Vladimir would be coming after us?"

The mix of pain and excitement made it hard to think straight, but one little detail came clear in James's head: he remembered Isla carrying the large case out to the car when they left the apartment.

"Boris and Isla might have escaped, but they must have known Vladimir would send men to the flat to grab *me*. They stitched me up. They walked out of that flat expecting that I'd be caught and tortured. I'm *glad* those bastards are dead."

"Nice story," Eric said, sounding like he wasn't quite ready to believe James's explanation.

James pointed at the laptop screen. "Give me one good reason why I'd sit around and wait for Vladimir Obidin to turn up?"

Eric smiled. "I have to admit, I've thought long and

hard about that and I haven't been able to think up a single convincing explanation, except that you'd been stitched up by a couple of rogue agents."

"I could have died," James said, shaking his head slowly.

"I reckon it's only down to your training and a healthy glob of luck that you didn't," Eric said, as he grabbed the computer off James's lap and snapped it shut. "And a helping hand from yours truly, of course."

Eric slid the laptop into a nylon pouch and came back to James holding a chunky satellite phone. Whereas a normal mobile requires local relay stations to work, satellite phones beam their signals into space and work anywhere in the world.

"I believe you wanted to make a call, young man."

James raised a tiny smile as he grabbed the phone. "Are you getting me out of here, or what?"

"The smart money's on what, I'm afraid," Eric said. "Within a few hours they'll have missed me back at the Obidin compound and someone will be out looking for me. My bags are packed, I'm driving to Moscow, and getting on the first flight back to the good ol' USA. I'm happy to be out of this, to be honest with you. I haven't seen my girls in near two years."

"Can't I come with you?" James asked.

"There's only one road out of town. It's lightly trafficked and the police are searching everyone. If they shine a flashlight in my car and see you in that state, we're both as good as dead."

"I thought you were helping me," James said, as he got the horrible feeling that he was back on his own.

"You're not my problem, kid," Eric shrugged. "I pulled you out and patched you up because I wanted to hear what you had to say. Your people have caused us a *lot* of trouble. I've done you a favor, but it's up to your MI5 chums to get you out of here. You Brits have that big jet-engine contract with Obidin. There might only be one road out of Aero City, but there are more than a dozen runways in town."

"I guess," James said.

"We won't be needing this apartment. You can stay here as long as you like. Keep drinking strong coffee and moving around. There's enough tinned food to last a month and there's fresh clothes in all sizes in the wardrobe. Whatever you do, *don't* fall asleep. I know you're coming round a bit now, but you could still lapse into a coma."

Eric grabbed his overcoat from the bedpost. "I'm taking the phone, so you'd better make that call."

James blinked a few times to clear his blurry vision before dialing the CHERUB campus emergency number.

A man with a Birmingham accent answered. "Unicorn Tire Repair."

"This is agent twelve-o-three," James said. "Can you put me through to Ewart Asker?"

The man sounded elated. "James, is that you? We've got a grade one missing agent alert out on you. Are you okay?"

"Snot and blood all over the joint," James said dryly. "But I seem to be alive."

CHAPTER 11

GLOOM

Lauren decided that she felt like being alone and went back to her room. She was sprawled over her bed with the soccer results coming out of her TV when her mobile rang. She guessed it was Bethany, who was playing in a basketball tournament off campus. She'd been calling between matches to see if there had been any news.

"Yep," Lauren answered, as she flipped her phone open.

"The emergency desk just got a call," Zara said happily. "It sounds like he's been badly beaten up, but he's alive."

"Oh thank *God*." Lauren leapt off her bed as tears welled up in her eyes. "That's *so* brilliant. Where's he been?"

"I don't have full details yet, but he's in Aero City and Ewart is on his way to pick him up."

"Can I speak to James later?"

"Maybe . . . Ewart has a satellite phone with him, so we can probably sort something out. But they're not completely out of the woods. The police are searching every car that leaves Aero City, so they're planning to smuggle him out via a small airstrip."

"But he'll be okay?"

"You can never be one hundred percent, but we know he's alive and he's being looked after."

"I feel like a massive weight got lifted off," Lauren grinned.

"Great," Zara said. "Now I've got some phone calls to make. Can I rely on you to tell Kerry and anyone else who might be worried?"

"No problem," Lauren said cheerfully. "I'll go right now."

She snapped her phone shut and ran out into the corridor. "Rat!" she screamed as she banged on his door, which was near the elevators at the far end of the eighth floor. "I got a call. He's okay."

Rat emerged and chased Lauren downstairs to the sixth floor, where Kerry and most of James's mates lived.

"Kerry, Kerry, Kerry," Lauren yelled as she ran onto the sixth floor and almost splattered James's mate Bruce against the wall.

"They found him?" Bruce grinned.

"Beaten up, but sounds like he's okay," Rat explained, as Lauren charged into Kerry's room.

She was surprised to find the room was empty, then noticed that the bathroom door was locked.

"He's all right," Lauren yelled, as she pounded on the door.

Kerry unbolted the door and pulled Lauren into a tight hug.

"I don't think I could have handled it if he'd been killed," Kerry sniffled.

Lauren wiped a tear from her face. "What's the betting that we'll both be back to yelling at him in a week's time?"

A Nissan Almera pulled up at a striped barrier. It was close to midnight and Aero City's power had failed for the second night running, but the corrugated metal hangar in front of the car was surrounded by security lights that were powered by a generator inside the airfield.

Ewart wound down the driver's side window and spoke to the security guard in bad Russian. "I'm Mr. Newman. They're expecting me."

The guard looked disinterested as he pressed the button to raise the gate. The front of the hangar was painted with the words *Hilton Aerospace* in three-meter-high letters. Ewart looked over onto the rear seat.

"Don't fall asleep back there," he said.

The clogged sinuses inside James's broken nose were giving him the worst headache of his life, and the clean shirt and tracksuit pants he'd taken from the CIA safe house were sticking to the partly formed scabs on his skin. He peeked out from under a blanket and spoke sourly. "I *know*; I'm not an idiot."

As they drove up to the hangar, a shaft of light appeared between its giant doors, wide enough for Ewart to drive through. A huge man in an coverall with a Hilton Aerospace logo on it shook Ewart's hand as he stepped out.

"Thanks for helping out at such short notice, Mr. Edwards," Ewart said.

"No problem—and call me Craig," the man smiled, as Ewart stared at the faded skull and crossbones tattoo on the back of Craig's hand. "Always happy to help a fellow Brit out of a tight spot. That's my missus, Irene, by the way."

Irene wore an identical coverall to her husband as she rolled a shabby wheelchair up to the rear of the car and opened the door beside James.

"I can walk okay," James said, as he sat up.

The woman shook her head, before speaking with a London accent. "The jet is coming in to land on runway two. It's over a kilometer along the taxiway, you're all beat up, and it's an ice rink out there."

"So what's our escape plan?" James asked, as he lowered his aching body into the chair.

Craig explained. "We wheel you out to the edge of the runway as the plane comes in. You and Ewart climb aboard the second it stops moving, the pilot does a one-hundred-and-eighty-degree turn, powers up, and she'll be back in the air within three minutes of touchdown."

"What about the flight plan?" James asked. "Won't Obidin's people know the jet is coming?"

"We've logged a flight plan for a Hilton Aerospace cargo plane to land at our regular airfield across town, but the pilot will divert here at the last minute. We've had cops sniffing around and searching our containers over there all day. We used to use this airfield when a big jet came in to have its engines serviced, but Obidin lost that contract and it's all done in Britain now."

"And the outgoing flight?" Ewart asked. "I assume we're not gonna get shot down by a couple of MiGs."

Craig shook his head. "The pilot will stay away from controlled airspace. If air traffic control does pick us up for any reason, she'll just claim that our office forgot to file the flight plan. That's no biggie: Private jets and the smaller Russian airlines use that excuse all the time."

"What's the latest on the arrival time for our jet?" Ewart asked, as Irene grabbed the blanket out of the car and wrapped it over James like a shawl.

Craig looked at his watch. "There's enough time for a brew, I reckon. Then you'd better head out toward the runway."

The hangar was mainly used by British mechanics doing repairs on airliner engines, and the walls were adorned with pinup girls and football posters. James felt a touch homesick as he dunked fruit shortcakes in his mug of tea. By the time he'd drunk half, he could hear the distant roar of his ride home.

"Better get our skates on," Ewart said, as he grabbed a small briefcase and laid it across James's lap.

James shook the Edwardses' hands and thanked them for their help, before Ewart wheeled him toward the gap in the hangar doors. They stepped into the night air and a gentle drizzle dusted James's face as he spotted the flashing wing lights of a corporate jet amid the stars.

"Oh, Christ," Ewart spat, as he looked toward the gate.

James snapped his head around and spotted a Japanese

pickup truck with blue lights on the top. "It's not my week," he said, shaking his head. "You reckon that guard tipped them off?"

He didn't get an answer because Ewart had run back inside the hangar. He reemerged with Craig and Irene, as James popped the catches of the briefcase on his lap.

"I could try holding them off," Craig said uncertainly.

Ewart shook his head. "We've got an eight-seat jet, you two will have to come with us."

"We *live* here," Irene protested. "We haven't got our passports or anything."

"If me and James get away, they'll arrest, torture, and quite possibly kill you," Ewart explained bluntly. "Start wheeling James toward the runway, I'll deal with these guys."

The security barrier went up as Ewart opened the briefcase. He pulled out a Glock 9mm automatic pistol and a stun gun.

Craig looked at Ewart. "You want help? I was SBS1 before I was MI5."

Ewart smiled as he handed Craig the Glock and a spare ammunition clip. "Navy man, eh? That's nice to hear. I'll go for the subtle approach. If things mess up, start shooting, head for the plane, and don't worry about me."

Irene snorted involuntarily, close to tears.

"We'll be okay, love," Craig said firmly. "You start pushing James. We'll be half a minute behind."

As Irene began the tricky task of wheeling the chair across the icy taxiway, James tried to reassure her. "Your husband's ex-SBS and Ewart has done similar training. Street cops will be totally outclassed."

Irene shook her head as the wheelchair gathered momentum. "I *knew* he was in the Navy, but I only found out that he had links with MI5 when Ewart turned up on our doorstep at lunchtime. Now I'm wheeling a fugitive toward a runway and Craig's waving a gun around . . ."

James smiled. "Not what you expected when you got out of bed this morning."

"Too bloody right. So how come you're all tangled up in this mess? Doesn't look like you're even shaving yet."

"I don't mean to be rude, Irene, but my brain's not up to spinning a lie and it's better for both of us if I don't tell the truth."

As the jet skimmed the chain-link fence at the airfield's perimeter, Ewart strode confidently toward the pickup. He spoke to the driver in his dreadful Russian. "Good evening, officers, is there a problem?"

"I think there is." The driver smiled, pointing up toward the jet. "I've never seen a flight come down here at this time of night before and my friend on the gate says he's never seen *you* either."

Ewart heard a second police car pulling up at the barrier as he tried to reassure the two policemen. "Hilton Aerospace. It's our regular cargo flight."

"No flight plan, no runway lights," the cop said, raising a single eyebrow to show that he didn't believe a word. "Maybe I'm Clint Eastwood and you're the Easter bunny."

"Evening, boys!" Craig boomed, surprising Ewart and the cops as he grabbed the door handle on the passenger side of the pickup. He ripped the door open and punched the cop out with his massive fist before dragging him into the snow.

Ewart realized that Craig had made a smart move: They had to take out the cops in the first vehicle before they were outnumbered. As the driver reached for his holster, Ewart pulled the stun gun and gave him fifty thousand volts. He dragged him out onto the tarmac and gave him a right-hander before snatching the cop's gun from its holster.

"Back it up," Craig shouted.

Ewart was surprised to find himself taking rather than giving orders, but Craig clearly knew his stuff. Ewart jumped into the driver's seat, belted up, put the gearbox into reverse and sped backward toward the second police car as it came through the barrier. It was one of the little Russian jobs, and the back end of the pickup reared up over its hood, severing the windshield pillars and concertinaing the roof.

Ewart crunched the pickup back into first gear, but the rear wheels were off the ground and it wouldn't budge from its position mounted on top of the little car. This was a pain: They could have used it to drive up the taxiway. He jumped out of the cab as he was deafened by the passing jet. The pilot had to apply full reverse thrust to slow her craft before it ran out of icy runway.

As aircraft tires squealed, Ewart peered into the little cop car with the pickup driver's pistol in his hands. The sudden reverse had taken the two men inside by surprise and their seat belts had kept them pinned in position as the rear end of the pickup crushed them. It wasn't something you'd want to look at twice.

Ewart looked around for Craig and spotted him smacking the guard's head against the Plexiglas inside the security booth.

"Plane's on the ground, Craig," Ewart shouted. "Let's move."

It was six hundred meters to the runway and the icy ground made it difficult to achieve anything faster than a brisk walk. Up ahead, the co-pilot opened up the small passenger jet and dropped a set of steps as Irene wheeled James alongside.

"Do you need a carry?" the co-pilot asked James, as Irene took off the blanket and helped him to his feet.

James shook his head as he stumbled forward and grabbed the railing at the edge of the steps. "We've got two more coming," he said.

The co-pilot looked surprised. "You were supposed be ready and waiting."

"The police turned up," Irene explained anxiously. "My husband and his companion should be here any second."

As soon as James was inside the cramped jet, he collapsed into the leather chair nearest the door and gasped for breath. The cockpit door was open and the pilot nodded from her position in front of a line of dials and computer screens.

"Hey," James said, smiling with relief.

"What's the delay, kid?"

"Two more coming," James said. He thought about adding *hopefully*, but didn't.

The runway was pitch black and he was alarmed to see two more sets of headlights coming up the narrow road toward the security barrier.

Irene stood out on the pavement, shouting her head off. "Craig, where are you?"

The pilot craned her neck to look backward out of the cockpit, before shouting to the co-pilot. "We've got snow and ice building up on the wing. De-icing is on, but if we don't get off the ground in a minute or two, someone will have to climb up there and give it a scrape."

As James watched the police cars turning through the security barrier, Irene finally heard a shout over the idling jet engines.

"It's Craig," Irene shouted. "They're coming."

But the headlights were coming faster.

"Get inside and pull up the steps," the pilot shouted. "I'm turning ready for takeoff."

The co-pilot practically shoved Irene up the steps. "You can't leave my husband," she begged.

James watched anxiously as the co-pilot grabbed the handrail to raise the steps a few centimeters, so that the pilot could turn the aircraft without them scraping along the ground. A deafening blast of air came through the door as the pilot gave a tiny boost to the right engine, enabling the aircraft to swing a hundred and eighty degrees.

The headlights looked even bigger when James stared out the opposite side of the aircraft, but he still couldn't see Ewart or Craig.

"We're going," the pilot shouted, as she started flicking switches and pressing buttons.

"You can't leave them here," Irene shrieked.

"They've got a gun," the co-pilot said firmly. "That gives them a chance of getting away. We've got three thousand liters of fuel in the wings and an auxiliary tank in the cargo bay. If one bullet hits us we'll go up like a bomb."

As if to emphasise the point, the muzzle of an automatic weapon sparked just outside the aircraft. It hit one of the cars, making it veer off-course. Then something thunked against a carbon fiber panel, almost directly beneath James's seat. After an anxious second, he saw Ewart scrambling to his feet after a dramatic skid under the belly of the aircraft. Ewart grabbed the rail at the bottom of the steps and lunged inside.

"Where's my Craig?" Irene screamed. A second blast of automatic gunfire sounded from somewhere behind the aircraft.

"Pull the steps up," the pilot ordered. "Now."

"Don't you dare," Irene shouted as Ewart scrambled down the aisle and collapsed into a seat at the back.

"I was alongside him till a few seconds ago," Ewart called. "I slid under, Craig ran around behind the tail."

The co-pilot leaned out of the doorway and sighted Craig, lying on the runway just a couple of meters behind the tail. The big man had slipped on the ice, crunched his knee, and was struggling to get up.

"What the *hell* are you doing?" the pilot shouted as the co-pilot jumped down the steps.

James could see the pilot's hands on the throttles, ready to take off the second she pushed them forward. Outside, the nearest car was less than two hundred meters away.

James leaned forward and peered through the door to try to see what was going on. Craig was hopping toward the aircraft with one arm around the co-pilot's back. He was tall enough to grab the railings near the top of the stairs. He pulled up his injured legs and swung himself into the aircraft. The co-pilot tripped over Craig as he came inside and sprawled across the cabin.

The pilot looked at James and screamed: "Get the door!"

Sheer terror gave James the strength to reach over the two men and grab the metal lever that retracted the steps. The pilot hit the throttles as soon as the steps were off the ground, and James had to grab hold of a handrail above the door to stop the blast of air from knocking him back.

A siren sounded in the cockpit and a voice warning blared out of a speaker above James's head. "*Danger, main door improperly secured. Danger, main door improperly secured . . .*"

Craig crawled along the aisle and the co-pilot got back to his feet as a hydraulically assisted bolt locked the door into place. The red warning light went out, replaced by a reassuring green bar with DOOR SECURED written across it.

James clicked his seat belt on as the co-pilot scrambled into the cockpit, but a quick glance out of the far side window showed him that the excitement wasn't over. The car that Craig had shot off-course was coming along-side them and the cop in the passenger seat was aiming a pistol. He remembered what the pilot said about a single stray bullet blowing the whole plane—but the cop only got one shot in before the twin jets gained an edge over the small Russian petrol engine.

The ice on the runway made the takeoff hairy. The pilot was fighting her tail rudder, trying to keep the air-craft from skidding off the runway. All James could see was her hand on the throttles, but her shaking arm and bulging tendons made it clear that this was no routine takeoff.

Then the nose lifted and everything went smooth. Everyone in the aircraft let out a collective gasp. James looked around and saw Craig, with ripped pants and a bloody gash over his knee, belting up in the leather seat behind him.

James peered out of his window and looked back at Aero City. There were a few cars moving along the roads and odd glimmers of light from buildings with their own generators. He felt relieved for about ten seconds, then his ears popped and his sinuses exploded with pain.

CHAPTER 12

NURSE

James opened his eyes slowly. It took a couple of blinks for his surroundings to come into focus. He was in a hospital bed. The back of his throat felt like it had been scoured and he had a tube up his nose, electrodes wired to his chest, a drip in his arm, and a port taped to the back of his hand for injections. He felt hungry and needed to pee *really* bad. Then he raised his head slightly and noticed Lauren.

"Hey," James croaked, as he watched his sister breaking into a giant smile.

"Kerry," Lauren yelled happily over her shoulder. "He's awake!"

"Where am I?"

"East Side military hospital, near campus," Lauren explained, as Kerry's boots squeaked toward the bed. She had her winter jacket and gloves on, as if she'd been about to leave.

"I'll fetch the nurse," Kerry said, before dashing off again.

James tried to sit up, but Lauren sat on the edge of the bed and pushed him down gently.

"You'll pull your tubes out."

"But I'm busting," James explained.

"Just go," Lauren said gently. "You're all wired up down there."

"Eh?"

"With a catheter and a bag."

James shuddered. He knew that catheters are inserted into the penis, and while he had no memory of it going in, he immediately realized that he'd have to endure the painful procedure of it being yanked out at some point in the future.

Even with covers over him, James felt weird having Lauren sitting next to him as the high-ceilinged hospital room echoed with the sound of his pee running into a bag.

"How long have I been here?"

"Since yesterday," Lauren said. "But you were in a hospital in Finland for two days before that."

"You mean, like a coma or something?"

"Not a full-blown coma, but you've been drifting in and out of consciousness. You're groggy now because they gave you a general anaesthetic this morning, before you went down to operating room."

"Operating room?"

"You've got a broken rib. They made a little incision in your chest and pulled out a loose bone fragment. They also did a bit more work on your broken nose while you were under."

"The last thing I remember is shutting the door of an airplane . . . And a bloke with a bloody knee and . . ."

"That was Saturday," Lauren nodded. "It's Wednesday now. You had a blood clot inside your nose. As the plane rose up, the atmospheric pressure dropped, the gas trapped inside your sinuses expanded, and the pain knocked you out. The pilot had to make an emergency landing in Helsinki."

Kerry came back into the ward, followed by a fat nurse. He gave James a huge smile and spoke with a Caribbean accent as he pulled a small flashlight out of his pocket.

"Nice having you back with us, James," he said. "Look at the light and try to follow it with your eyes."

James obediently tracked the narrow beam as it moved in front of his face.

"Great stuff." The nurse smiled as he pushed a few buttons on a monitoring device beside the bed. It hummed as it spat out a length of curled-up paper.

"This looks fine," the nurse said as he studied the figures. "How do you feel?"

James shrugged. "I just feel a bit dull, like I'm all wrapped in cotton balls or something."

"Anything else?"

"My nose hurts and I'm *completely* starving."

Lauren looked at the nurse. "Is he okay?"

The nurse nodded reassuringly. "He'll be confused for the next couple of hours. But his heart rate and blood oxygen levels are healthy. Doctor Packard should be here shortly and I expect he'll run a few tests before he's satisfied, but it all looks fine to me."

"Your blood oxygen level was dangerously low when you arrived in Helsinki," Lauren explained. "They were worried that you might have brain damage."

"I'll come back tomorrow," Kerry said, smiling, as the nurse headed out of the room.

"Can't you stay a bit longer?" James asked.

Kerry shook her head. "It's midnight. I was on my way out ten minutes ago. My cab driver will be blowing his top."

"Night then," James said, as Kerry reluctantly headed for the door. Then he turned toward Lauren. "What about you?"

"Nah," she said, shaking her head. "I'll sit with you as long as you like. When you arrived here yesterday I told them that I wasn't leaving the hospital until you did. Zara got cross with me, but when . . ." Lauren stopped talking and gave a massive sob. "When . . ."

James reached out from under his sheets and put his hand on Lauren's knee.

"At first, when you were missing I was *so* scared," Lauren sobbed. "Then they found you and I was okay. But then they said about the emergency landing and you were drifting in and out of consciousness and they didn't know how badly injured you were. So when you got back here I . . . I told Zara that the only way I'd leave your side was if they dragged me out kicking and screaming."

James felt his eyes blurring with tears. "Come on, sis, I'm gonna be okay."

"I know we have our own friends and that, James, but you and me are special. We go all the way back to when Mum was alive. I mean, I can remember when I could barely walk and I used to drive you nuts by following you *everywhere*."

If it hadn't been for tubes, bruises, and a complete lack of energy, James would have sat up and hugged her. "Brothers and sisters are weird," he croaked. "Somehow you end up loving each other but making each other crazy at the same time."

CHAPTER 19

BRIEF

Two days after his operation, James was still in the hospital and going stir-crazy. The bruises and swellings were reducing, all of his tubes and sensors had been removed, and he was eating normally and using the toilet down the hall. Lauren agreed to return to campus once she saw that her brother was on the road to recovery, but she still traveled to the hospital after lessons every day, usually accompanied by Kerry and a couple of James's other mates.

The daytime was worst. James watched TV, played on his PSP, and read motorbike magazines, but it did his head in having nobody around, so he was pretty grateful when Ewart and Zara Asker turned up just after he'd eaten lunch.

Zara had smartened up since becoming chairwoman

and sported a gray pinstripe business suit, but Ewart looked the same as ever. Ten years younger than his wife, he wore ripped jeans and a T-shirt with the poster from the 1960s *Planet of the Apes* film on it.

"So what's this in aid of?" James smiled as the couple sank into the green armchairs alongside his bed.

Ewart spoke first. "I've been going through the recordings I made when I interviewed you about the mission yesterday. And—there's no way to sugarcoat this, James—we're really not sure how much of your testimony we can believe."

James was shocked. "Are you saying I'm a liar?"

Zara shook her head. "Not so much lying, James, as confused. You took a severe beating, you spent a night out in the cold, and you were under a huge amount of stress."

Ewart took over. "The thing is, James, two well-respected undercover operatives are dead. I've discussed the situation with senior MI5 officials and they're not buying your story that Boris and Isla were killed after murdering Denis Obidin."

"Ewart, I told you yesterday. The CIA guy took me back to the safe house, he put the laptop in front of me, and I watched the whole thing on video."

"Are you *completely* sure it was Boris and Isla?"

James tutted. "Absolutely sure. I saw them getting dressed before they went out. They were wearing the right clothes and everything."

Ewart wagged his finger. "But in the testimony I recorded yesterday, you said that you had a pulsing headache, your eyes were swollen, and the video footage was blurry. Can you *really* be sure?"

"I felt rough," James nodded, "but I wasn't *blind*. It was CCTV footage. It was black and white and a bit blurry, like every other bit of CCTV footage I've ever seen."

"So you could positively identify Boris and Isla on the clip?" Zara said.

Ewart interrupted before James got to answer. "The thing is James, MI5 are saying that this video clip is what the CIA, or whoever this Partridge dude really works for, wanted you to see. It could have been staged with actors, or real footage could have been manipulated by computers."

"I guess," James said. "All I know is that it looked real to me when I saw it and we've since confirmed that Boris, Isla, and Denis are all dead."

Ewart nodded. "Point taken."

"Can't you contact the CIA and see if you can get hold of the footage?" James asked.

Zara smiled. "James, we're certainly going to try, but it's a delicate business. You can't just ring up CIA headquarters and say, 'Hey we're a bunch of British spies who don't officially exist, you know that top secret undercover mission you've got going on in Northern Russia . . .'"

"Well, *obviously*," James nodded. "But the Americans are our friends, right? I mean, I worked with the CIA and the FBI in Arizona two years ago. That's how they knew who I was."

"Espionage isn't a world of black and white, James," Ewart said. "In some instances, such as the Arizona situation, British and American interests are the same and we work together. In Aero City, things are more complex. Denis Obidin was a massive presence in the Russian aerospace industry. His contract with Hilton Aerospace to fit British jet engines and maintain Russian airliners is worth *billions*. Even though it's a declining market, the big American aeroengine companies would still love to get hold of that contract and gain a foothold in the Russian aerospace market."

"In fact," Zara said, "if two British agents *did* charge into Denis Obidin's office and kill him, it might very well push several lucrative defense contracts into the hands of the Americans. It could be exactly what the CIA wants the Russians to believe."

"Well, I guess . . ." James wasn't entirely convinced by Zara's argument. "I mean, what you're saying isn't impossible, but what if the version the CIA man told me is true and it turns out that MI5 are covering their backs and refusing to accept the blame?"

Zara nodded. "At this stage we're just gathering evidence. We're ruling nothing in and nothing out."

"Anyway," James said, "why are us Brits so keen to do business with the Obidins? I thought the whole point of my mission was to gather evidence and put Obidin behind bars for selling illegal weapons."

"We certainly wanted the evidence," Ewart smiled. "But MI5 might have achieved a better outcome by using it to blackmail Obidin. That way, he stops selling weapons to people our government don't like *and* three thousand British jobs are guaranteed."

James shook his head. "Sounds pretty shady."

Zara nodded. "It is shady, but the Russian courts can be as corrupt as their police force. Even if we'd gathered cast-iron evidence against Obidin, there's no guarantee that a crooked judge or a bribed jury wouldn't have acquitted him."

Ewart spoke again. "Another aspect of your testimony is causing me some concern. . . ."

"Hang on," James said angrily. "How come it's *testimony* all of a sudden? Yesterday afternoon, you came in here acting all casual and asked if I felt well enough to answer some questions. You said you'd record the conversation so you didn't have to write it all down. I thought it was just a debriefing, but now you're asking me all this extra stuff, sounding like a lawyer and picking apart what I said."

"James, there has to be a comprehensive investigation into what went wrong," Zara explained. "Two agents are dead, you were lucky to get out alive. We're not saying that you're a liar, but we can't just carry on as if nothing has happened. Ewart is going to conduct a thorough investigation into every aspect of the Aero City mission. He'll obviously be on the lookout for evidence that confirms your version of events, but he has to be impartial. That means he'll have to investigate your conduct during the mission and ask you some difficult questions about it."

James shrugged wearily. "Well, whether you believe me or not, everything I told you yesterday is what I honestly believe is true."

Zara sat up in her chair and adopted a grave tone. "The thing is, James—and I came along with Ewart today because I wanted to tell you in person—CHERUB has to appear completely fair and honest. As well as Ewart's investigation, MI5 will be conducting a separate inquiry into the events in Aero City, and both organizations have been asked to report back to the intelligence minister as soon as possible. In the meantime I'll have to suspend your status as an active CHERUB agent."

"Eh?" James gasped furiously. "After everything I went through out there? Are you taking the piss?"

"None of us likes it, James, but until the inquiry is complete and you're cleared of any responsibility, I have no option but to suspend you."

"But I haven't done *anything*."

"It's not a punishment, James," Zara said softly.

"What a crock of *shit*," James yelled.

"Hey, watch your mouth," Ewart shouted.

"Ewart, don't start," Zara said. "James, I know this is really rotten for you, but we have to obey certain rules. One of those rules is that we can't send agents on a mission while their conduct on a previous mission is under investigation."

"I nearly died," James screamed. "Those two MI5 traitors stitched me up. Now *you're* stitching me up."

"James, I'm sorry," Zara said. "I know you're upset, but we're not stitching anybody up."

"You know what? Screw it. Why should I risk my life on another mission for people who don't trust me or stick up for me? I *quit*—send me off to live with a set of foster parents or whatever."

"Come off it, James," Zara said. "I can see how this might seem like we're kicking you when you're down, but try to keep things in perspective. The investigation will probably take one or two months. You wouldn't have been sent on another long mission until you were feeling better and you'd caught up on your schoolwork. The difference to your CHERUB career will probably be minimal."

James thought for a second. "Maybe that's true, but everyone on campus is gonna know I'm under investigation and I know how these things drag out. You say one or two months now, but it's just as likely to be four or five."

Ewart rolled his eyes. "James, you're not the first agent ever to be suspended pending an investigation and I'd bet that you won't be the last."

"Besides," Zara said, "if you leave, you'll end up at some other school with no friends and about half of the facilities you've got on campus."

"I guess," James sighed. "And I didn't mean to swear at you. It's just, I could do without this after everything I've been through in the last week. . . ."

Zara reached into a carrier bag she'd brought in with her and pulled out a big box of fancy chocolates.

"Continental selection." Zara smiled. "Kerry said you liked them. They're a personal gift from Ewart and me. And this second one is a get well present from CHERUB itself."

As James grabbed the box of chocolates, Zara reached back into the carrier bag and pulled out a box with an Apple logo on it.

"I'm not really up on these things," Zara explained, "but Kerry said you were on about getting an iPod for when you go running. I gave it to Kyle last night and he said he's loaded on some music and a couple of audiobooks."

James was pleased with the gifts, but they left a bitter taste. It felt like they were buying him off.

CHAPTER 14

QUESTIONS

Two weeks later

James broke off the cross-country trail and sprinted across a soccer field, heading toward the rear entrance of the main building on CHERUB campus. It had been raining for most of the last three days and mud spattered up his legs as he ran.

When James reached the double doors, he looked at his running watch and pressed the stop button before flipping through the settings: time 22 minutes 17 seconds, distance 5.03 kilometers, heart rate 139 beats per minute. It was only half a minute outside his personal best and he'd set that when the ground was hard.

As he leaned against the wall and pulled off his soggy

sneakers, James spotted his mates, Kyle and Shak, running across the field behind him. He thought about waiting, but his T-shirt was wringing with sweat and he didn't want to get cold.

The back hallway on the ground floor smelled of the muggy air that wafted out of the laundry. The elevator always took ages and James felt sprightly, so he jogged toward the staircase.

"Mr. Adams," a man called sternly.

James's heart sank as he turned around and saw his geography teacher Mr. Norwood. Norwood was an ex-cherub in his mid-thirties. Like many CHERUB staff that didn't have families, he lived in an apartment on the fourth floor of the main building. He approached James holding a plastic laundry basket filled with folded shirts and jeans.

"Been for a run I see." Mr. Norwood smiled as he glared at the muddy sneakers hooked over James's middle fingers.

"Yes, sir."

Mr. Norwood tapped his chin thoughtfully. "And yet, I seem to recall you telling me that you were still recovering. You said you'd been told to take things easy for a while and not overtire yourself with homework."

James tried to sound sincere. "It's true, sir. I nearly *died*."

Kyle and Shakeel staggered through the doors. "You came out of nowhere, James." Kyle grinned as he slapped James on the back.

Mr. Norwood looked at Kyle. "So, you'd say James is in good health now?"

Kyle and Shak both nodded.

"He's got strong legs," Kyle explained. "He's not fast, but

he blasted past us when we were coming up the last hill."

James's friends kept on walking and James turned to follow them. "Nice talking, Mr. N," he said hurriedly. "I'd better take a shower before I stink the joint up."

"Good-bye, James," Mr. Norwood said. "I'll see you on Tuesday morning, with the homework on rain forest ecosystems."

"I still get headaches, sir."

Mr. Norwood shrugged. "I'll give you a choice, James. Either bring your homework, or an excuse note written by your handler."

James realized he'd been cornered. "All right, I'll do it," he said miserably.

"And, James, I don't appreciate you trying to con me."

James walked toward the staircase and found Shak and Kyle cracking up on the first landing.

"Bus*ted*," Shak grinned.

"Shut your face," James tutted. "I don't care anyway. It's only some piddling question-and-answer sheet and Kerry's in my class, so I'll copy off her."

"Cool," Shak nodded, as the three boys started up toward their rooms on the sixth floor. "I've got Norwood in another set, can I copy Kerry's off you?"

When he reached his room on the sixth floor, James noticed that his answering machine was flashing at him. He tapped the play button and listened to the messages as he stripped off for a shower.

"*You have two new messages, first message left today at nine seventeen a.m.*"

James recognized Ewart's voice. "Hi, James. Listen, I know it's Saturday, but I got another call from MI5.

They'd like you to come down to London to answer some more questions. If it's okay, I'll try setting it all up for Thursday."

James threw his T-shirt down and groaned to himself. "What's the point of more questions, you penis? I've been down there and gone through everything twice already."

James could refuse to cooperate with the investigation if he wanted, but it wouldn't look good on his record. On the upside, a Thursday in London would mean he'd get away without handing in his GCSE History coursework for a few more days.

"Second new message left today at eleven thirty-seven a.m."

"James, it's Meryl," the voice barked angrily. "I want your sorry little hide down here in the second-floor conference room as soon as you've finished your run and taken a shower. And don't bother putting your good clothes on."

"No more messages. To listen again, press one, to repeat messages, press two. . . ."

James shut off the answering machine and shook his head as he hooked his muddy shorts over his big toe and flicked them up in the air, narrowly missing his dirty clothes basket. As he headed for the shower he racked his brains trying to work out why Meryl sounded so angry.

Mr. Norwood couldn't have complained in the time it took him to walk up the stairs, and Meryl's message had been left more than an hour earlier anyway. Whatever he'd done, the request to put on old clothes was a bad sign. It could only mean oven cleaning, ditch digging, or some other thoroughly unpleasant way of spending your Saturday afternoon.

* * *

Two floors up, Lauren Adams had just finished Saturday morning lessons and was in a much better mood. She had a wheeled suitcase and a mass of clothes spread over her bed, and System of a Down blasting from her mini hi-fi.

She jumped out of her skin when a man's voice sounded in her ear. "Sorry," he shouted. "But I knocked three times."

It was John Jones, a dome-headed mission controller who'd worked with Lauren and James on several previous missions. He wore a smart brown suit and shoes, with a waistcoat that made him look like a country gent.

Lauren rushed across the room and switched off her music. "Sorry, John. You frightened the life out of me."

"Give me Elvis Presley any day." John smiled. "Where are you off to? I was hoping you'd be able to help out on a mission."

"Oh," Lauren said. "Well, I'm only away for one night, with a few friends. Some fancy spa-hotel type deal."

"Very swish," John said. "I'd like to have someone in place as soon as possible, but it can wait for a day or so. I need a young agent who speaks decent Russian and is capable of working solo. To be honest, you're the only candidate I feel I can totally rely on."

"Right." Lauren was slightly embarrassed by the compliment. "I haven't got any other missions lined up. Do you want me to come to your office on Monday morning or something?"

"No," John said, as he pulled some stapled sheets of paper from his jacket pocket. "I've got a photocopy of the briefing here. The mission isn't hugely complicated, but I have a young daughter myself and it's an issue I'm particularly passionate about."

"So what are we talking about?" Lauren asked.

"Human trafficking."

```
   **CLASSIFIED MISSION BRIEFING
        FOR LAUREN ADAMS**
   THIS DOCUMENT IS PROTECTED WITH
A RADIO FREQUENCY IDENTIFICATION TAG.
 ANY ATTEMPT TO REMOVE IT FROM THE
   MISSION PREPARATION BUILDING
        WILL SET OFF AN ALARM
  DO NOT PHOTOCOPY OR MAKE NOTES
```

```
Human Trafficking & Slavery
Talk of slavery often brings forth
images of Africans being shipped
to colonies in the Americas during
the eighteenth century. Few people
realize that it is still a problem
in both rich and poor countries. In
2004 a United Nations report stated
that slavery was the world's third
largest source of criminal income
after drugs and the illegal weapons
trade. Furthermore, the growth in
slavery has been so rapid that it
could become the biggest earner
within twenty years.

Modern Slavery
Modern slavery takes many forms. The
common feature is that poor people—
usually children or young adults—are
kidnapped or tricked into traveling
to a wealthier part of the world,
where they are held captive and
```

forced to work against their will.

In poor countries, it has long
been common for youngsters to be
captured and taken far away to work
in sweatshops, to fight as soldiers,
or to work in the sex industry.
Some poor parents willingly sign
their children over to people who
promise to offer them a better life
in another part of the world, while
others hand their children over
to crime syndicates and are too
terrified ever to contact the police.
Most disturbingly, many child slaves
are street children or orphans who
are sold into slavery by the police
officers and care workers who are
paid to protect them.

In rich countries, such as the
UK and the United States, the vast
majority of slaves are teenage girls
who are forced to work within the sex
industry. Girls as young as twelve
are smuggled into the UK, beaten,
terrorized, and often injected with
heroin or other narcotic drugs to
make them docile, before being forced
to have sex for money.

The problem is vast. It is
estimated that there are more than
25,000 forced sex workers in the UK
(500,000 within the European Union)
and that over 90% of these are girls
under the age of twenty. A few of
these girls have been smuggled from
Asia and Africa, but the majority are
from Russia and the poorer parts of
Eastern Europe.

The CHERUB Mission

In early September a high-speed
passenger ferry collided with a small
motor launch during a storm in the
English Channel. Despite the launch
being severely damaged, the captain
refused all offers of help and tried
to escape.

Appalling weather meant that search
and rescue resources were stretched
to the limit. The authorities were
unable to pursue the boat, but
several hours later a customs officer
on a routine patrol spotted the
launch tied to a small jetty, two
kilometers from the seaside town of
Worthing.

At first, the boat appeared to
have been abandoned, but further
inspection revealed that a twelve-
year-old girl was trapped at the end
of the jetty. Two customs officers
braved high seas washing over the
jetty to bring her back to shore.

The officers suspected that the
girl was being trafficked to work
in the sex industry, and a search
team sent onto the boat when the
storm subsided revealed clothes and
personal items belonging to as many
as ten teen and preteen girls.

Since September, the young girl
rescued from the pier has been
staying at a children's home near
Brighton. She has been questioned by
police and social workers, but has
adamantly refused to admit anything,
except that her first name is Anna.

Police have been unable to trace any sign of the people who were running the smuggling operation, or of the other girls who escaped from the damaged boat. Although all human trafficking investigations are given a high priority, the police are particularly concerned in this instance because it is thought that up to half of the girls on the boat were aged thirteen or under and are likely to have been trafficked to pedophile gangs.

All attempts to question Anna have so far proved fruitless. However, police psychologists are hopeful that she may open up to a trusted friend.

Although Anna's English is improving, it is thought that a girl aged 11-13 with a decent command of Russian will have the best chance of winning Anna's confidence and unearthing information about both Anna herself and the criminal gang that smuggled her into Britain.

Arrangements will be made for a CHERUB agent to move into the Brighton children's home and share a room with Anna. The aim is to make friends and get as much information as possible about her background and the people who smuggled her to the UK.

NOTE: THE CHERUB ETHICS COMMITTEE APPROVED THIS MISSION BRIEFING, ON CONDITION THAT ALL AGENTS UNDERSTAND THE FOLLOWING:

This mission has been classified LOW
RISK. The agent is reminded of her
right to refuse to undertake this
mission and to withdraw from it at
any time.

   This mission is likely to last one
month or less. Its primary goal is
to gather information from the victim
of a crime. The danger to the agent
should be minimal.

"My god," Lauren said, after she'd read the briefing. "Those poor girls. Of *course* I'll do the mission, I had no idea it was such a big problem. I always thought prostitutes had sex because they made loads of money. I didn't realize that they were forced into it."

"Sadly an awful lot of them are," John said. "It's starting to get more publicity these days, but people still don't care much about the women. I mean, you open up your Sunday paper and hear that some soccer player slept with a prostitute and a lot of men just laugh and say 'good on yer, son.' They don't understand that many of these women are being drugged and terrorized."

Lauren nodded. "I bet that's exactly what James and his stupid mates would say. Speaking of which, I've gotta run downstairs. Can I give you a call on my mobile and we'll sort this out later?"

"Fair enough," John said, as Lauren scrambled toward the door. "I'll be in my office for a few more hours and my mobile will be on all night—don't you want your suitcase?"

"Not right now," Lauren said, as she sprinted off down the corridor.

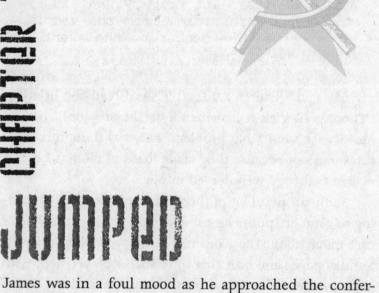

CHAPTER 15

JUMPED

James was in a foul mood as he approached the conference room on the second floor. He still couldn't think of anything he'd done that would explain why his handler, Meryl Spencer, had sounded so annoyed on the phone.

He'd only ever been to the conference room once before, to watch an extremely boring video on the safe use of stab-proof vests. He pushed the door open and was baffled to find that the windowless room was pitch black.

"Meryl?" James asked curiously.

Suddenly all the light tubes started flickering and a great shout came up from under the conference table.

"Surprise!"

After a brief jolt, James spun around and saw close to

a dozen of his friends clambering from beneath the long table. A PowerPoint graphic appeared on the screen at the end of the room. It had a picture of a birthday cake with a fifteen at the bottom. Beneath it was written, P.S. SORRY IT'S A BIT LATE.

Kerry stepped up and gave him a kiss. "Happy birthday, James."

Meryl emerged from behind the door, where she'd activated the light switches. "So, you got my message then?"

James turned and pointed at her with his mouth hanging open. "You . . . ," he spluttered.

"I bet you were crapping yourself on the way down here." Bruce grinned.

"I *was*." James nodded. "I was doing my head in trying to work out what I was in trouble for."

Meryl gave James a quick kiss as Lauren burst into the room.

"*Aaaarghhh*," she moaned, as she placed her hands on top of her head. "I can't *believe* I missed it. What did he look like?"

"It was good," Kerry's best mate, Gabrielle, giggled. "He was totally stunned."

"Does he know what we're doing yet?" Lauren asked.

"You mean this isn't it?" James said.

"Oh no," Meryl smiled. "You've had a pretty rough time of it lately, what with getting beaten up, being suspended from missions, and having Ewart and half of MI5 giving you the third degree. So Zara suggested that we use up some of CHERUB's abundant supply of hotel points and take you on a magical mystery tour."

"Sweet, where are we off to?"

"It wouldn't be a magical mystery if we told you," Kerry said, as she glanced at her watch. "I've packed a bag for you and we'd better get on the road if we're gonna make it on time."

Luckily, the twins Callum and Connor were the only good mates of James's who were away on a mission. Lauren, Rat, Kyle, Bruce, Kerry, Gabrielle, Shak, Mo, and Gabrielle's new boyfriend, Michael, all piled into the minibus with their overnight bags. Somehow Lauren had also managed to get Bethany invited, despite the fact that James hated her guts.

Kyle had made a compilation CD of James's favorite music and they had it turned up loud as Meryl blasted down the highway at over a hundred miles an hour, knowing she'd never get a speeding ticket in a vehicle registered to CHERUB.

"Hood him," Meryl said, when she turned off the highway.

Shak produced a woollen balaclava. Kerry and Lauren held James in his seat while it was pulled over his head, with the eye and mouth holes at the back.

"It itches like hell," James complained, but Kerry just jabbed him in the ribs and told him to stop being a baby.

It was already starting to turn dark when they pulled up in a gravel parking lot. James couldn't see, but could hear two-stroke engines buzzing in the distance and hoped it was something to do with motorbikes. The sounds got louder as they led him across the parking lot and through a gate, before ceremoniously removing the hood. He was slightly disappointed when he looked out over a floodlit track covered with small, four-wheeled dune buggies. But he didn't want to seem ungrateful and broke into an appreciative smile.

"Cool," he grinned, watching a buggy lift off the ground as it sped over a massive hump and ploughed through a muddy puddle.

This explained why Meryl had asked him to wear old clothes. Maybe it wasn't motorbikes, but it still looked like a lot of fun.

They headed toward a shelter with a corrugated metal roof and some benches underneath. Meryl approached a weedy teenager with a clipboard, but he was surrounded by drunk blokes who all wore identical T-shirts saying KEVIN JONES STAG WEEKEND 2006.

"You can't go out there in that state," the teenager was explaining, as five drunken men stared him down.

"Then we want our money back."

"I can't do that," the teen spluttered. "It's in the terms and conditions, but anyone with half a brain cell could have worked out that you can't turn up drunk at a place like this."

"You're going the right way about getting a slap," the largest of the drunks said.

The five men looked like rugby players, and even the smallest one was twice the width of the teenager.

Meryl interrupted. "Party of twelve, booked in the name of Spencer."

"Tickle my *titties*," one of the drunks spluttered, as he pointed at Meryl. "I know you, you're that Kenyan bird who won the hundred meters in the Olympics. Me sister had a poster of you in her bedroom. How about a kiss?"

Meryl scowled. "How about a punch in the face?"

As the man who'd asked for a kiss lunged toward Meryl, the largest of the five drunks shook his head and opened his enormous mouth. "She's too muscly to shag, looks more like a geezer to me."

Meryl restrained the man lunging at her by grabbing his hand. As his thumb crunched, she wrenched his arm behind his back, then deliberately tripped him up and sent him sprawling toward the giant who'd accused her of looking like a man.

"I suggest you leave," she said tautly.

"That's not a nice way to speak to a gentleman," the giant said, as he reached around to grab Meryl's bum and suggestively flicked his tongue in and out.

All her life, Meryl had put up with blokes calling her butch and making jokes about how often she shaved, or how she probably had testicles. She used her powerful physique to give the giant an explosive shove. He stumbled back and lost his footing as he tripped on a curb stone.

"Try touching me again and see what you get," Meryl shouted.

The other four men looked warily at Meryl as they started backing up toward the parking lot.

"Lesbian," the giant shouted.

"If all men were like you I would be," Meryl yelled back.

Meryl sounded a touch upset and the eleven cherubs stifled their laughter as she turned toward the teenager with the clipboard. He looked shaken up.

"You okay?" she asked.

The kid shook his head. "I hate this job. You wouldn't *believe* the crap I put up with for minimum wage. I wish I'd got the job at McDonald's, you get so much less hassle there."

"Drunk blokes are all dickheads," Kerry said sympathetically.

The teenager shook his head. "Hen parties are even worse. Half a dozen women saying that you're a nice boy and trying to pinch your bum. They're complete animals."

James and Kyle couldn't help giggling.

"Anyway," the teenager said as he looked down at his clipboard. "You lot aren't due on for another twenty minutes, but I owe you one for getting rid of that bunch of idiots, so you might as well grab some gloves and helmets and use their slot to have a couple of extra races."

The dune buggies were less than two meters long. They only had small motorbike engines mounted behind the driver, but their open chassis and aluminum roll cage weighed less than fifty kilos, enabling them to accelerate from dead stop to their 30kph top speed in less than three seconds. With rock-hard suspension, tiny steering wheels, and seats less than fifteen centimeters off the ground it felt much faster.

"This is awesome," James grinned, flipping up his visor as he stepped out of his buggy and used one of the cloths standing on the edge of the course to wipe his helmet.

Like everyone else, Kerry was wet and covered in mud.

"I'm freezing," she groaned, as she bounced on tiptoes and tucked her hands under her armpits.

James looked concerned. "Don't you like it?"

"It's ace," Kerry grinned. "But next time I reckon we'll do it for someone who has their birthday in the summer."

Meryl and all the others were getting out of their buggies and coming toward them. The course was divided into three sections. The first was a muddy paddock with a few little bumps where you drove around in circles getting a feel for the buggies. The second section, which the CHERUB group had just completed, was a time trial on a winding course. It started off easy, but ended up with three large jumps that landed you in deep water if you didn't take them at full speed.

"Okay, everyone," the skinny teen said, adopting a slightly formal tone. "Results of the time trial for the Spencer party. In third place, with a time of seven minutes and sixteen seconds, car number eight, James Adams."

A few cherubs clapped, but they all had thickly padded driving gloves on, so it didn't make a lot of noise.

"In second place, seven minutes fifteen and a half seconds, car number three, Meryl Spencer."

"In your face, kiddywinks," Meryl screamed.

"And our winner—with a time of six minutes and thirty-six seconds that wouldn't shame some of our regular visitors—Bethany Parker."

James tutted as the teen presented Bethany with a plastic trophy that looked like it cost about fifteen pence to make.

"Champion of the world," Bethany yelled, as Gabrielle snapped her picture with a camera phone.

"Drop dead, you stupid cow," James mumbled.

Kerry and Mo were standing closest to James and couldn't help laughing. "You love her really," Mo whispered.

"Okay," the teen with the clipboard shouted. "I'm gonna open the gate and I want you to drive through to the competition track. You normally get ten laps, but we've got some time in hand, so I'll let you have fifteen.

"In this race you'll be in direct competition with each other. Anyone who is overly aggressive will be red-flagged by the marshals and *must* pull into the pits. Any questions . . . ? Okay then, get back in your buggies and make sure that your safety belts are fastened securely."

The noise was deafening as the twelve buggies drove down a narrow alleyway. They had to wait a couple of minutes while the stewards wheeled off a broken-down buggy from the previous race and straightened up the tire walls.

The twelve drivers were lined up on the grid in the order that they'd finished the time trial. The floodlit course was built into a hillside and dozens of daily races had turned it into a mud pit. James lined up in third, with Meryl and Bethany in front and Kerry alongside him.

He turned to Kerry and shouted over the drone of the engines. "Gonna kick your arse, girlfriend."

Kerry turned and flicked James off. "Don't think I'll let you win, just 'cos it's your birthday."

James revved as the three red lights came on and slotted the transmission into drive the second they went out. But he felt a sharp jolt as Kyle—who must have started before the lights went out—rammed into his back.

The shunt actually gave James momentum and he

got ahead of Kerry. Unfortunately, Bethany's buggy was driving its wheels into the mud and he was about to smash into it. He snapped his steering wheel left to avoid the collision, but in the process he swerved into Kerry's path and sandwiched her against the red-and-white-striped curb.

A couple of cars swept past James on the outside as he tangled with Kerry, but he had the racing line into the tight first corner and came out with only Meryl Spencer ahead of him.

For the next two corners, James raced a couple of meters behind Meryl's rear light. He fought to see through the mud spraying off her back tires, while Kerry, Bruce, and Bethany's headlights blazed in his rearview mirror.

James's adrenalin level surged as he spotted Meryl going into a corner too fast. Her back end jiggled out—and while it didn't look dramatic, she lost a lot of momentum. James and the three cars on his tail eased past her on the next straight.

James was thrilled at being in the lead, but a gentle bend gave him his first glimpse of the craziest part of the course. The back straight was four buggies wide, but it ran from top to bottom of the hill, starting off almost vertical before flattening out at the bottom as it tapered into a straight with two steep ramps.

The buggy was out of control on the steepest part of the slope and James found the steering wheel slipping through his hands as he battled to keep going.

With gloomy lighting and an uneven surface, there was an element of luck in going down the hill. While James hit a bump, Bruce got a better run over on the right-hand side and managed to glide past Kerry and take the lead off James.

But Bruce's extra speed was his downfall. As the slope straightened out and the track narrowed to lead into the ramps, his buggy aquaplaned into the tire wall and spun the width of the track, missing James by centimeters, before crashing into the tire wall facing backward. By the time Bruce had found space to turn back the right way, he'd dropped to last place.

Kerry and James were side by side as they flew over the two jumps, but in their anxiety to stay ahead they entered the final corner of the circuit too fast. Both buggies skidded out wide, enabling Bethany to power-slide through on the inside. She led by more than ten meters as they crossed the finish line for the first time.

James tried to get back at Bethany, but she was too talented. While James skidded and occasionally touched the tire wall, Bethany seemed able to judge her speed and, braking perfectly, edged farther into the distance with every corner.

By the end of lap eleven, Bethany was out of sight. James and Kerry were still battling for second, with Meryl, Kyle, Mo and Lauren bunched up twenty meters behind, waiting to pounce on any kind of mistake. Michael had spun and was about fifty meters behind the pack, while Gabrielle and Rat were hopeless and had both been lapped by everyone except Bruce, who'd embedded his car in the tire wall during a reckless attempt to fight his way back to the front of the field.

With two laps remaining, James caught a nose full of fumes as he turned onto the finishing straight. He was delighted to see Bethany standing in a smoky pit lane, furiously undoing the buckle on her helmet.

Perfect, James thought to himself, as he skimmed past Gabrielle on the outside to lap her for the second time. His fingers ached from clutching the steering wheel. As he turned into the first corner, he had to slam his brakes to avoid ploughing into Lauren, who'd been allowed through on the inside by Rat.

James was furious with Rat for showing Lauren such blatant favoritism, but he shut it out of his mind because he was now sandwiched tight between Lauren and Kerry. He was delighted when he saw Lauren mess up the line into the third corner and he retook the lead, with Kerry right up behind him.

After the gentle curve, James found himself bouncing down the steep back straight, with Kerry coming out of his slipstream and pulling up alongside him. They stayed side by side as they got nearer to the bottom, where the course narrowed for the first ramp.

James was on the racing line and smiling inside his helmet because Kerry would have to brake and drop in behind him unless she wanted to plough into the tire wall.

But she *didn't* back off. With less than twenty meters to the jump, Kerry pulled up wheel to wheel with James and turned in to nudge him aside. If James gave way, they'd both make it over the jump, but Kerry would have had the best line for the second jump and the final corner. He'd effectively be handing Kerry the lead into the final lap and that wasn't going to happen.

At the last second, Kerry realized that she'd got it wrong. She hit her brake and steered left, but it was too late and she slammed into tires at the point where the course tapered, clipping the rear of James's buggy as she did so.

As Kerry disappeared amid the tires, James felt his back end slide out as he hit the front of the mud ramp. The change in direction had a dramatic effect on his speed, and instead of skimming over the puddle on the opposite side, his buggy careered off the edge of the ramp and landed on its side atop a pile of tires. He came to an unceremonious halt, crashing into a foam barrier that had been erected to stop flying buggies from rolling clean over the tire wall and hitting the trees on the other side.

James's engine cut automatically when his buggy tipped over, but insult was added to injury as Lauren's buggy and the three behind it skimmed over the ramp and sprayed him with muddy water as they nosedived into the puddle beyond it. Once the first batch of buggies was past, James hurriedly unbuckled his seat belt, before rolling over the slippery tires and dropping down into the mulch on the opposite side.

"Why didn't you move over, you idiot?" Kerry yelled, as she jumped off the tire wall and angrily flipped up her visor.

"*I* had the racing line," James said, as he fought with his helmet buckle.

"But you must have known I'd crash into the tires."

James grinned. "How's that my problem?"

"Pig," Kerry yelled, as she hurled her helmet at James. "I thought you loved me. If you loved me, you'd have let me win."

James started to laugh as he tugged off his helmet and unzipped his foam neck brace. "Love is one thing, buggy racing is another."

Kerry put her hands on her hips and scowled at him. "Wipe that smile off before I thump you."

"You gonna make me?" James stepped closer to Kerry. "You know, even with your hair all wild and mud all over your clothes, you're still sexy."

Kerry tried keeping up her scowl, but she couldn't help smiling at the compliment. "You're lucky it's your birthday."

"Knew you couldn't stay mad for long," James said, as he leaned forward and gave Kerry a kiss.

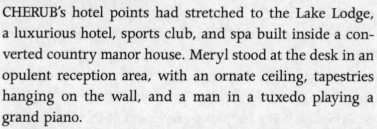

CHAPTER 16

ROOMS

CHERUB's hotel points had stretched to the Lake Lodge, a luxurious hotel, sports club, and spa built inside a converted country manor house. Meryl stood at the desk in an opulent reception area, with an ornate ceiling, tapestries hanging on the wall, and a man in a tuxedo playing a grand piano.

The guests were mostly middle-aged and elderly couples, heading into the restaurant in evening gowns and smart suits. They all looked surprised when they noticed the eleven muddy youngsters standing by the revolving door in their socks.

As the receptionist tapped her keyboard, swiped Meryl's credit card, and offered her a long form to fill in with the names of all the kids on it, the lanky hotel manager raised the counter flap and swept up alongside her. "Geraldine, perhaps you can give this party their room keys now and Miss Spencer can come downstairs and complete the formalities when they've cleaned up. The young guests are *dripping* on the carpet."

The manager rapidly programmed sets of room keys and handed each one to a pair of kids.

"And one room is supposed to be a suite," Meryl said. "It was part of the offer when you booked more than five rooms."

As the birthday boy, James got the suite and was seriously impressed. It was four times the size of his room on campus, with a king-sized four-poster bed, a separate living room with a giant TV hanging on the wall, a real fire, and a steaming plunge pool outside on the balcony.

He took his second shower of the day, then put on a hotel robe and slippers before calling Kerry on her mobile.

"Hey, sweetcakes. This room is the dogs, what's yours like?"

"Pretty snazzy," Kerry said. "Not as fancy as your suite though, I bet."

James picked a couple of grapes out of the crystal fruit bowl beside his bed. "The only thing is, the porter was supposed to be bringing my bag up. He hasn't left it with you, has he?"

"We had it brought to Lauren's room," Kerry explained. "I'm waiting for Gabrielle to finish doing her hair, then we're all heading your way."

"Can't I come and get my clothes?"

"You can *wait*," Kerry said stiffly and James immediately guessed why.

"Oooh, am I getting presents?"

"You'll find out soon enough."

James crashed out on his massive bed and smiled as he brushed his cheek on the soft hotel robe. The buggy racing had been superb and now he was all clean and relaxed in this incredible hotel room. It was exactly what he needed after the last few weeks. The only downer was that his nose wasn't fully healed yet and it always seemed to ache when he came in out of the cold.

Meryl was first to knock, dressed in her hotel robe and trailed by a room service cart stacked with chocolate biscuits and insulated jugs of coffee and hot cocoa.

James was warming his fingers on a mug when his ten companions arrived en masse. Lauren—who had her race winner's rosette pinned on her hotel robe—was wheeling a snazzy Samsonite case, which she placed on James's bed before giving him a kiss.

"Happy birthday, bruv."

"Is this my bag?" James asked, slightly confused.

"It is now," Meryl nodded, as the kids poured out cups of coffee and cocoa. "Compliments of CHERUB. You've only got that tatty backpack you use on training exercises, and I thought you could do with something decent when you go on short missions."

"If I'm ever allowed on another mission," James sighed, as he leaned over and unzipped the bag.

"Of *course* you'll go on more missions," Meryl said. "The investigation will be over in no time."

James was slightly stunned as he flipped back the lid.

He'd expected to find a present on top of his stuff, but he didn't recognize a single thing inside the case.

"Whoa," James gasped, as he pulled out a bag of expensive-looking gents' toiletries, complete with a fancy shaving brush and mirror. "Body Shop toiletries and Paul Smith eau de toilette, very chic."

"I know you don't shave yet," Kyle grinned. "But it won't be long."

"Cheers." James began removing a neatly pressed white shirt and a pair of chinos. They were pretty nice, although they weren't the kind of things he'd usually wear.

"Us girls got together and decided that you needed a makeover," Lauren explained.

"And we're going down to the restaurant for a meal later," Kerry added. "We didn't want you lowering the tone by sitting there in an Arsenal shirt and a pair of Nikes like you usually do."

"Thanks," James said with a grin, as he took out some new pairs of socks, a striped silk tie, a couple of Gap T-shirts, a pair of flashy swimming shorts, and a pack of Calvin Klein briefs. None of the items were hugely expensive, but it made him feel good because all his friends had clearly got together and planned out the best way of making his birthday celebration special.

"I know you wear boxers, but I think you've got the right kind of body for those," Kerry explained, as James inspected the briefs.

"You can come over to my room in them anytime," Kyle offered.

"I'm sure I will, Kyle," James said, shaking his head as Bethany and Lauren made eww noises. He wasn't quite sure if the noises were because Kyle was gay or at the thought of him in a pair of CK briefs.

The last items in the bag were a pair of shoes and a 2007 Manchester United album.

"They're your shoes," Kerry explained, "but we gave them a polish."

"The first they've ever had, judging by the state of them," Gabrielle added.

"And this *thing*," James said, his voice full of mock disgust as he held the Manchester United album between his thumb and forefinger at arm's length.

"That's from me." Bethany grinned innocently. "I thought you *liked* Man United."

James huffed. "I suppose it might come in handy if I ever have to scrape up some vomit."

The dinner in the Lake Lodge restaurant was a bit fancy for James's taste. He usually counted cheeseburger and fries or a good breakfast fry-up as his favorite meal, but it was a nice setting with candles on the table in a dining room overlooking a lake. He liked the fact that everyone was dressed up, especially Kerry in a black off-the-shoulder dress and the gold necklace he'd got for her birthday earlier in the year.

After profiteroles and hot chocolate sauce, Meryl said she was going to the bar and told the kids that she trusted them to behave themselves. They all decided to try out the plunge pool on James's balcony.

As they headed upstairs, James found himself behind Lauren and Rat. Lauren—who wouldn't have been seen dead in a dress six months earlier—wore green stockings and a black microskirt and Rat had his hand around her waist.

Lauren was only twelve, but her bra had a purpose these days, and her hips had started to widen out so that she was beginning to get a proper woman's bum. James didn't like it one bit. It was okay when he used to tease her about having a boyfriend, but he felt differently now that she actually had one.

They were stepping off the third-floor landing when James realized why it made him uncomfortable. Until now, he'd been able to go after girls and rely on the fact that his little sister would always be there for him. But in a few years, he'd leave CHERUB, Lauren would probably get a serious boyfriend, and they'd slowly grow apart.

Lauren's miniskirt was almost like a sign hanging off her butt saying that she was looking for someone to replace James in her affections.

"What are you looking so miserable for?" Kerry asked, as she whacked James across the shoulder.

"Am I?" James said, pretending to be mystified.

Ten minutes later everyone except Kyle was in the bubbling spa pool on James's balcony. It felt beautiful because the water was really hot; the November air was crisp and the balcony looked out over a highway, with headlights snaking along it and a nearby village with a huge church lit up in the center.

"Where's Kyle got to?" Gabrielle asked, as she popped up in the middle of the pool and ran her hands through her long braided hair.

James shrugged. "He took my spare room-key and said he had to go fetch something from the van."

Kyle arrived a few minutes later, holding a cardboard box and still dressed in his shirt and jacket from dinner.

"What's that?" James asked as Kyle put the box down and ripped into the cardboard.

"Champagne," Kyle grinned, before leaning over the pool and passing a bottle to James. "Mind you, it's not actually champagne. It's Australian sparkling wine, six ninety-nine a bottle in Sainsburys."

"Don't let Meryl see that," Lauren said nervously. "She'll skin us alive."

"I think there's a tray of glasses by the minibar," Kerry said.

Kyle tutted. "And what did your last servant die of, Miss Chang?"

"I seem to remember kicking his head in after he refused to fetch a tray of champagne flutes." Kerry smirked.

As Kyle fetched the glasses, James popped the cork out of his bottle and downed a few mouthfuls before passing it along to Kerry.

"There you go, cow face," Kyle grinned as he set the glasses down at the edge of the pool beside Kerry. He threw off his jacket and started unbuttoning his shirt.

Kerry poured glasses of fizzy wine and passed them around the pool as James popped another bottle and Kyle pulled down his pants, revealing a complete absence of underwear.

"Go put something on," Gabrielle yelled as she covered her eyes in mock disgust. "I don't wanna look at that *thing* all night."

Kyle broke into a smile as he stepped into the pool.

"Sorry dudes, but the Kyle bathes naked. At least, he does when he forgets to pack swimming shorts."

"Perfect." Lauren grinned as she furtively sipped her sparkling wine. "Now all we need is for James to start farting."

By 1 a.m. James's skin was wrinkled, the empty bottles were hidden under the bathroom sink, and everyone except Kerry had gone back to their rooms.

"You're all shriveled like a prune." James giggled as he lay on his bed kissing Kerry's back.

"You're just Mr. Smooth aren't you?" she said, as she rolled over.

They were both a little drunk. James reached across to his bedside table and grabbed a small foil package. "I looked in the bathroom cupboard," he explained. "This hotel doesn't miss a trick."

Kerry was shocked. "Put the condom down, James, you *won't* be needing it."

"Come on," James said gently. "Why not?"

Kerry groaned. "We've had this conversation a million times already. If we have sex before we're sixteen, we'll both get kicked out of CHERUB."

"Who's gonna know?"

"They'll know if I get pregnant."

"That's what *this* is for," James said sarcastically, as he jiggled the condom.

"I'm fourteen years old and they're not a hundred percent effective."

James tutted. "I'll be really gentle, Kerry, I swear. Just do this one little thing for me."

Kerry's eyebrows shot up and she shoved James away furiously. "One little thing? What the hell is all this?" She spread her arms out wide. "I shopped for your presents, I looked up this hotel and the dune buggy place on the Internet. I even polished your rotten bloody shoes."

"I know, Kerry, but . . ." James couldn't think what to say. "It's not as if we'd be the only underage cherubs ever to have sex."

Kerry pointed at the bottom half of her swimsuit. "My body, my decision. Maybe, if we're still together when I turn sixteen. But right now I don't even know if we'll still be together tomorrow morning. I'm *sick* of you always pestering me. You're like a dirty old man."

James heard Kerry sob as she picked her hotel robe off the floor. It made him feel really guilty.

"Come on, Kerry, don't cry. You've had a few drinks. You're tired and a bit overemotional."

"You're not even worth crying over." Sniffing, Kerry knotted her robe and began hunting for her slippers. "I've been planning this for weeks. Everything was supposed to be *perfect*. You don't have any respect for me or my feelings."

"I can't help it," James said desperately. "I've really had fun today. I do love you and I want to be a fantastic, wonderful, caring boyfriend who understands your feelings and all that stuff. But I'm also a fifteen-year-old virgin and I really, *really* need a shag."

Kerry wiped her eye on the sleeve of her gown and James thought he heard her laugh as she stepped toward the door.

"Good night, Casanova," she tutted.

CHAPTER 17

BRIGHTON

James was woken by the buzzer on his door. It went off again as he scrambled around in the nude looking for his robe.

"Hang on, I'm coming," James shouted.

He was surprised to see Lauren standing in the door-way. She was fully dressed, with her jacket on and her wheeled suitcase behind her.

"Hello," he said curiously. "What time is it?"

Lauren glanced at her watch. "Eight minutes past seven," she said as she stepped into the room.

James had been up worrying about what had happened with Kerry. He'd had less than four hours' sleep and the wine had left him feeling groggy.

"What's going on?" he asked. "I didn't think we had anything planned for this morning."

"You don't," Lauren said, as James sat down on the corner of his bed and rubbed his eyes. "I think you've got a session in the spa booked for later, massage and that. I was well looking forward to it, but I've got a mission and John Jones is waiting downstairs."

"Oh," James said, surprised. "When did this happen?"

"I found out yesterday, but I didn't mention it last night 'cos it always feels a bit sad when someone's going away. I didn't want to spoil the mood."

"How long for?"

"Less than a month and it's only down in Brighton so we'll probably see each other."

"Who's with you?"

"John's the mission controller, but I'm the only agent."

"Oooh, black T-shirt and going on your first solo mission at twelve years of age," James said, a touch sarcastically. "You're quite the little superstar, aren't you?"

Lauren flushed and looked down at the carpet as she realized that she was being insensitive. "I hope your inquiry and everything works out, James," she said awkwardly. "I mean, nobody can fault your record on missions until now. You're the only agent who was on *both* of the missions that knocked out Help Earth. I've heard loads of people say that you should have got the black shirt for that."

"I expect it'll all turn out okay in the end," James said unconvincingly. "Anyway, good luck with your mission and keep safe."

"It's categorized as low risk, so there's no need to

worry." Lauren grinned, as the two siblings hugged. "And do me a favor and keep an eye on Rat for a few days. He was a bit choked last night when I told him I was going away. He's not been at CHERUB for long and I think Andy's his only close mate."

James nodded. "I'll invite Rat along if something's happening. I like him anyway, although it's awkward when Andy's around. He's still sore because I beat him up that time."

"Hardly surprising." Lauren grinned.

"I've apologized about eighty-six times." James shrugged. "You can only say it so much."

"Anyway, John's waiting in reception. I'd better skedaddle."

"One last thing. You haven't spoken to Kerry, have you?" James asked. "Only, we had a bit of a row late last night."

Lauren stared pointedly at the condom on the bedside table. "I wonder what that was about," she said.

"I feel really bad," James muttered. "I mean, you and Kerry set all this up and I end up rowing with her. Plus she'd had a few glasses of wine and you know how she gets."

"Haven't spoken to her," Lauren said. "But I'd recommend groveling and lots of it."

James couldn't get back to sleep. He ended up ordering tea and toast from room service and sitting on his bed reading the Sunday paper he'd found outside his door.

Kyle called just after nine. "Everyone seems to be up and about. We're heading down to breakfast and we're booked into the spa for ten o'clock."

"Righty ho," James said. "I'm not sure about this spa thing though. Have you ever been to one? It looks girly to me."

"Can't say I have," Kyle said. "But you should have seen the girls cooing over the brochure when we booked up."

"So you're going?" James asked.

"I know it's not your cup of tea, James, but the girls went to the dune buggy place because they knew you'd like it."

"I guess," James said, clearly not convinced.

"Besides, there's five of us lads, so I expect we'll just stand around taking the piss out of each other."

"Who knows, maybe I'll even like it, eh?"

"Exactly," Kyle said. "See you down at breakfast."

After waiting for Kerry and the others to head off to the dining room, James crept down the back stairs to the lobby and stole a rose from the floral display. When he reached the dining room, he put it between his teeth and knelt in front of Kerry.

"Good morrow, my sweet," he said, making a poor attempt at a posh accent as he handed her the rose. "Please accept my apologies for my caddish behavior last night."

Kerry smirked. She twirled the rose between her thumb and forefinger and addressed the whole table.

"Who thinks I should kiss and make up?"

Everyone started to laugh, and comments flew around the table ranging from "kick his arse" to "marry him" and "get it over with." James was a little bit scared because he'd left himself open for Kerry to humiliate him if she wanted to.

"I tell you what," Kerry said, as she leaned forward and kissed James on the cheek. "I'll accept your apology, so long as you go and fetch me another piece of toast from the counter."

It was early Sunday afternoon when Lauren arrived at the Aldrington Care Center, or the ACC. She'd spent the entire drive with a set of detailed paperwork spread across the backseats of a Range Rover Sport. As well as ploughing through a series of briefings on human trafficking, she had to read and remember all the details of a background story that had been carefully prepared by John.

Her name was Lauren Yuran, daughter of an English mother who'd died in childbirth. She'd lived in eastern Russia with her father until the age of eight, but had been sent back to live with her British grandmother when he was imprisoned for his role in an armed robbery. Unfortunately, her grandmother died of a heart attack within a year and she'd spent the last three years living in children's homes and with a succession of short-term foster parents.

She was returning to Aldrington Care Center following an unsuccessful placement with foster parents in Croydon, and as she spoke Russian, the chief supervisor at the care home—who knew nothing about the CHERUB operation—had agreed to place her in a room with the mysterious Anna.

Lauren Adams's previous experience of a care home had been in London, in the time between her mum dying and her being accepted into CHERUB. She'd expected a similar type of building with shabby corridors and mildew in the bathrooms. But ACC was less than two years old and modern care facilities are built quite differently.

There was a small office and a central kitchen where main meals were prepared, but the home itself consisted of five self-contained units. Each unit was built like a terraced house, with a kitchen and living room downstairs and six large bedrooms upstairs with accommodation for two children in each.

John had packed a large bag of Lauren's things, and with Lauren in tow, he wheeled it across a deserted playground and up to the front door of unit three.

"It's open," a kid shouted.

Lauren pushed the door and stepped into a large kitchen, with two washing machines running and notices taped everywhere: YOU MUST CLEAN THE WORKTOPS BEFORE PREPARING ANY FOOD. STACK ALL CUPS AND PLATES INSIDE THE DISHWASHER AFTER MEALS, and in giant orange letters, NO SNACKS OR OTHER TREATS BEFORE HOMEWORK IS COMPLETE AND SIGNED OFF BY THE HOUSE PARENT ON DUTY.

The kitchen was extremely hot and Lauren was slightly flustered by the bare chest of a good-looking teenager sitting at the dining table reading the latest Caroline Lawrence book.

"I'm looking for Chris Powell," John said hopefully.

"He's off today," the kid explained. "Madison is on duty. She's in the front room playing video games."

Three little kids sitting on the carpet all turned around when Lauren and John stepped into the room. Madison appeared to be in her thirties. She wore a pair of inexplicably large glasses with red plastic frames and a T-shirt with Lego men on it.

"Hi, Lauren," Madison said brightly, as her giant earrings jangled. "I'm one of your house parents. Welcome to ACC. These three are Luke, Seb, and Oonah, and you're going to be upstairs sharing a room with Anna."

Lauren gave the three little kids an awkward wave as they glanced away from the Playstation to acknowledge her.

"And you must be John Clarkson," Madison continued, as she reached out to shake John's hand.

"That's right," John lied.

"Have you worked at Croydon social services for long?" Madison asked.

"I'm retired actually," John said. "I'm doing a few weeks' cover for someone on maternity leave."

"Well, feel free to stop in the kitchen and make yourself a cup of tea. I'll show Lauren up to her room."

John shook his head. "I'd better get going. I want to watch the four o'clock match on Sky."

As Madison stepped out of the room, John made a telephone shape with his hand and mouthed the word *later* to Lauren.

As Lauren and Madison jointly carried the big case up to the first floor, the house parent began explaining various rules and rotations and asked if there were any kinds of food she particularly liked.

"And this is your roommate, Anna," Madison said brightly as they stepped into a comfortable-looking bedroom with a giant black stain in the middle of the carpet. "I'll leave you two to get acquainted. If you've got any questions, I'm just downstairs."

The two beds were space savers, with wooden ladders

leading up to the sleeping area. There were child-sized wardrobes, chests of drawers, and pullout desks underneath.

"Hey there," Lauren smiled, as she went up on tiptoes and peeked at Anna.

Anna sat on her bed playing with a bead necklace kit. There wasn't much of her. She was ten centimeters shorter than Lauren, with a tiny waist, china-white skin, and fragile hands and feet. Lauren was chunky like her brother and imagined that she'd be able to lift Anna over her head as she might have done when playing with a toddler.

When Lauren had to read some massive computer hacking textbook, or found herself melting on some brutal training exercise in high summer, she used to consider quitting CHERUB. But she knew it was worth it when she saw someone like Anna and realized that her mission might help save her and other girls just like her from being abused.

"You stare for?" Anna stuttered. She'd only been learning for a few weeks, so her English was pretty terrible.

"Sorry," Lauren said, before switching to Russian. "You sound Russian."

Anna brightened up as she turned to face Lauren. "Do you speak Russian?"

"Not much since I moved to England, so I'm out of practice, but my father was Russian. I lived there until three years ago."

"Amazing," Anna grinned, as she clapped her hands together. "I only speak when the translator comes and then all they talk about are my problems, so I don't answer."

"I know that feeling." Lauren nodded. "The carers just keep going *on and on*. Sometimes I just want to stick my iPod on and tell them to get stuffed."

Anna burst out laughing. "I can't believe you're a Russian."

"I can practice my language with you." Lauren grinned. "What a *weird* coincidence. . . ."

CHAPTER 18

TRAINING

It was late Sunday night and James was back at campus. He was watching TV in bed when Lauren called.

"Yo, bitch," James grinned. "How's it hanging?"

"Not bad, gay boy," Lauren said softly. "The girl I'm supposed to be chumming up seems nice, but she's *really* quiet. I spent the afternoon showing her how to make Scoubidous."

"Why are you whispering?"

"I'm in our bathroom, Anna's in the next room. Did you make up with Kerry?"

"Pretty much," James nodded. "I think she cut me some slack 'cos it was my birthday bash."

"And how was the spa?"

"Good." James grinned. "This *gorgeous* woman gave me a massage and it was bloody hilarious because Bruce got this dirty great fat bloke with hairy knuckles. Then we all got kicked out of the steam room for throwing buckets of cold water around. And *then* I saw this beauty therapist and she put this mudpack on my face and gave me a manicure."

"I can't believe I missed it," Lauren moaned. "I've *always* wanted to go to one of those places."

"You know how my nails are usually all broken and dirty? They're all neat and shiny now and she gave me some tips and a bottle of this special lotion to put in the bath. It's supposed to dry my skin out and stop me from getting spots."

"So all you boys enjoyed it?"

"Except Bruce." James laughed. "I didn't expect to, but I'd definitely go again if someone else was paying. And you should have seen Kerry and Bethany in the beauty shop afterward. They spent a *fortune*."

"On what?"

"I dunno, it all just looked like expensive pots of smelly gunk to me. We got you a little present, 'cos you missed out. It's like a gift set of all these different oils and this wooden ball thingy for massaging your back. Oh and don't worry, I checked before we paid, and they said it didn't contain any animal products or stuff that was tested on animals."

"Thanks, James," Lauren said. "By the way, I've got some great photos from last night on my phone. There's a superb shot of that old colonel waving his walking stick when we mooned him off the balcony."

James had a 7 a.m. combat training session on Monday mornings, so he was knackered when he reached the dining room at quarter past eight. Meryl cornered him as he headed toward Kerry and Kyle at their usual table.

"Nice healthy start." Meryl stared pointedly at James's tray, which was stacked with bacon, eggs, beans, fried bread, and hash brown.

"Don't you start on that," James moaned. "You know Zara's made them turn the Coke machine off until lunchtime now?"

Meryl shook her head. "You drank Coke with *breakfast*?"

"Not every day. . . . And I only ever drank diet 'cos the normal kind makes me fat."

"Anyway," Meryl said, looking mildly horrified. "I've noticed that you're only studying for five GCSEs and a Further Maths A-level at the moment. Your schedule looks *very* light, so we're going to have to make some adjustments."

James tutted. "But I've already got Maths and Russian A-levels, miss. My Spanish is good enough to pass an A-level already, and I'm so good at maths that I'll ace Further Maths and Physics when I get around to taking them. Five A-levels will get me into whatever university I want."

"James, I'm fully aware that CHERUB language training and your exceptional ability in mathematics means that you'll have no problems getting into university. But that *doesn't* mean I'm going to allow you to spend the next three years coasting. All cherubs are bright and we expect you to push yourselves. Kerry should be able to get three easy language A-levels when she takes them next summer, but she's still studying for nine GCSEs and she's almost a year younger than you."

"Yeah, but . . . ," James stammered. "I mean, Kerry's a good all-rounder. I'm rubbish at anything where you need to do loads of reading and writing. She can write an essay in half the time it takes me."

"Well, if you don't want any more academic work, there is one other option."

James perked up. "Is there?"

"Our head training instructor, Mr. Pike, is always on the lookout for kids who are willing to help prepare some of the red-shirts for basic training. Especially at the moment, what with Mr. Large recovering from a heart bypass and Miss Smoke on maternity leave."

"Oh," James said, clearly not keen on Meryl's suggestion.

Cherubs were often asked to help out with training younger kids, but training instructors were some of the least popular staff on campus and helping them out didn't win you many friends. Plus, training instructors often worked as hard as or even harder than the trainees themselves.

Meryl smiled. "If you don't want to help Mr. Pike with training, James, I'll have to enroll you on a couple of extra academic courses. I hear that Mr. Reddit is starting a new Latin for Beginners and there are GCSE courses in sociology and economics that started a few weeks back. Once you've caught up on the backlog, you'll probably find them quite enjoyable."

"No," James gasped. "Come off it, Meryl, you know I'll hate every minute. And Latin? I mean, what the hell use is that unless you want to grow up and become a Latin teacher?"

"How about helping Mr. Pike then?"

James looked sullenly at his tray of breakfast. "I suppose it's the lesser of two evils."

"Great," Meryl smiled. "You've got an appointment to see Mr. Pike after lessons this afternoon."

"But . . . ," James spluttered. His heart sank as he realized that Meryl had stitched him up.

"I didn't think you'd go for the Sociology and Latin," Meryl said. "Now you'd better go eat your plate of grease before it gets any colder."

Lauren would have to attend a Brighton secondary school, but it was going to take a few days to sort out a place and that didn't exactly break her heart. When all the other kids in her unit had eaten breakfast and gone off to school, she pushed open the door of her room and began going through Anna's stuff.

It was a pitifully brief search. Anna had stepped off the boat with nothing but the clothes she stood up in and had collected only a few items of clothing and knick-knacks in the weeks since she'd arrived in Britain.

Lauren flipped carefully through a collection of notebooks filled with Anna's felt-tip drawings. She had a deliberate style, with thick black outlines carefully colored in. Some pages were doodles, while others documented Anna's attempts to learn English, with rows of tiny pictures and hand-drawn images with descriptions written in English and spelled out phonetically in the Russian alphabet beneath them.

After going through the desk drawers, Lauren climbed up the ladder to Anna's bed. A tiny picture caught inside a plastic key fob had been taped to the bedpost. The photograph had water damage around its edges and showed Anna in a photo booth. She looked eight or nine years old and was propped on the leg of a very young-looking mother. On the woman's other knee was a stern-faced baby, with straight dark hair and a pacifier in its mouth.

Lauren had seen an enlargement of the picture among the paperwork she'd read on the drive down, but seeing this tiny fragment of Anna's past still made her feel sad.

She began a careful inspection of Anna's bed, first holding up the pillows and looking to see if anything had been slipped inside and then working her way around the edges of the mattress. Besides dust, crumbs, and a grubby sock, Lauren found a bunch of papers with Anna's writing on them.

The sheets had been torn from lined exercise books. They had no drawings on them, just neat lists written in Russian with a purple gel-ink pen. Each list started off the same. Point one was always *keep identity secret*, and point two, *work hard in school and learn good English*.

After that the lists diversified. Some lists continued sensibly:

(3) *Get a well-paid job.*
(4) *Find Georgy and bring him to Britain.*
(5) *Start my own business (Hairdressing or Car Dealer).*
(6) *Become rich and buy a nice house.*

(7)   Get married and have a boy and two girls.

While other lists were outpourings of Anna's wildest fantasies:

(3)   Go to loads of clubs in London.
(4)   Make friends with rich and famous people.
(5)   Marry a hunky football star and move to Barcelona.
(6)   Find Georgy and buy him a house next to ours in Spain.
(7)   Start my own airline with my husband's money.
(8)   After a difficult start, I become richest woman in the world.
(9)   Pay men to go back home and kill everyone I hate. Slowly!!!

Some of Anna's lists were funny, while others made Lauren sad. Lauren had never actually written out lists like this, but she occasionally did something similar when she couldn't fall asleep, lying in bed and plotting out her future.

Anna's lists were vague, but they still told Lauren a lot. First of all, the police psychologists suspected that Anna hadn't spoken about her past because she was traumatized. But the lists made it clear that that she was deliberately keeping her identity a secret. Second, Anna only ever mentioned rescuing Georgy, who Lauren guessed was the toddler in the photograph. This meant that Anna's mother was either dead, or had no contact with her daughter.

It wasn't the kind of concrete information that Lauren would need to unearth the traffickers, but she'd made a start.

CHAPTER 10

INSTRUCTORS

CHERUB's training instructors worked from a ratty pre-fabricated hut outside the basic training compound. James rapped on the metal door.

"Come in," Mr. Pike shouted.

The room had threadbare carpet and a few shabby desks and was littered with dirty sportswear and damp towels. The tang of old sweat and body spray hung in the air.

Mr. Pike sat at the head of a long table, with his deputies Mr. Speaks and Mr. Greaves along the sides. James was surprised to see that Mr. Greaves had his camouflage pants rolled up and his feet in a bowl of water.

"Pull up a seat, James," Mr. Pike said, as he pointed to an insulated jug in the middle of the table. "Coffee?"

James nodded as he sat down. He felt extremely odd seeing the three powerfully built instructors off duty. Normally you only had close encounters with these men when you were terrified or exhausted, yet here they were at the end of a day's training looking like three middle-aged blokes who just wanted to go home and fall asleep in front of the TV.

As James took a mouthful of his coffee, he noticed that the confidential files of eight red-shirts and three new recruits were spread over the table.

"There's a new session of basic training starting in a month's time," Mr. Pike explained. "This is our preliminary meeting. We discuss the strengths and weaknesses of each candidate, try and pair them off into evenly balanced partnerships, and also finalize the exact nature of the exercises we'll be taking them on, without overspending on the travel budget."

James was surprised. "I always thought you paired kids off at random."

"Quite the opposite," Mr. Pike said. "CHERUB is always short of agents, and the powers that be put us under a lot of pressure to get everyone through basic training."

"Without lowering our standards," Mr. Speaks added, as he ran a length of grubby towel between his toes.

"I want you to take a look at this young fellow," Mr. Pike said, as he slid one of the folders across the table toward James. "You're pretty confident on the height test obstacle these days aren't you?"

James nodded. "I've been over it that many times now, I don't even think about it."

"The little fella in that folder is having some serious problems."

James flipped the file open and saw a black-and-white picture of a red-shirt boy who'd turned ten three weeks earlier. His name was Kevin Sumner. James didn't know him, but he'd seen him around campus.

"So he's scared of heights?" James asked.

"Terrified," Pike nodded, "and he hasn't got a hope of getting through basic training unless he combats his fear. Kev's a tough young fellow, with a good head on his shoulders, but he went on a rollercoaster when he was seven years old. The emergency brake came on when he was halfway around a three-sixty-degree loop and he spent three hours hanging upside down before the fire brigade got him out. He's been petrified of heights ever since."

"So, you want me to take him through it gently?"

Mr. Pike shook his head. "We've been there, tried that and Kevin's thrown up all over the T-shirt. I want you to use a different technique. Remember how you learned to swim?"

James would never forget. When he first arrived at CHERUB, he'd been terrified of water, and a month of intensive swimming lessons had made no difference. In the end, it took two bullying sixteen-year-olds repeatedly throwing him in the deep end of a swimming pool to combat his fear.

"You'll have to be ruthless, James," Mr. Pike said. "Pick one of your mates to help you. You can both take whatever time you need out of lessons, and if you can get Kevin to go across that obstacle unassisted, I'll make sure you get a passing grade in any subject you choose."

"You mean I get out of having to do my History coursework?"

"I can set that up if that's what you want." Mr. Pike nodded. "But remember, the technique only works if that kid is more frightened of you than he is of plunging off a fifty-meter drop."

James looked at the photo and wondered if he had the cruel streak necessary to become a CHERUB training instructor. But then again, it was totally worth it if it got him through GCSE History.

John Jones was staying at a guest house less than a kilometer away from the Aldrington Care Center. When Lauren got bored of sitting around waiting for Anna and the other kids to get back from school, she arranged to meet John in a nearby café and told her carer that she was going for a walk.

The café was in the back of a baker's and the smell of warm bread filled the air as Lauren and John drank mugs of tea and ate doughnuts.

"I'm starting to wonder if young Anna's as innocent as she seems," John said.

"Why's that?" Lauren asked.

"Those lists you read show that she's determined not to reveal her identity. That's a pretty smart move if you want to stay in England."

"How come?"

"If Anna had revealed her name and told the authorities where she was from, she probably would have been deported back to Russia within a matter of days."

"But we know she's Russian now," Lauren said.

John nodded. "Yes, but the rules don't permit the authorities to simply stick a child back on the first plane to Russia. They have to know who she is, where she came from, and that someone will look after her when she returns. We've checked with the Russian police and nobody has reported Anna missing. If she can keep silent for a year or so, she'll be settled in Britain. Anna can say that she has friends and wants to stay here. The local authority will launch formal care proceedings, Brighton council will become Anna's guardian, and she'll be given British citizenship."

"That sounds quite manipulative," Lauren said. "And she's only eleven or twelve."

"But the lists demonstrate that she's thinking about her future. I suspect that one of the other girls inside that boat had been trafficked before and told Anna how to behave if she was captured."

Lauren gasped. "Trafficked before?"

"That's common," John explained. "Once a girl is captured, the criminal gangs who traffic the girls regard them as their property. Girls caught by the British authorities are usually deported straight back to Russia. With no home and no job, the gangsters frequently pick the girls up on the streets again and send them straight back to Britain."

"Doesn't the government do anything to stop that happening?"

John shook his head. "It's all to do with politics. A large proportion of the general public doesn't like immigration. The government is more popular if it's tough on immigration, and any system the government puts in place to support these girls will be open to abuse. If they start giving special treatment to women who are forced into prostitution, then thousands of other illegal immigrants will start claiming that they were forced into prostitution."

"I guess," Lauren said weakly. "But how can they send girls home with no protection from the gangsters?"

John shrugged. "It's just one of those horrible situations where there aren't any easy answers."

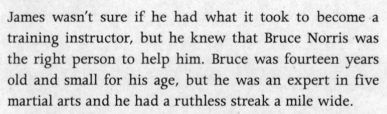

CHAPTER 20

WOLF

James wasn't sure if he had what it took to become a training instructor, but he knew that Bruce Norris was the right person to help him. Bruce was fourteen years old and small for his age, but he was an expert in five martial arts and he had a ruthless streak a mile wide.

"Remember," James whispered, as they crept down a dark corridor on the second floor of the junior block. "We've got to scare him shitless, but we can't actually hurt him. . . . Not badly anyway."

"I know," Bruce said. "I'm a peaceful person, James. I might have finished fifty or sixty violent brawls, but I've *never* started one."

The two boys wore boots, combat trousers, black jackets,

and black gloves. The carer who'd let them into the junior block had told them that she didn't want all the red-shirts woken up by screaming, so they had to take their victim silently.

As they stepped through an open door into the bedroom Kevin Sumner shared with his best friend, James and Bruce pulled furry werewolf masks over their heads.

"On three," James whispered, as he stared down at the peaceful face of a sleeping ten-year-old. "One, two . . . three."

As James swung his knee across and pinned Kevin to his bed, Bruce pinched his nose. The youngster's scream was muffled as Bruce crammed a dirty sock into his mouth, but his eyes shot open wide, clearly petrified at being woken up by two wolfmen.

"Time for walkies, squirt," James said, as he picked Kevin out of bed and slung him over his shoulder.

Kevin kicked and screamed into the vile-tasting sock as James carried him along the hallway, down four flights of stairs, and out into the night air. After a two-hundred-meter jog across muddy ground, James ripped the sock from Kevin's mouth and dumped him into a deep puddle.

"On your feet, scum," Bruce shouted, as he and James switched on head-mounted LED lamps.

Kevin sobbed as he scrambled up, barefoot and with nothing but a vest and pajama bottoms to protect him from the cold.

"Too slow," Bruce shouted, as he kicked the back of Kevin's legs. He crashed face-first into the puddle.

"Get up again," James yelled.

"Quickly this time," Bruce added.

Kevin was crying and shivering.

"Look at the little baby," Bruce said nastily, as he pressed his boot down on Kevin's bare foot.

James closed up behind, so that the shivering boy was sandwiched with the white lights blazing down on his sodden hair.

"What do you want?" Kevin asked weakly.

James didn't answer the question. "You're now the property of the wolfmen," he grinned. "Mr. Pike has told us that you're a little snot-nosed scaredy-cat. He says you'll never make it through basic training because you're afraid of heights and won't go over the obstacle. Well, until you pull yourself together and stop acting like a pussy, we're going to make your life a living hell."

"If you run away, we'll catch you," Bruce said. "If you cry, we'll laugh. If you even think about taking a swing at us . . ."

Instead of finishing his sentence, Bruce placed his black gloved hands around Kevin's neck.

"Leave me alone," Kevin screamed, as Bruce pressed down on his shoulders until his knees buckled.

"Kiss our boots," James said.

"Get stuffed, queers," Kevin shouted defiantly.

Bruce produced a length of nylon rope from his pocket and held it in Kevin's face. "If you don't start showing me some respect, Mr. Sumner, I'm gonna tie this around your ankles, hitch you into the nearest tree, and leave you hanging upside down until morning."

They knew from the file that hanging upside down was Kevin's worst nightmare.

"*Noooooo*," Kevin squealed, as Bruce grabbed his ankles. "I'll kiss your boots."

"Get on with it then," James barked. "And thank me for it."

James didn't know what to feel as Kevin crawled pathetically through the puddle and planted his lips on the end of James's boot. He knew exactly how miserable being bullied like this made you feel, but on the other hand, James never would have made it as a cherub if he hadn't been through it himself.

"Thank you," Kevin said, after kissing Bruce's boots.

"Mr. Wolfman, sir," Bruce shouted.

"Thank you, Mr. Wolfman, sir," Kevin said weakly. He was soaked in near freezing water and his teeth were chattering as James grabbed the back of his vest and hitched him out of the mud.

"You need warming up," James barked. "Start running toward the basic training compound, *quickly.*"

Kevin tried to control his sobbing as he started running into the darkness, with James and Bruce a few paces behind him.

"There's only one way to get away from us, Sumner," Bruce said, as they ran. "We're gonna be on your case until you make it across the obstacle without me or James giving you one finger of help."

James looked angrily at Bruce. "Don't use my name. I'm wolfman number one."

Kevin looked back over his shoulder. "I know who you are," he said defiantly. "James Adams and Bruce Norris. I'm ten years old, I'm not a complete moron."

Bruce ripped off his mask and scowled at James.

"I *told* you the wolfman thing was stupid."

"I really *hate* red-shirts," James moaned as he tried to peel off his mask. "They're all lippy little smart arses."

James's mask was stuck half on and half off. He couldn't see where he was running and had to stop. "Give us a hand, Bruce."

"I guess that proves you've got a big head," Bruce grinned as he eased James's mask off, but his mood changed when he realized that Kevin had cut into the trees and was out of sight.

"Come back here, you little git, or I'll break every bone in your body," Bruce snarled.

They could hear Kevin's feet splattering in the mud less than twenty meters way. Then the noise stopped.

"He must be hiding in the trees," James whispered.

They fitted their lamps back on their heads before throwing the masks away, then switched off the beams before creeping into the trees.

"I'm giving you until ten, Kevin," Bruce shouted. "We're working for Mr. Pike, so you're gonna have to face us sooner or later. But if you come out before I reach ten, you won't have to spend two hours hanging upside down from a tree."

"Get stuffed, gonad breath," Kevin shouted, as Bruce started to count.

Unfortunately for Kevin, James was less than three meters from where he'd shouted and made a lunge at him. Unfortunately for *James*, Kevin had found a thick branch, and he swung it at James as he approached. The piece of wood hit James's knee with such force that it cracked in two.

"You little pecker," James yelled, clutching his leg as Kevin sprang out of his position huddled against a tree trunk.

James managed to grab Kevin's muddy foot as he tried to escape. The pain in James's leg made him angry and he mercilessly crushed the small foot and twisted his ankle. As Kevin wailed in pain and crumpled onto the ground, James let go of his foot and knelt over him.

"I could splat you like a bug, you little freak," James shouted.

"Let's tie the little bugger up," Bruce said enthusiastically. "I reckon he'll show us more respect after a few hours dangling in the freezing cold."

"Please," Kevin sobbed, as James watched the boy's desperate expression and fresh tears welling up in his eyes.

James realized that he absolutely hated doing this. "Do you *want* to pass basic training?" he said, eyeballing Kevin.

"Yes," Kevin sniffled.

"And you're not going to do it until you get over your fear of heights, are you?"

"No."

"I'm here to help you get over that fear," James said. "I know this works, because I've been on your end of it myself. Okay?"

Kevin nodded.

"So get your arse out of the dirt and we're gonna get you through this."

As James hauled himself off the ground using a hanging branch for leverage, Bruce grabbed Kevin out of the dirt. "You're lucky he got to you before I did," Bruce growled. "If you'd whacked me with that stick, it'd be halfway up your arse by now."

Lauren was having a slightly quieter evening in Brighton. After coming in from school and changing out of uniform, Anna sat quietly and did her homework, which mostly comprised English comprehension exercises set by her special needs teacher.

After an evening meal cooked in Aldrington Care Center's main kitchen, the two girls went back to their room and gossiped while they watched TV and played cards. The conversation ranged from lightweight stuff about pop music and boys they fancied through to deeper stuff about their past lives.

Anna freely told anecdotes about funny things she'd seen in Russian schools and stories she'd read in newspapers, but she clammed up when it came to specific details about her past. All she'd confirm was that the people in the picture stuck to her bed post were her mother and little brother Georgy.

Attempts to find details of where Anna had lived in Russia and how she'd come to Britain were either ignored or brushed aside with a swift change of subject, and queries about Anna's mother produced a pained expression that suggested she was close to tears.

Lauren wasn't sure if Anna's reluctance to talk was because she was genuinely traumatized, or part of a carefully contrived shield that would stop her from being sent back to Russia. Either way, a few hours with Anna were enough for Lauren to realize that her young companion was extremely intelligent.

The two girls went to bed after staying up late to watch a movie on Channel Five. About half an hour after the lights had gone out, Anna stepped out of bed onto her ladder and whispered to Lauren.

"Are you awake?"

Lauren opened one eye and thought about answering, but didn't because there was something suspicious in Anna's tone. She closed her eye as she heard Anna creeping down the ladder and walking across to Lauren's side of the room.

Anna grabbed something from Lauren's desk and Lauren recognized the sound of her mobile phone flipping open as Anna stepped gingerly toward the bathroom. Lauren panicked: The mission had been planned in a rush and while she'd fitted a new SIM card inside her phone, she hadn't cleared all her text messages and the phone's memory card was stuffed with pictures and video clips from James's birthday weekend. If Anna saw any of them, her cover would be shot.

"Ahem," Lauren said, clearing her throat as she switched on the spot lamp clipped to the metal frame of her bed.

Anna froze like a bunny caught in headlights.

"Do you need my phone?" Lauren asked.

"No, no," Anna said, smiling uncomfortably, as Lauren rolled over the side of her bed and dropped barefoot on to the carpet.

It was a shame in a way: Lauren realized that Anna's call might have provided a major clue about her identity. But Lauren couldn't risk her finding the pictures and clips.

"I don't mind you using it," Lauren said, holding the phone out to Anna. "Provided you don't yak on for hours and use up all my credit."

But Anna shook her head, sheepishly refusing the offer. "Who would I call? I just wanted to look. Please don't be angry at me."

Lauren shrugged. "Forget it."

"I've never had a mobile," Anna said, shaking her head frantically. "You're lucky."

"Just ask next time," Lauren said, as she climbed back up to her bed with the phone in her hand. She tucked her phone between her mattress and the wall for safekeeping and turned out the light.

"Climb on there," James ordered, pointing at a wooden barrel that went up as high as his nipples.

"Quickly," Bruce shouted.

The barrel was weighted down with sand and didn't budge as Kevin hauled himself onto the lid and sat down.

"Stand *up*," James yelled.

It was the kind of instruction you'd expect a ten-year-old to follow easily, but Kevin's hands were shaking as he got to his feet.

"Don't look down, just jump into the mud."

"I can't," Kevin quaked as he tried to squat back down.

"You bend those legs one more millimeter and I'll stand on your balls," Bruce shouted. "Now jump."

"I've seen four-year-olds jump from higher up than that," James yelled.

A tear ran down Kevin's cheek as he sat down.

"I'm giving you until three to stand up and jump off

that barrel," Bruce said fiercely. "One . . . two . . ."

"I can't," Kevin whined.

"Three," Bruce roared.

Bruce furiously hauled Kevin off the barrel. He splattered him face-first into the mud and rested his boot against the side of his head.

"What do you reckon, James?" Bruce asked. "Time for something radical?"

"The little wimp's left us with no choice."

"You see that building over there?" Bruce pointed at a flat-roofed shed used to store gardening equipment. "We're gonna take you up there and throw you off the roof."

"No," Kevin sobbed desperately, as he curled up in a ball. "Don't make me go up there."

James grabbed him out of the dirt. "You'd better start putting some effort into this, sissy. We're not going anywhere. You can cry and whine and fight with us all night long, but it doesn't hurt us one little bit. We're going to keep doing this, night after night, until you show us some guts."

Kevin tried to bargain as Bruce dragged him toward an aluminum ladder. "Let me try the barrel again."

"Nope," Bruce said, as Kevin tried to wriggle free. "We gave you three tries with the barrel. Now we're throwing you off the roof."

"Please," Kevin howled.

He was kicking and screaming way too much to be forced into climbing the ladder, so Bruce climbed on to the roof and leaned over the side, then James held Kevin up so that Bruce could grab him. As Bruce dragged Kevin across the flat roof, James ran around the building to an area on the opposite side that had a crash mat beneath it.

"Jump," Bruce shouted as he pushed Kevin up to the edge of the roof.

James stood on the edge of the crash mat with his arms spread out wide. "Come on, you little chicken. What the *hell* are you scared of?"

Bruce gave Kevin a shove that left him dangling over the edge. "Please," Kevin sobbed. "I think I'm gonna be sick."

"Oh, give over, you little pussy." Bruce sneered. "*Jump.*"

But Kevin retched and violently spewed the contents of his stomach onto the crash mat. James stepped back but didn't get clear before some of the puke hit his outstretched arm. Bruce was so shocked that he let Kevin go.

The ten-year-old screamed as he flopped onto the crash mat, landing in a mixture of rainwater and his own vomit.

"Nice landing, pansy," Bruce said.

Kevin rolled over, his vest and pajama bottoms covered in his own vomit. James felt really sorry for him, but he knew that this technique would only work if he showed no mercy.

"I hope you're proud of yourself, loser," James said. "Maybe next time we'll throw you off where there's no crash mat."

"Get stuffed," Kevin shouted. "I hate you both."

"Now all we need is for the baby to piss his pants." Bruce grinned as he dangled his legs off the side of the roof and jumped down, carefully avoiding the crash mat.

"Right," Kevin snarled, as he jumped to his feet. "I'll show you two pricks."

Kevin steamed away from the mat. For a second, James thought he was going to try running off again. But he headed for the ladder and started climbing up.

"I'll jump," Kevin screamed madly, as he ran across the roof and leapt off with such force that he almost cleared the landing mat.

"Blimey," James said, resisting the temptation to say *well done* as he gave Kevin a hand up.

"Not bad for a pansy boy," Bruce added.

"You want me to do it again?" Kevin snarled. "You want me to jump off the roof again?"

"Once more," James said, trying not to show that he was delighted.

James and Bruce smiled and gave each other a high five as Kevin scaled the ladder.

"Poor little sod," Bruce whispered.

Kevin took his second jump more cautiously, curling his toes over the edge of the roof and landing on his feet.

Bruce hitched Kevin up by his muddy vest and James eyeballed him.

"Not bad," James sneered. "Wash yourself up and go back to bed. We'll see you tomorrow after lessons, by the main obstacle."

"And don't be late," Bruce added with a snarl.

CHAPTER 21

BREAKFAST

It was past midnight by the time James had showered and climbed into bed. Unless he had to get up early for combat training, James always slept in for a few minutes after his alarm. And every so often he'd drift back to sleep. . . .

"AAARGHHH!" James gasped, when he looked up and saw that it was twenty to nine.

He vaulted out of bed and scrambled into a clean uniform before taking the elevator down to the dining hall. He was delighted to see Bruce, Kyle, Shak, Gabrielle, and particularly Kerry sitting at their usual table, finishing up their breakfasts.

"I need to copy your geography, Kerry," James said.

Kerry calmly sipped her grapefruit juice. "Good morning to you too, James."

"Seriously," James said, glaring at his watch. "You know what a hard-ass Mr. Norwood is."

"Haven't you heard?" Kyle said gravely.

James looked confused. "Heard what?"

"Mr. Norwood was in a car accident last night. He's dead."

"Oh my God," James gasped. "That's terrible."

But he was actually relieved about the homework, until he saw Kyle breaking into a smile.

"Had you for a minute," Kyle grinned.

James scowled at Kerry as all his mates started laughing. "So can I *please* copy your homework?"

"There," Kerry said, as she ripped the question sheet out of her backpack and slammed it on the table. "Would you like a pen and paper too?"

James felt around inside his pant pockets. "Um, I would actually, yeah."

Kerry shook her head as she produced the pen and paper. "And don't copy it word for word, it's too obvious."

"Cheers," James said. "I'd better run and get some breakfast before they pull the shutters down."

The good thing about being late for breakfast was that there wasn't a line. The bad thing was that all the decent food had gone. After considering a sweaty-looking egg-and-bacon croissant, James settled on a mug of coffee and some fruit, which he'd be able to eat with one hand while he copied the homework.

He sat at an empty table so that he could concentrate.

Unfortunately, he'd only done seven out of fifteen questions when the bell rang for first lesson.

"I need my work back," Kerry said, looming over James as more than a hundred cherubs filed out of the dining room.

"Just give me a minute."

Kerry tutted. "We'll be late. You've had the whole week to do it."

"You go," James spluttered, as he realized that his answer to question nine was more or less illegible. "Tell Norwood that I'm upstairs speaking to Meryl or something."

"Okay. But it's gonna look obvious if I haven't got my homework and then you turn up with both sets."

"I only need five minutes and he always collects homework at the end."

Kerry tutted again. "See you in there."

Within another couple of minutes, there were less than a dozen kids left in the dining room. James was scribbling his answer to the final question and eating the last mouthful of his banana when a shadow loomed over his page.

"I'll just be a sec," James said, without looking up from his page. He assumed it was one of the dinner ladies wanting to clear the table.

But a gruff boy's voice came at him. "All right, *nark*."

James looked up and saw a gray-shirt kid about a year younger than himself. His name was Stuart Russell and they were in a couple of lessons together, but the only thing James knew about Stuart was that he'd snogged Gabrielle at a Christmas party.

"You what?" James asked.

"I called you a nark," Stuart said. "Helping the training instructors."

James shook his head. "What's *your* problem?"

"Kevin Sumner's my cousin. He told me what you did last night."

James stood up warily. Stuart was smaller than him, but his confident air made James suspect that Stuart knew some moves.

"Look," James said, raising his hands, "he's a nice little dude and we're trying to help him. Gotta be cruel to be kind, you know?"

Stuart raised a finger. "Well make sure he doesn't get hurt, because I'll hurt *you* if he does."

"You gonna hurt Bruce Norris, too?" James asked.

Stuart suddenly looked a lot less sure of himself. He turned to face a friend of his who was sitting on a table a few meters away. "I thought you said it was Bruce Clark."

The kid at the table shrugged. "Kevin just said the name Bruce . . ."

James couldn't help smiling: Bruce Clark was a shy eleven-year-old who wouldn't harm a fly. Bruce Norris was a campus karate champion who would probably enjoy harming the fly and then go after its brothers and sisters for the hell of it.

"Cat got your tongue, Stewey?" James grinned. "Shall I pass your threat on to Bruce Norris?"

"It's still bogus," Stuart said, as he stepped back. "You screwed up and got two MI5 officers killed. I don't know why you're even on campus, let alone training other kids."

James was better at turning the other cheek than he'd been when he first joined CHERUB, but the comment about the suspension riled him.

"What do you know?" he snapped. "You're talking out of your arse."

"I know enough," Stuart mocked. "I bet they kick your butt out of here when the investigation finishes."

James's temper snapped and he lunged toward Stuart. His first punch slammed against Stuart's nose, but the second only glanced the top of the gray-shirt's head as he ducked out of the way. Stuart charged forward, butting James in the stomach. Chairs and tables grated across the floor as Stuart pushed James backward and pinned him to a tabletop.

James was terrified that Stuart was going to punch his partially healed nose and was actually quite relieved when the chunky fist smacked him on the lips. As James tasted blood in his mouth, he punched Stuart in the ribs with enough force to unbalance him.

"Break it up," one of the dinner ladies yelled, as James brought his knee up and knocked Stuart onto the floor.

As Stuart scrambled to his feet, the overweight dinner lady placed herself between them and brandished a soup ladle.

"Show's over," she shouted. James realized that everyone else in the canteen was watching them. "Get to your lessons."

Stuart and James were both muscular and could have easily shoved the dinner lady aside, but while they were both furious, neither lad was prepared to assault a member of staff.

As Stuart skulked off to collect his bag, James straightened up his clothes and realized that he'd been lucky: If a teacher or a member of the care staff had broken up the fight instead of a dinner lady, he'd probably be on his way to the chairman's office instead of first lesson.

James turned back to the table he'd been working at and saw that his coffee mug had tipped over in the melee. His hastily scribbled homework was fine, but the top half of Kerry's was soaked in a massive brown stain.

She was going to kill him.

Lauren phoned John as soon as Anna and all the other kids had cleared off to school.

"I messed up," she confessed meekly.

"What do you mean?" John asked.

"Anna wanted to use my phone and we could have logged her call, but I had to stop her 'cos I've got loads of personal messages and pictures on there."

John tutted. "That's the kind of mistake I'd expect from an agent on their first mission. You really ought to know better."

"Sorry."

"I guess it's partly my fault: I should have set you up with a clean phone for the mission. These modern smart phones retain all kinds of data, even when you supposedly wipe the memory. Now, let me think. . . ."

John continued after a moment's pause. "Okay, we obviously want Anna to get access to your phone and have a record of everything she says. I'll go into town and get you an identical replacement, then I'll get the boffins on campus to tap into the cellular network and record all your calls. The only thing is, you'd better tone down the dirty talk with your boyfriend."

"Very funny," Lauren said dryly.

She liked working with John: Some mission controllers would have gone on and on about not deleting the stuff from her phone, but John just accepted the apology and got on with it.

"I'll meet you in the baker's at about two o'clock with the new phone, okay?"

"Fine," Lauren said. "But there's one other thing I was thinking about."

"What?"

"Suppose we uncover this trafficking ring and put the baddies behind bars. Will they stick Anna back on the first plane to Russia?"

"Anna's future is down to the immigration authorities."

"Yeah," Lauren said, "but if I uncover who she is and she gets sent back home because of me, that's . . . It's like, I'm a cherub because I want to help people, but I won't be helping Anna, will I?"

John sighed. "I see what you're saying, but I'm not sure what I can do."

"Come *on*, John," Lauren said. "With all CHERUB's resources, you're telling me that you can't swing it so that one little girl gets taken into care?"

John sighed. "I guess you're right. I'm not promising anything but I'll look into it."

CHAPTER 22

BREAK

"It wasn't deliberate," James yelled, as he barged two of his classmates out of the doorway and sprinted down the corridor with Kerry on his tail.

"You're *dead*, Adams," Kerry screamed, as two little red-shirts jumped out of her way.

James sprinted around a corner, but dropped to a brisk walk when he saw two teachers stepping out of a classroom. He didn't want to get yelled at for running. Kerry slowed down too and the chase continued at walking pace until James reached the staircase that led up to their rooms.

"Come on, Kerry!" James said, as he leapt up the stairs two at a time. "Give us a break."

Speed had always been James's weakness and Kerry cornered him on the fourth-floor landing.

"Dickhead," she snarled as she gave him two powerful beats to the upper arm. "I've got enough to do without getting a stupid detention because of you."

"It's not my fault," James whined, as he rolled out his bottom lip to show where it had scabbed over. "Stuart Russell is a total moron."

"It's nothing to do with that," Kerry snapped. "You copied it word for word."

"It wasn't exactly the same."

"It took Mr. Norwood all of two seconds to figure out. That's the last time you ever copy my homework, James. I don't care how much you beg."

James anxiously ran his hand through his hair, which needed cutting. "How about we go back to my room and patch things up?"

"Don't push your luck," Kerry snarled. "I've got another lesson and *you've* got History coursework to do."

"Nah," James grinned. "Mr. Pike's getting me out of that, as long as Kevin Sumner makes it across the obstacle."

"That's your problem, James," said Kerry. "You're always trying to wing it. I bet that's why your mission went tits up as well."

James was stunned. "Pardon me?"

Kerry knew James was sensitive about being under investigation and realized she'd overstepped the mark. "Just ignore me, James. That was a stupid thing to say."

"Stuart said something about that as well. Is that what everyone's saying about me?"

Kerry turned to head back downstairs, but James grabbed her arm. "Don't walk away from me."

"James, I've got a lesson to go to."

"I want to know, Kerry."

Kerry looked down at the floor. "There's a rumor going around that you were filmed planting the bugs and that that's why the two MI5 agents got killed."

"Who told you that?"

"I don't know," Kerry shrugged. "It's just campus gossip, everyone's talking about it."

"Do *you* believe it?"

"Of course I don't."

"But you just said 'I bet that's why your mission went tits up.' It's hardly a ringing endorsement."

Kerry squirmed. "I didn't mean it like that."

James felt like he'd been stabbed through the heart. "Then what *did* you mean?"

"It was . . . James, I'm gonna be late for my lesson."

Kerry backed away and started down the stairs. When she was out of sight, James bunched his fists and considered punching the wall, but he'd tried it once before and discovered that it hurt a lot more in real life than when people did it in the movies.

He started heading up toward his room, but changed his mind before he reached the next landing. He'd not heard from Ewart since his answering machine messages on Saturday morning and he wanted to know what was going on with the investigation.

The mission preparation building was one of the most modern on CHERUB campus. Ewart Asker's office had a smart maple desk with framed photos of his family hidden behind teetering stacks of paperwork.

"Take a seat," Ewart said, pointing James toward the two suede sofas by the window. "Have you come up with any new information?"

"Afraid not," James said, as he sat down. "I haven't heard from you in a few days and I was wondering what was going on."

Ewart shrugged. "We're going nowhere fast."

"Wasn't I supposed to be going down to MI5 in London to answer some more questions?"

"I knocked that on the head," Ewart said. "To be honest I had a blazing row with them. They're asking you to go back to London and go through the same testimony for a third time. As far as I can tell, the only reason for them to do that is if they're trying to trip you up and discredit your evidence.

"Meanwhile, MI5 are stalling and refusing to send me a large amount of information that I requested on Boris and Isla. So I've told them, they're not getting another interview with you until they start full cooperation with me."

"How did that go down?"

"Like a hungry Rottweiler in a chicken coop," Ewart said. "The head of MI5 has been on the phone to Zara complaining about my conduct. The intelligence minister doesn't like the fact that CHERUB and MI5 are conducting separate inquiries and is talking about sending in an independent investigator. But it's not like some failing secondary school or the post office, you can't just give an outsider open access to the intelligence services."

"The thing is, Ewart, there are all these rumors going around on campus that I'm going to cop the blame for the two MI5 agents being killed. Which means I'll either be booted out of CHERUB, or spend the rest of my time here doing recruitment missions and crappy little security checks."

Ewart shrugged. "You'll just have to develop a tough skin where gossip is concerned, James. You know how it is, you start off with two plus two and by the time it's spent a few days in the campus rumor mill, kids are making it add up to four hundred and fifty."

"But even Kerry believes it—or at least half believes it."

"I told you at the start, James, this investigation is probably going to take months. Any rumors that you hear are completely baseless. Our problem is that we have *nothing* to go on, apart from Boris's and Isla's dead bodies and your testimony."

"How do you rate your chances of getting the video from the CIA?"

"We're trying our best," Ewart said. "But it could take weeks and there's always a chance that we won't get it at all."

James smiled awkwardly. "Do *you* believe me, Ewart?"

"I've no reason to think that you're lying," Ewart said. "You've had a few discipline problems, but your record as a CHERUB agent is rock solid. The trouble is, MI5 are saying the same thing about Boris and Isla. They'd put in more than forty years' loyal service for MI5 between the two of them and their personnel records are unblemished—not that they're allowing me to see them.

"Basically, James, MI5 are saying that their agents are

clean. They're trying to tell the intelligence minister that you're to blame for everything that went wrong in Aero City. I'm trying to tell the intelligence minister that we've got no reason to distrust you and that MI5 are holding back information and refusing to cooperate with my investigation."

"Nightmare," James said.

"You're telling me," Ewart nodded. "It's like the old question: What happens when an irresistible force hits an immovable object? We're completely stuffed unless we get some solid evidence."

"What about if I went through your files on the investigation?" James asked. "You never know, a fresh pair of eyes might make a difference."

Ewart shook his head. "Sorry, James, that's a *big* no. I'm already getting flak from the MI5 bods saying that I'm unfit to investigate because I was involved in the operation and I'm the chairwoman's husband. Letting MI5's prime suspect sift through all my investigative work wouldn't go down well at all."

"I guess I'll leave you to it then," James said, as he stood up. "I've got a fitness session in the gym at eleven."

"I'll try and keep you informed," Ewart said. "And don't let rumors get under your skin. They're baseless: nothing but flights of fancy."

"Just one other thing." James stood in the doorway. "Suppose that there's no more evidence two or three months down the line when the investigation finishes. What happens to me?"

Ewart looked uncomfortable. "We have to be completely above board, James. You know that."

"Meaning?"

"Two people are dead and MI5 are doing their best to lay the blame at our door. If we can't prove that you're innocent, Zara won't have much option but to ask you to leave CHERUB."

"So the rumors aren't so far from the truth after all," James said dejectedly.

CHAPTER 29

CONFESSION

Lauren was lying on her bunk reading a problem page when Anna came in from school. She stood on the bottom rung of the ladder and waved a Toblerone.

"For you," Anna smiled.

"Cheers," Lauren said, as she grabbed the bar. "What's this in aid of?"

"Last night, with the telephone . . . ," Anna trailed off.

"Don't worry," Lauren said, as she offered Anna two bits of Toblerone. "You've never had your own phone. To be honest, I'd forgotten all about it."

This wasn't true. Lauren had spent half an hour trying to find a good place to put her replacement phone. She wanted it where Anna would be able to find it, but not somewhere so obvious that it made Anna suspicious of a trap.

"Last night, I lied," Anna said. "I took your phone to call a friend in Russia."

"Why didn't you use the phone in the hallway downstairs?" Lauren asked, secure in the knowledge that this was also bugged.

Anna looked suspiciously over her shoulder, then stepped off the ladder and pushed the door shut. "I don't want the care workers to trace the call," she whispered. "I lived in a children's home in Russia. It wasn't nice like here, no good clothes, not even a warm place to wash, and they'll beat me if I go back. But I want to call my friend and see if Georgy is okay."

"Well, I guess you can use mine," Lauren said. "It's in my desk drawer."

"You're a good friend," Anna smiled. "My English is rotten, it's so nice having another Russian to talk to."

Anna pulled the phone out of the drawer and flipped it open, but then stood staring at the keys. Lauren jumped off her bed with the last triangle of chocolate bulging in her cheek.

"Give us," Lauren said. "Tell me the number."

"Two, six, one, two, seven, one."

Lauren shook her head. "That won't work, that's just the local number. You need the area code and the country code for Russia."

"Pardon?"

"Extra numbers," Lauren explained.

"Where from?"

"I can get them from the operator, as long as you know where the place you're dialing is."

Anna smacked herself on the forehead. "I'm so stupid," she gasped. "I've tried before from the phone box near school; *that's* why it didn't work."

It took Lauren a couple of minutes to call the operator and get the correct codes for Nizhniy Novgorod and dial the number.

"It's ringing." Lauren handed the phone across to Anna.

"Hello," Anna said, putting on a deep voice.

John Jones sat in his bed-and-breakfast half a kilometer away. He listened to Anna's conversation, with a laptop spread on the bed in front of him. The computer was doing a reverse search of the Russian telephone directory, via a secure link to CHERUB campus.

"Who is this?" a woman asked.

"My name is Yasha," Anna said. "I'm a school friend of Polya's. Can I speak with her?"

"Polya isn't here anymore," the woman answered sourly.

"Oh," Anna said, slipping into her normal voice for a moment. "I have a book she lent me. Can you tell me where she is?"

"I don't know," the woman snapped. "I'm not a secretary."

An address flashed up in Cyrillic letters on John Jones's laptop:

Underage Care Unit 7
The Municipal Building
Main Square

"She lent me a book," Anna repeated. "I'd like to give it back to her."

The woman made a sound like a door creaking and followed it with a knowing laugh. "Anna," she said slyly. "I thought I'd seen the last of you."

The call abruptly went dead.

Anna turned ghostly white as she snapped the phone shut.

"My friend is gone," she choked. "I hoped she'd tell me about Georgy, but I suppose they sent her away too."

"If it's a children's home, they'll look after him, won't they?"

"Georgy is cute," Anna said, matter-of-factly. "Not many people want kids our age, but now I'm out of the way he'll be adopted easily. I'll never see him again."

Lauren put her arm around Anna's back as a tear ran down her face.

"They mustn't send me back there," Anna sobbed. "So keep quiet about this, okay?"

It was dark and bitterly cold as James headed out of his last lesson and toward the training compound. Bruce ran up behind and slapped him on the back.

"How's your gob?" he asked.

"Not bad," James told him. "Bit of a fat lip."

"Stuart Russell's in my woodwork class," Bruce grinned. "I grabbed hold of a chisel, went up to him, and said: 'You got a problem with me, sunshine?' All the color went out of his face. I swear, he looked like he was gonna shit his pants."

"Is Stuart hard?" James asked. "He was acting pretty confident."

Bruce shook his head. "Stuart's all mouth. Lauren could probably take him."

James laughed. "Lauren could probably take me. She might be little, but you just try getting hold of her."

"Anyway," Bruce said, "stop smiling. We've got a job to do."

Kevin was waiting when they reached the wooden obstacle, dressed for the cold weather in a thick jacket, gloves, and woolly hat.

"Think you're pretty smart, don't you?" Bruce said, as he grabbed Kevin by the scruff of his jacket and squeezed him against a wooden post. "Telling your cousin all about us. Trying to make trouble."

"I was just talking." Kevin squirmed. "I didn't know he'd come after you..."

"You pull another stunt like that and I'll personally find the most disgusting toilet on campus and shove your head down it. Understand?"

"Yes, sir," Kevin said meekly.

"We saw progress last night," James said, as he reached into his jacket for a key Mr. Pike had given him and slotted it into a gray box on the post above Kevin's head. "Now let's see how you get along with this baby."

As James turned the key, banks of floodlights came on, illuminating the wooden framework of CHERUB's sprawling height obstacle. The mixture of towers, planks, poles, and rope swings built amid tall trees was a tough challenge for anyone. If you were scared of heights, it was your worst nightmare.

"Looking a bit pale there, Kev." James grinned.

He felt bad as Kevin fought back a sob. James's instinct was to give him a hug and tell him that he'd be okay, but they'd already made one breakthrough by being ruthless. They couldn't drop the façade now.

"Crybaby," Bruce sneered, pinching Kevin's cheek. "How are you ever gonna make it as a cherub if you start bawling before you even try?"

James was pleased to see Kevin choke back his tears, grit his teeth, and show the same defiant expression as he'd done after jumping off the roof the night before.

The obstacle started with a line of rope ladders, each of which led up to a wooden platform suspended between two huge trees more than twenty meters off the ground.

"Don't look down," James said, as Kevin nervously planted his boot on the bottom rung.

James remembered how frightened he'd been the first time he'd gone over the obstacle. As Bruce raced ahead on another ladder, James followed a few rungs behind Kevin. He was a little slow and he stopped moving when the wind made the ropes sway, but James thought he was doing okay for a first timer.

In some ways, it was easier going over the obstacle in darkness because you were much less aware of your surroundings.

"Where's the railing?" Kevin asked, when he reached the platform.

"There ain't one," Bruce said, with a flourish in his

voice that made James wonder if Bruce actually enjoyed making Kevin suffer.

James could remember his own first time on the platform, twenty meters up and less than two boot lengths wide. "If that plank was on the ground, you'd walk up and down it all day long and not fall over," he explained, as he rested a reassuring hand on Kevin's shoulder.

Bruce took the lead onto the next section of the course, which comprised two long scaffold poles stretching across the ten-meter gap to the next platform.

"Rest a hand on each pole and hook your boots around at the back. Then crawl," Bruce explained.

"Are there nets under here?" Kevin asked.

"You'll find out if you fall off," James barked. "Move your skinny butt."

Again, Bruce led the way across and onto the next platform, which was square and had a wooden fence built around two sides. The metal poles were freezing cold on James's fingers. Kevin moved quickly, until he was about two-thirds of the way across and his right boot slipped. He managed to tighten his grip and hook his ankle back around the pole, but it had spooked him and he froze up and started sniffling again.

"Jesus Christ," Bruce screamed. "We know who we'll have playing the fairy in this year's nativity play."

James was concerned because Kevin had stopped moving. If he fell, he would hit a net before the ground, but it would wreck his confidence and the branches would cut him to pieces on the way down. And it wasn't just that James felt sorry for Kevin and wanted him to succeed: His History coursework was at stake as well.

"Shift it," James said, as he took his hand off the rail and gently tapped Kevin on the bum.

Kevin shuffled forward again, but he was crying his eyes out. Bruce grabbed hold of him as soon as he was within reach and slammed him against the wooden fence.

"If I hear one more sob," Bruce said, as he pinched Kevin's nose and twisted it out of shape, "I'll give you something that's worth sobbing for."

"I can't do this anymore," Kevin squealed. "Please let me down."

Bruce grabbed the collar of Kevin's jacket and dangled him over the open side of the platform. "You wanna get down?"

"Don't let me go," Kevin screamed. "*Please* don't let me go."

"Baby," Bruce said, "I can't put up with your racket any more." And he let go of Kevin's jacket and shoved him off the platform.

James gasped as he heard the small body screaming through the branches. "What are you *doing*?"

Bruce shrugged. "He'll hit the nets."

"But they're for emergencies. He could easily put his back out or something."

Bruce tutted. "James, we're supposed to be ruthless. You're carrying on like you want to marry the kid."

"But there's ruthless and there's *this*, Bruce. You threw him off the platform, *psycho*."

"Me and Kyle used to do it all the time when we were red-shirts," Bruce said dismissively, as he put his foot out over the edge and leaned forward. "Nighty night."

James watched Bruce disappear through the branches.

As James looked down, he was relieved to catch a glimpse of Kevin stumbling out of a net to safety, crying but apparently undamaged. Then Bruce screamed out in pain.

"Bruce?" James yelled frantically as he looked down. "Are you okay?"

"Do I sodding well sound okay?" Bruce yelled back.

James crouched down and felt under the platform for one of the emergency ropes. Once he'd undone a leather buckle, a length of knotted rope dropped down toward the ground.

"I'm coming," James shouted, as he lowered his boots off the side and stepped down onto a knot.

Bruce kept moaning as James scrambled down the rope. He raced up toward Bruce, who was crumpled on the ground.

"What happened?"

"God knows," Bruce groaned, "but my leg is killing me."

Kevin stepped up behind James. "I saw," the younger boy sniffed, as he pointed up toward a section of black netting with a gap in it. "His boot got caught in the hole and his leg made this massive crunch."

"Run to the medical unit and get someone to drive straight up here," James said. "I think it's just a dislocated joint, but it might be broken."

"Gotcha," Kevin said, before he sprinted off.

James knelt over Bruce and grimaced when he realized that Bruce's boot was almost pointing backward.

"Actually, I think that is broken," James said, recoiling at the thought that it was probably even more painful than it looked.

"If you . . . ," Bruce croaked weakly.

"Eh?" James said, as he moved his ear closer to his friend's mouth.

"I've jumped off that platform a hundred times," Bruce moaned. "And if you say *I told you so*, I swear to God I'll kick every single tooth out of your head."

James broke into a giant smile. "I told you so, Brucey boy."

CHAPTER 24

CALLS

Lauren was woken by her MC Hammer ring tone at three in the morning. She leaned way over the side of her bed and grabbed the phone off her desk. It was a man's voice, someone she didn't know, speaking in Russian.

"Is that Anna?"

"No," Lauren said. "But she's here, do you want to speak with her?"

Anna whispered anxiously from across the room. "Hang up!"

"Sorry, Anna doesn't want to speak to you," Lauren said.

"I'm Anna's friend and I want to help her. I can tell her where Georgy is."

Lauren looked up from the phone. "He says he knows where Georgy is."

The room was dark, but there was enough light for Lauren to see Anna twisting her face uncertainly as she crossed the room and grabbed the mobile.

"Hello," Anna said nervously.

"Anna," the man said in a gentle voice.

Anna made a choking noise. "Mr. Broushka."

"You made us a promise, Anna. We took a lot of risks and paid a lot of money to take you to England. All we asked was for you to come and work in our factory to pay off your debts."

Anna didn't answer; she just gawped at the phone.

"I know where Georgy is," the man said reassuringly.

"Where?"

"I'll tell you all about it when I come to collect you."

Anna smiled. "So you don't know where I am?"

"You owe us money, Anna. You should have called us sooner. You shouldn't have run away."

"I *didn't* run," Anna said. "They left me on the boat."

"Where are you, Anna?"

Lauren shook her head frantically.

"If you don't tell me, Georgy might have a fall," Mr. Broushka purred. "Or maybe he'll reach up and pull a saucepan of boiling water down on himself."

"I'm—" Anna spluttered, but she snapped the phone shut and threw it back at Lauren. She collapsed against the bed and started sobbing. "They . . ."

"Who was he, Anna?"

"Mr. Broushka was an old man who used to fix things at our children's home. They didn't have any money for

209

maintenance, so he'd help out, mending broken windows, replacing lightbulbs. He used to be friendly to all the kids; not like the staff who were as mean as hell. Sometimes he'd bring us hot pies from the bakery and cheap toys for Georgy and the little kids.

"After a while, he started telling us about this cousin who had a factory in England. He said it was very hard for them to get staff. He asked if some of us girls wanted to work there, almost joking at first. But we kept asking him about it, practically begging him to fix us up with jobs in England when we were older.

"It went on for ages. Mr. Broushka laid it on thick, telling us how we'd live in nice houses and have lots of money in England. He said there were lots of English men who'd marry such beautiful girls and then we'd get citizenship. Then one night, he told us that his cousin was in town and that we could go and meet him if we wanted to.

"There was me and eight other girls and we all broke curfew and got on a bus to the riverfront. When we arrived, Mr. Broushka told all of us to get inside a truck. A couple of the older girls wanted to know what was going on, but there were other men there—gangsters—and when two of them tried to get away, the men started slapping and kicking them. They pulled out baseball bats and bundled us all in the truck. They said we were going to be traveling for several days and that if any of us made a fuss we'd be . . ."

Anna stopped to sob and Lauren grabbed her hand.

"The men said that they would rape us."

James woke up at 6 a.m., to ice on his bedroom window and a severe weather warning on the radio. He peeked between the slats of his blind and was delighted to see the trees and lawns of CHERUB campus under a layer of white frost. This meant he could go back to bed for another hour and a half.

James grabbed his telephone and called the main campus switchboard. "Hi, I need to be put through to Kevin Sumner's room in the junior block."

After three rings, a young boy answered with a yawn and a hello.

"Is Kevin there?" James asked.

"Nah, he's had to go off to the training compound."

"Already?" James moaned. "But I'm not supposed to be meeting him there for another forty-five minutes."

"Well, he's not here."

"Does he have a mobile?"

"Yeah, but it's here on the table."

James shook his head and tutted. "Listen, if you do see Kevin tell him that it's James and I'm cancelling his training session. It's too dangerous to climb up the obstacle in this weather. It'll be covered with ice."

"I'm telling you he's already gone," the kid insisted.

"Okay, cheers. I'll take my mobile with me, so if he does turn up, make sure he gives me a call so I don't have to go all the way out there."

After putting the phone down, James wondered if he'd got the time mixed up in his head. But he'd discussed it with Kevin on the walk back from the medical unit and he could distinctly remember saying 6:45.

"Oh well," James muttered to himself. "You can stand out there and freeze your butt off for half an hour if you want."

James listened to the news and sports on his radio as he used the toilet, got dressed, and blasted some instant porridge in his microwave, all the while hoping for the call from Kevin that would mean he could get back in bed instead of going out into the cold.

When it didn't come, he wrapped up warm in a CHERUB-issue green skiing jacket, thick gloves, and a hat with ear flaps. He was in a foul mood as he jogged in the crisp morning air, knowing that he could have gone straight back to bed if Kevin hadn't left the junior block so ridiculously early.

It took twelve minutes to reach the height obstacle, but there was no sign of Kevin. James figured that the cold might have got to Kevin's bladder and made him disappear into the trees for a leak.

"Hey?" James shouted. "Kev, are you out there?"

"Yoo-hoo," Kevin shouted, from up high.

James looked toward the sky and was shocked to see Kevin's outline silhouetted against the rising sun. He'd made it across the scaffold poles to the second platform.

"What the *hell* are you doing?" James yelled.

"What the hell does it look like I'm doing?" Kevin yelled back.

"Don't move, you lunatic. It's too icy."

"The scaffold poles *were* pretty hairy." Kevin grinned.

James noticed that the rescue rope he'd used the night before was still dangling down from the platform. "Come down on the rope," he called. "Seriously, it's not safe up there."

"We've got nets," Kevin said, starting to walk toward the third platform. This involved crossing a series of wooden planks and leaping over gaps between them. "Maybe I'll break a few bones. Well, so what? Why do you care, bully boy?"

"Come down *now*," James screamed. "I'm ordering you."

James couldn't look as Kevin leapt a meter and a half between the ends of two planks.

"If you want me, come and get me!"

James thought about Bruce screaming his head off in the medical center the night before and the sight of his horribly twisted leg. It had freaked James out, but had apparently had the opposite effect on Kevin.

James considered staying on the ground, but he was worried that Kevin might freak out or slip and need help, so he reluctantly began clambering through the netting, until he reached the dangling rope.

By the time James got to the platform, Kevin had made a series of jumps and was more than thirty meters ahead of him. He was shocked to see that the planks were slippery with frost and ice, broken only by Kevin's boot prints.

James didn't fancy it one bit, but he'd come this far. He made the first two jumps easily enough, but the third was onto a plank that was slightly offset and he felt his boot skid alarmingly as he landed. With more luck than skill, James managed to stay on by grabbing hold of an overhanging branch and countered his sliding boot by leaning in the opposite direction. James had been through so much on missions that it wasn't *the* most frightening moment of his life, but it ran the leading contenders pretty close.

"Careful, old timer," Kevin shouted cockily, from his position on a square platform at the end of the jumps.

James steamed along the next plank and made a simple jump onto the platform. He adopted a bullying tone. "What do you think you're doing, you nutter? It's like a skating rink up here."

"I want my gray T-shirt," Kevin yelled. "I want to get through basic training and become an agent more than anything else in the world."

James crouched down and felt under the platform. He was relieved to find an escape rope, identical to the one he'd climbed up. He was still shaken from his skid and couldn't manage to keep up his training instructor persona.

"We can come back tomorrow, Kev. It's great that your confidence has built up so quickly, but——"

"I'm going heel to toe," Kevin said, referring to the final section of the course.

When James first went over the height obstacle three years earlier, it had ended with a sheer drop onto a large gym mat. But the tree that supported the final platform had rotted and Mr. Large had used the repair work as an opportunity to design a much scarier final section.

It now involved walking down a steeply sloping plank that was narrower than a CHERUB combat boot, before whizzing down a rope slide to the ground. Just to make life even more difficult, a large pond had been dug and you had to jump off the swing while you were still several meters off the ground. Jump too soon and you'd break your legs, jump too late and you got a soaking. And to make sure that the soaking didn't appeal on a hot day, the pond had been stocked with glutinous brown algae that smelled like rotting meat.

"You can't go down the ramp in this weather," James said, grabbing Kevin by his sleeve. "It's lethal."

But Kevin twisted and broke free. Like everyone who'd been at CHERUB for a few years, Kevin had spent hundreds of hours in the dojo learning combat skills. James towered over the ten-year-old and was probably double his weight, but he still didn't fancy tussling with him on an icy wooden platform thirty meters above the ground.

"Sod you then," James snarled. "Ignore me. Show me how brave you are. Just don't blame me if you get tangled in a net and end up like Bruce."

"I'm not brave," Kevin shouted, somehow managing to sound sad and defiant at the same time. "I've never been so scared in my life. But I want to be a cherub. If I can get over here when it's all iced up, any other time is gonna be a piece of cake."

"I wash my hands," James said, as he theatrically rubbed them together. "There's not much I can do short of punching you out and lowering you down on a rope."

"You can wish me luck," Kevin said as he stepped off the platform and placed a boot onto the steeply sloping beam.

James could hardly bear to look as Kevin balanced precariously on the slippery plank. James had been over it dozens of times, but when it was dry you could take a short run up and make it down in eight nervous steps. With ice on the plank your boot would skid off sideways.

After three steps, Kevin's front boot slipped. After controlling a wobble, he looked back toward the top and realized that he'd bitten off more than he could chew. James frantically reached under the platform to unbuckle the rescue rope. It was meant for getting to the ground, but he reckoned he could throw the end out for Kevin to grab hold of.

As the rope dropped through the branches, James looked up and saw that Kevin had turned around and now had one knee resting on the plank. Next, the youngster rested his hands on the wood and let his feet slip over the sides so that he sat astride it.

James couldn't help but smile. If you came up with a group, the instructor would scream abuse and make you run punishment laps if you shuffled along a plank instead of walking, but it wasn't actually breaking any rules. The only rule was that Kevin had to get across the obstacle without any assistance.

With his chest resting against the beam and his arms wrapped around it, Kevin tried to control his descent. But the angle was steep and the rough wood shredded his sleeves. When he thumped into the base of the final platform, he screamed—then swung his leg around, before stepping off and looking over his shoulder. James was on the previous platform ten meters away, but he could see the giant splinter of wood sticking out of Kevin's bum.

"Don't pull it out," James yelled. "Leave it there, in case you've ruptured a vein or an artery."

Kevin limped to the front of the platform and grabbed a meter of damp nylon rope out of a plastic garbage can. He slung one end over the main rope that led down to the ground and gripped the rubber handles on each end.

"Wait until you clear the last tree," James shouted.

"Then count two seconds and let go, or you'll crash into the pond."

"Gotcha," Kevin nodded.

James had no intention of following Kevin over the icy beam. He grabbed the escape rope and was lowering himself over the side as Kevin launched himself off the platform.

"SHIIIIIIIIIIIIIIIIIIIIIIIIIIIIIIIIIIIIIIIIIIIIIIIIIIT," Kevin screamed, picking up speed as the branches skimmed against his legs.

James was less than halfway down when everything went silent. Desperate to know if Kevin was okay, he clambered through fifty meters of undergrowth, before breaking out onto the flat expanse of grass where the rope slide ended.

"Kevin!" James called anxiously. "Are you okay?"

Lots of kids mistimed letting go of the rope the first couple of times they tried it. Although injuries were usually restricted to sprained ankles and cut knees, Kevin's silence was giving James visions of shattered limbs and concussions.

"Over here," Kevin shouted.

James sprinted toward the pool. Kevin had let go a little bit late and ended up with his legs in the stinking water, but he was already on his feet and limping breathlessly toward James.

"I bloody did it." Kevin grinned. "Basic training here I come!"

James knew Kevin still had a mountain to climb: During basic training he'd be expected to complete the obstacle in less than three minutes with a fifteen-kilogram pack on his back. But this was a moment for celebration, not harsh reality.

"Well done, mate." James grinned back. "Not bad. In fact, I'd go so far as to say it was pretty damned impressive for someone who wouldn't jump off a meter-high barrel two nights ago."

"I want to be a cherub," Kevin said. "When Bruce shoved me off the platform last night, I was *so* scared. I actually wet my pants on the way down."

James grimaced. "Nice."

"But when I bounced off the net I looked up at the obstacle and it was like, *is that all you've got?*"

"When the weather's better, I'll take you over a couple more times, so you get used to it," James offered.

"I'm sorry I went up when it was icy," Kevin said. "But after last night I just *had* to do it."

"I should report you," James said.

Kevin looked up pleadingly, knowing that the instructors could punish him hard if they knew he'd disobeyed James's orders.

"I won't this time," James relented. "But you saw what happened to Bruce. I'm glad you're not scared anymore, but it's dangerous up there."

"Thanks," Kevin said, as he stared up at the obstacle. "I hated you and Bruce that first night, but I reckon I owe you one now."

"Just doing my job," James said happily, as he considered all the History coursework he'd just got out of. "I guess I'd better piggyback you over to the med unit so they can take that splinter out of your arse."

CHAPTER 25

PIKE

Lauren was pleased that she was getting good information out of Anna, but she woke up in a mood because she was facing a third boring day sitting around in Aldrington Care Center.

To make matters worse, one of the house parents came to Lauren's room after breakfast and told her that they'd found her a place at a school in Burgess Hill, starting the following morning. On top of the stupid green uniform and the fact that settling into a new school was always a nightmare came the news that she'd have to leave at six thirty in the morning and walk to a bus stop two kilometers away before taking a thirty-five-minute bus ride.

"You sound like you got out of bed on the wrong side

this morning," John said cheerfully, when he rang Lauren on her mobile.

"Seriously, don't wind me up," Lauren moaned. "I might really lose my temper."

"What's the matter?"

"Thick gray tights, a hand-me-down pullover with a dirty great rip in the elbow and an hour a day on a bus full of strange school kids."

"Blah," John said dismissively. "You should count yourself lucky. When I first joined MI5, they had me staking out a gents' toilet on Hampstead Heath."

"Nice," Lauren said, cracking into a smile.

"You've not suffered until you've spent a week crawling around in an asbestos-lined roof cavity and coming home to your wife smelling like a public toilet. It's no wonder I'm divorced. . . ."

"Oh," Lauren added, "and to make my life even more perfect, this idiot boy—the dude who was at the dining-table when you dropped me off—found out that I'm a vegetarian and hid a piece of bacon in my cornflakes."

John laughed.

"It's *not* funny," Lauren said firmly. "I've got a piece of dead animal inside me. It makes me queasy just thinking about it."

"Got lots of bits of dead animal inside me," John said. "The landlady here does a cracking cooked breakfast."

"Anyway, I take it you heard the calls last night?"

"Yep, and the messages you left with my assistant on campus. You must have called while I was in the shower."

"So what are we going to do with the information?" Lauren pressed.

"MI5 runs an anti-trafficking task force. We can pass the information on about Mr. Broushka and the children's home in Nizhniy Novgorod, but I'm not hopeful."

"Why not? I bet you could track him down easily enough."

"Probably," John said. "But it's a question of resources. It would probably take a team of two or three officers to track him down and then we'd have to find evidence compelling enough to get the Russian police to prosecute him."

Lauren tutted. "So why are we even bothering?"

"We've got to hope that Anna knows a few more details that will enable us to get our teeth into the British end of the organization. Keep pumping her gently for names, places, descriptions of the men, and any snippets of conversation she might have overheard while she was in the truck or on the boat."

"The guy on the phone sounded creepy," Lauren said. "Maybe he'll ring again. He certainly sounded keen to get his hands on Anna."

"I'm not surprised. They must have spent a lot of money smuggling Anna across Europe and into Britain and they probably had a buyer lined up ready to pay good money for her."

"How much is a twelve-year-old girl worth?" Lauren asked.

"It depends upon the buyer: twenty, thirty, or maybe even fifty thousand pounds."

"It makes me shudder just thinking about it," Lauren said. "But why would they pay so much? Couldn't you just pick any girl off the street?"

"You could," John said. "Trouble is, the girl would probably have family and friends. It gets in the paper, on the TV, and the police mount a full-scale manhunt. If you take a girl like Anna from a children's home in Russia and smuggle her in, she just vanishes. Nobody's looking for her because nobody even knows she's here."

James put his head inside the training instructor's hut. He'd knocked, but hadn't got an answer.

"Mr. Pike?"

Pike emerged from a tiled area at the back of the hut, with wet hair and dressed only in a pair of alarmingly skimpy underpants.

"Thanks for coming by during your lunchtime," Pike said.

"No bother," James said. "I was coming up this way to see Bruce. The nurse asked me to bring his portable DVD player and some clean clothes."

"How's he doing?"

"About what you'd expect, I guess," James shrugged. "It's a bad break. When I left him last night they'd given him a load of sedatives and he was dead to the world."

"Too bad. We've had a couple of bumps and sprains where kids have bounced off a net and hit a tree, but that's the first broken bone we've had in my time here."

"I guess it's just a freak thing, getting your foot caught in the net like that."

"Anyway," Pike said, as he pulled on a clean pair of combat trousers. "I asked you up here to say thanks. I wasn't totally convinced that Kevin would respond to bullying tactics, but it seems to have worked out."

"He's even a bit the other way, sir. I'm worried that he might go too far and start thinking he's indestructible."

"I've got him for a hundred days of basic training, starting in just over three weeks," Pike smiled. "I reckon we'll have his head straight by the end of that.

"The other reason I wanted you to come up was to ask if you'd be interested in helping us out a bit more. There are always kids to be trained. We can always do with a hand on weekend exercises and of course, if you're helping us out on a regular basis, we'll make sure that your own training and academic requirements are lightened."

James nodded. "Meryl said I had a choice between helping out with training and doing heaps more academic stuff. The only thing is, if they lift my suspension I'll probably be out on missions most of the time."

Mr. Pike was now dressed, except for his boots. He walked over to a coffee percolator. "Drink?"

"Nah, I'm fine."

"So how's Ewart getting on with the investigation?" Pike asked.

James shrugged. "I went over there, but Ewart won't tell me what's going on. He says there's a big row going on with MI5. It looks like it could drag on for months and I could be the one who gets stitched up."

"That wouldn't surprise me," Pike said. "Once upon a time, me and Ewart were best mates."

"Really?" James said. "I've never seen you speak to each other."

"That's 'cos I hate his snidey guts. I completed my basic training a few months before Ewart. We had rooms next to each other; I had your girlfriend's room actually."

223

James smiled. "Kerry's room. I never knew that."

"We even went on our first couple of missions together. But the third time out, Ewart stitched me up big time. We were both still gray-shirts, thirteen years old. Some of our mates had got their navy shirt and we were both getting desperate. Anyhow, like you I hated writing essays and reports. The only things that interested me were skirt, rugby, and punch-ups. So when our mission came to its end, Ewart generously volunteered to type up my report as well as his own. We'd both done a decent enough job, but I see him two days later and he's wearing a navy shirt.

"When I read the reports, it was like everything Ewart had done was perfect and everything I'd done was half-arsed. I did my nut, but I couldn't complain unless I was prepared to admit that I hadn't written my own mission report."

James shook his head. "Some best friend."

"I dragged Ewart out of his room and kicked him from one end of the sixth-floor corridor to the other, but the damage to my career was done. Ewart was part of the elite, going off on all the best missions. It took me another eighteen months to get my navy shirt, but I was never regarded as anything other than an average agent."

"Do you get on with him now?"

"Barely," Pike shrugged. "Zara's a nice lady and she invited me when her kids were christened. I put my good suit on and acted civil, but Ewart still leaves a bitter taste in my mouth. He's a snidey little so-and-so and if I was in your position, I'd be worried. I'd bet you my left nut that what comes out of that investigation isn't what's best for you or for CHERUB, but whatever's good for Ewart bloody Asker."

James wasn't sure what to think. Maybe Ewart had set Mr. Pike up, but the incident must have taken place more than fifteen years ago and they'd both been kids. It hardly seemed like grounds for believing that Ewart would do the same to him. And what did Ewart even have to gain by stitching him up?

"You know what?" Pike grinned, as he pulled a blue plastic card out of his wallet and handed it to James. "That's for the mission preparation building, full access."

"What am I supposed to do with it?"

"The mission controllers don't usually work late," Pike explained. "Go into Ewart's office and have a good snoop around."

James tentatively grabbed the card. "I dunno, sir."

"You only get one shot at a CHERUB career," Pike said. "Ewart ruined mine; don't let him do it to you."

"Thanks," James said, as he tucked the card in his pocket.

"Just be careful," Mr. Pike said. "I could lose my job for giving you that. If they catch you, I'll have to say that I lost it."

CHAPTER 26

ESCAPE

The Aldrington Care Center's newest resident was a four-year-old lad named Carl. He'd arrived the night before, sporting ragged clothes, a swollen right eye, and a layer of filth. After a thorough scrubbing, a night's sleep, and a morning being interviewed by police, Carl was allowed to explore his temporary home and found Lauren killing time on the Playstation in the living room.

She felt sorry for the gloomy youngster and was happy to break the monotony by entertaining him. After some games of snap and a few laps chasing around the sofa, they put on coats and gloves and headed to the play area outside the unit. The young lad clearly hadn't spent much of his short life in playgrounds and got ridiculously excited, screaming and laughing as he bounced on the seesaw and begged Lauren to push faster on the swings and roundabout.

She was following him up the steps of a slide when her mobile rang. She didn't recognize the number on the display, but the call was coming from Britain.

"Hello, are you Anna's friend?" the man asked. He spoke in Russian, but it wasn't Mr. Broushka and there was a lot of background noise, like he was traveling in a car or train.

"I am," Lauren said. "But she's not here. She's at school."

Carl slid down as Lauren sat at the top of the metal ramp.

"That doesn't matter," the man said. "I wanted to talk to you anyway."

"*Me?* What about?"

"Anna won't talk to us. We'd really like to speak to her. She's got it into her head that we want to hurt her, but she's mixed up. We're her people, she needs to be with us."

Lauren heard a second voice, speaking in English away from the phone. "Got it."

"Sorry to trouble you," the first speaker said abruptly. "I've got to go now. I'll call back later when Anna's out of school."

The phone went dead before Lauren could answer.

"Come down," Carl demanded, as he looked up at her from the base of the slide.

Lauren pushed herself off, but her phone was ringing again before she'd reached the bottom.

"Lauren," John said urgently. "We've got a *big* problem.

A tracking request was sent during your call and the local cell responded just before they hung up."

"You mean those guys know where I am?"

"They know which radio cell your phone is operating within, so only to within a couple of kilometers," John explained, as Carl balanced himself on Lauren's sneaker. "It's more primitive than the triangulation system that we can use to track mobiles."

Lauren patted the youngster on the head. "Play on your own for a minute, Carl."

"Who's that?" John asked.

"Just a little kid I was messing about with. How did they trace my phone?"

"Probably through an online location service. You're supposed to have permission from the person who owns the phone—like for parents who want to track where their kids are—but you can usually get around it by making a false declaration when you sign up."

"At least they can only pinpoint us to within a two-kilometer radius."

"But they know you're in a children's home," John explained. "All they've got to do is look up children's homes in a local services directory. I'm not sure but ACC is probably the only one around here."

"Do you think they're coming after Anna?" Lauren gasped.

"Definitely," John said. "Why else would they try and trace the call?"

Lauren looked at her watch. "She'll be coming out of school in under half an hour."

"A23," John said.

Lauren was confused. "Eh?"

"Sorry, I've asked the campus control room to put a trace on the mobile phone that called you. The Russian's signal has jumped two kilometers in two minutes, so my guess is that they're on the fast road into Brighton."

"How come they're so close already?"

"They knew Anna was picked up on the coast a few kilometers from here. She was bound to be somewhere in the Brighton area."

"How long till they reach us?"

"Fifteen or twenty minutes," John said. "Depending upon the traffic and how long it takes them to track down the care homes."

"Do you think they'll try snatching Anna straight-away?"

"Snatching her from inside the home is too risky. They'll either try picking her up shortly on her way home, or on her way to school tomorrow morning. . . . The car just moved about a kilometer west. Looks as if they've turned onto the A27 and they're not hanging about."

"So what do we do?" Lauren asked. "Can we get the police here to protect her?"

"We can't get the local plods involved without blowing our cover and a lot of long-winded explanations. In the longer term, we can either get Anna moved to another home, or I can have an MI5 surveillance team out here by tomorrow morning. But if they're planning on scooping her up now, it's down to you and me."

Lauren realized that she had to start preparing. "Carl, I'm going inside," she yelled, as she dashed toward her unit.

Carl screamed and ran after Lauren, but she didn't have time to listen.

"Where are you, John?" she asked, as she bolted up the stairs.

"On the way out of my room," John said. "I'm taking the car, I'll be outside the ACC's front gate within ten minutes."

Lauren was relieved to hear that John would get there before the baddies. She raced into her room, shut her door and grabbed her case from the wardrobe under the bed. After lifting out a stack of clothes, she found the hidden catch. A flap opened up, revealing a few pieces of emergency equipment.

Lauren pocketed a small can of pepper spray and pulled down her leggings before strapping a concealed knife to her thigh.

"Young lady," a man said stiffly, as he burst into the room.

Lauren jumped with fright as she straightened her clothes. "Haven't you heard of knocking?" she demanded. "I'm undressing here."

It was Ronald, one of the house parents. "What's going on with Carl?" he asked.

"I dunno," Lauren said, mystified.

"You were outside playing with him. Then you stormed off and locked him out in the dark."

"Oh," Lauren gasped. She'd forgotten that the front door had a catch that locked if you shoved it hard. "Sorry."

"That's not a very respectful way to treat one of our youngest guests, Lauren. He's a vulnerable human being, not a toy that you can abandon in a dark playground the instant you get fed up with him."

"I'm sorry," Lauren repeated, as she pointed at the open phone on her bed. "I got excited, my best mate just rang me."

"Well, don't do it again."

Lauren flicked Ronald off as he closed the door behind himself. She grabbed her phone off the desk. John was still on the line.

"I know where Anna gets off the bus from school," Lauren said. "I'll wait at the end of the street. I should be able to get to her before she's in sight of ACC. I'll tell her that I'm treating her to a burger or something."

Twenty minutes later, Lauren stood nervously on a dark street corner as the kids started to filter down from the main road in their school uniforms. John had parked up outside ACC's main gate and was keeping a suspicious eye out for any car with two men inside it.

The wind was bitter. Lauren started getting paranoid when it got to ten minutes past four. Finally, she looked down the main road and saw Anna stepping off a double-decker bus.

"Hey," Lauren said, smiling with relief. "You're late today."

"I have special English class at the learning support unit in town. What are you doing out here? It's freezing."

"I had another call from your Russian friends," Lauren explained. "They said they knew you were here and that they're coming to get you."

"You're joking," Anna said as she glanced around nervously. "How can they know?"

"I don't know," Lauren lied. "But they do."

"You haven't told anyone else about this, have you?"

"No," Lauren said. "But I'm worried sick. I think we'll have to tell someone. They could grab you off the street. I came out here because for all we know, they're waiting outside the ACC gates right now."

"What can we do?"

"I've got twenty quid," Lauren said. "The longer we stand around here, the more chance that they'll spot us. We'll find a McDonald's or somewhere warm and think everything through."

"I guess," Anna said, as she spun around.

Lauren's phone rang as they started walking. It was John.

"Pretend like you're speaking to your best friend," he said.

"Hi, Bethany," Lauren said enthusiastically.

"I've thought it through," John said. "I've had a good look around and I can't see the bad guys, but the mobile phone signal says they're less than three hundred meters away. Head for the café on the corner. I'll be your social worker, same as when you arrived on Sunday. When I come in, you tell Anna that you got scared and told me what was going on. I'll tell her that she can have full British citizenship and protection if she tells us everything she knows."

"Can you do that?" Lauren asked.

"I had a word with Zara; she says the easiest thing is to fill in the paperwork as if we're recruiting Anna into CHERUB. Then we'll reject her application and send her out for adoption."

"What if we kept the item?" Lauren was trying not to let Anna tag onto the conversation. Fortunately, she didn't speak much English anyway.

"I considered that," John said. "You said Anna's bright, but she's twelve already and there's not much of her. By the time we've taught her enough English to get through basic training and toughened her up a bit, she'd be too old."

"That's a shame," Lauren sighed. "I would have loved to come to your birthday party."

"I won't be able to park on the main road," John said. "So I'll be walking right behind you. I've got a gun, just in case they show their faces."

"I'll send you a nice card," Lauren said. "Speak soon, bye."

"Who was that?" Anna asked, as Lauren pocketed her phone.

"Mate of mine," Lauren explained, switching back to Russian. "Wanted me to go to her party, but didn't realize that I'd moved down here."

"Pity," Anna said.

Lauren pointed out the café on the opposite corner. "We can cross over and go in there, they do nice cakes."

They were approaching the no-parking zone leading up to a pedestrian crossing when a battered Toyota sedan screeched to a halt alongside them. Lauren turned and saw two burly men staring right at her.

"Run," she screamed, giving Anna a shove as the back of the car opened and a Reebok sneaker stepped into the gutter.

To Lauren's horror, Anna only managed two steps before the momentum from the push sent her sprawling across the pavement. Realizing that Anna wouldn't be able to outrun two grown men, Lauren went on the offensive. As the man in the Reeboks stood up, Lauren charged forward and kicked him in the balls. He crumpled over as she slammed her palm into his solar plexus, punched him in the face, and crunched his arm in the car door.

Meanwhile, the driver stepped into the road, sprinted around the car, and grabbed Anna off the pavement. He shouted to Lauren in English: "Hey, little girl."

Lauren caught the light glinting from the saw-toothed blade at Anna's throat.

"Get in the car or I cut her head off."

Lauren looked over her shoulder, but there was no sign of John. A woman screamed "hey" from the opposite side of the road as her stroller-pushing friend dialed the police on her mobile.

The man Lauren had beaten groaned as he grabbed the car door and used it to lever himself out of the gutter. Meanwhile, his knife-wielding companion bundled Anna into the front passenger seat. Once the knife was away from Anna's throat, Lauren considered going back on the attack, but within a second, she had a gun pressed against her temple.

"Little bitch," the bloody-nosed man spat, as he grabbed Lauren's jacket and thrust her inside the car.

Lauren ended up straddling the backseat and the man sat on her, crushing her legs as he pulled shut the rear door. As the driver slammed his door and dropped the hand brake, his companion shoved Lauren's legs from beneath him, before banging her head against the door trim and cracking his hand across her face.

"Kick me in the balls, eh?" he shouted, as Lauren collapsed across her seat. "You wait till we arrive. Then I'll show you who's boss."

"What the *hell* happened?" the driver said, as the car sped away. "It was supposed to be fast and clinical."

"This one came at me," his bloody-faced companion answered, as he stared Lauren down.

"Abby will go nuts. Half a dozen people saw us. We're gonna end up with the cops on our tail and you know what it's like with kids: It'll probably end up on the news."

"Don't blame *me*, arsehole. You told me it was one skinny little girl. You didn't mention that she had Bruce Lee's kid sister for a bodyguard."

The tires squealed as they took a sharp right turn. Anna was sobbing hopelessly in the front passenger seat.

"Do you think they got our number plate?" the driver asked.

"We were parked there for over a minute, you can bet somebody did."

"Call someone and get them to pick us up in another car. We've got to ditch this crate."

As her captors argued, Lauren felt inside her jacket. She still had her mobile phone, which meant that John would be able to track her. The only trouble was, they'd probably search her and confiscate it as soon as they had time to think straight, so she slipped it out of her pocket and pushed it down the back of her knickers, between the cheeks of her bum. It made sitting uncomfortable and it wasn't a nice way to treat a new phone, but they'd be unlikely to find it on a casual search of her pockets.

CHAPTER 27

CURIOSITY

School had finished for the day and James was sitting on Kerry's bed in his socks. Kerry pulled two mugs of hot chocolate out of her microwave, handed one to James, and grabbed a bag of miniature marshmallows off her bedside cabinet. After dropping a few into each mug, she leaned over and kissed James on the cheek before running her finger over the scar above his left eye.

"You look like Harry Potter." She grinned. "So how did your meeting with Mr. Pike go?"

"It was weird," James said, as he slid the blue card out of his pocket. "He gave me this."

"What's that?"

As James sipped his cocoa, he told Kerry about the

card giving access to the mission preparation building and the story of Ewart and Mr. Pike being best friends.

"So," he finished, "what do you reckon?"

Kerry shrugged. "I think that seventeen years is a long time for Mr. Pike to hold a grudge."

"I meant, what do you think about the idea of me sneaking into the mission preparation building?"

"Isn't the security in there supposed to be mental?" Kerry asked.

"They never got that biometric system working. In the end, they decided that campus is pretty secure so they've replaced it with swipe cards."

"What was Ewart like when you spoke to him the other day?"

James shrugged. "He seemed okay to be honest. But I was thinking in class this afternoon—"

"First time for everything," Kerry butted in.

"I'm trying to be serious," James said irritably. "Remember two years back when we were on our drugs mission and Nicole got expelled for snorting cocaine? Ewart was charging around the house that day, giving us all drug tests and it was like he *wanted* more of us to get expelled. I've had a few other run-ins with him as well, and the more I've thought about it, the more I've come to agree with Mr. Pike: Ewart wouldn't lift a finger to help anyone."

"Ewart's strict," Kerry said. "He doesn't stand for any nonsense, that's for sure. But it's a big leap from that to saying that he's actually dishonest."

James slowly turned the blue card over in his hands. "I'd really like to know what's going on with the investigation. I definitely don't think that Ewart is telling me everything he knows."

"It's the most sensitive area on campus, James. You're already suspended from missions. If you get caught sneaking around mission preparation you might as well pack your bags and start saying your good-byes."

"I know, but if what Mr. Pike says about Ewart is right, I'm doomed anyway."

"Yeah, *might* be, based upon an ancient grudge. Taking a risk based upon solid information is one thing, but this doesn't make any sense."

"But Mr. Pike's always fair. He was the one who stood up for us when Mr. Large kept bullying Lauren."

Kerry nodded. "Pike is a decent bloke, there's no denying that."

"Which is why I think I need to go in there—and I'd really like you to come and be my lookout."

"Na-uh," Kerry said. "No way. It's a massive risk."

"But you're smart, Kerry, I really need your help on this."

"James, if you're really concerned about Ewart, speak with Meryl or go to a member of the ethics committee."

"Ewart will smooth-talk his way out of it. And let's face it, he's married to the chairman."

"You know what I think?" Kerry said. "I think your curiosity is getting the better of you. You're not really worried about Ewart. It's just that this investigation is preying on your mind and you want to go into his office and have a good snoop around."

"Fine," James snapped. "If you're not gonna help me I'll ask Kyle."

Kerry shook her head. "Can't, he went off on some mission this morning."

"Shak then."

"Training," Kerry said.

James thought it through: Callum and Connor were away on a mission, so was Lauren, and Bruce was in the medical unit with a broken leg.

"Please, Kerry," James groveled. "You're the only one."

Kerry grabbed James's bicep. "I'm begging you, James, don't do this. I know you're worried about the investigation, but this is going to make things worse, not better. Even if you do start sneaking around Ewart's office, there's no guarantee that you'll actually find the information you're looking for."

James huffed. "I guess you're right. I'll give Mr. Pike his card back and tell him that it didn't work out."

"You know it makes sense," Kerry said, as she went up on her knees and swung her leg across James's waist.

James pulled the front of Kerry's T-shirt out of her pants and blew a raspberry on her stomach as he grabbed hold of her bum.

"You know, your new look with the scar and the slightly bent nose is very cute." Kerry giggled, as they started snogging. "It's like I've got my own personal thug."

The Toyota swung into a desolate alleyway. There'd been no sign of the police coming after them, but the driver and his companion—who Lauren now knew were called Roman and Keith—both wanted to abandon the car as soon as possible.

A lad of about twenty waited on the curb as they pulled into an open garage. He took the keys off the driver and swapped them for a set belonging to an aged Nissan Micra parked a few meters down the cobbled road.

"Are you sure it's small enough?" Roman asked the youngster, as he snatched the keys.

"I only had fifteen minutes' notice," the kid said. "That's my nan's car, so don't mash it up."

Roman gave the teenager a friendly pat on the cheek. "Don't worry, you saved our lives. Keep the Toyota locked up till dark, then drive it onto the Downs and burn it out."

"No sweat," the teenager said, as he eyed Lauren and Anna. "Those two are young even for you ain't they, Keith? And what happened to your nose?"

"Mind your own," Keith snapped back, squeezing Lauren's knuckles as he yanked her out of the car. "But the person who did it will be crying herself to sleep tonight, I guarantee you that."

They were squeezed inside the Nissan and back on the move within a minute. There wasn't much room in the rear and Keith's legs were spread out wide. He placed his hairy hand on Lauren's knee.

"We've got a buyer lined up for the princess in the front," he whispered. "But you're a little bonus. You belong to me."

Lauren shuddered as Keith blew her a kiss.

"Come on, baby," he grinned. "Don't I get a smile from my little Lauren? Just a teensy weensy one?"

Lauren turned to look out of the window and tried to think of all the painful ways she could slice Keith up with the knife strapped to her leg.

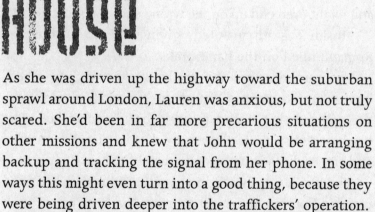

CHAPTER 28

HOUSE

As she was driven up the highway toward the suburban sprawl around London, Lauren was anxious, but not truly scared. She'd been in far more precarious situations on other missions and knew that John would be arranging backup and tracking the signal from her phone. In some ways this might even turn into a good thing, because they were being driven deeper into the traffickers' operation.

Anna sat in the front seat looking shocked, with red eyes and a blank face. Lauren wanted to reach between the seats, rest a hand on her shoulder, and tell her that things weren't as desperate as they seemed.

Lauren's problem was that escaping from a moving car is extremely dangerous, because overpowering the driver can easily cause an accident. On the other hand she didn't want to wait until they were inside a building, so her plan was to bide her time until they arrived, then pull her knife and grab Keith's gun before running off down the street with Anna.

The plan would have worked if they'd stopped outside a house, but to Lauren's horror they pulled through a set of electrically operated security gates at the back of a Victorian warehouse. She looked around the yard as the gates clanged shut behind them. The high walls were topped with coils of barbed wire and clusters of CCTV cameras hung from metal brackets.

Lauren reckoned she could still grab Keith's gun, but with no clear escape route it would be a risky move. She'd probably end up having to shoot someone in order to escape and might even end up on the wrong end of a bullet herself.

"Inside," Keith grunted, giving Lauren a shove as Roman pulled on the hand brake.

The warehouse had appeared old as they'd approached, but as Lauren stepped out of the car and looked inside, she realized that it had recently been refurbished. The brickwork was clean, there were double-glazed windows, and the back door had trendy metal fittings.

The inside continued in the same vein, with stripped wooden flooring and a red staircase that rose up through the center of the building. Music thumped as they passed the entrance to a concrete-floored storage area stacked with crates and bottles. Lauren glanced through a set of doors at the back of this space and saw a lively bar, with leather and chrome fixtures and customers dressed in their work clothes.

As they clanked up to the first landing, a scowling woman emerged from a small office. She was tall, with a red dress stretched over a lumpy frame and a pair of severely battered Converse sneakers on her feet.

"What *is* this?" she growled, pointing at Lauren. "Another mistake?"

"The one with the phone," Roman explained. "We had no choice but to take her."

"The heat we'll get on this will be unbelievable," the woman shouted. "Nobody would have made much fuss about a Russian quietly disappearing from a kids' home, but you muppets decide to snatch two girls, on a *main* road, in the *middle* of the afternoon. The police are going to be all over this."

"Don't sweat it, Abby," Roman said. "They won't track us back here. We rang Nicky boy and switched cars."

"And I'm out of pocket for a burned-out Toyota," Abby snapped. "We can't keep them here for long. The customers can't see them. I don't even want the other girls seeing too much of them. Take them upstairs and put them in separate rooms."

As they passed by, Lauren glanced inside Abby's office at banks of LCD screens showing everything that was going on inside the building, including the bar and a deserted nightclub. As Roman led the way toward a white door at the end of the corridor, Lauren was surprised to find herself being tapped on the bum.

"What's sticking out of there?" Abby asked.

Lauren cringed. She was wearing leggings and the phone had steadily slid down her bum, leaving an obvious bulge.

"Mobile phone," Lauren said.

Abby glowered angrily at the two men. "Didn't you search these two?"

Neither man had the balls to answer. They looked like small boys being told off by their mum.

"You knew she had a mobile phone," Abby screamed, snatching it from Lauren. "You know you can track them. Have you got one brain cell between you?"

She pulled off the battery before flipping it open and breaking the two halves apart. "If the cops got hold of her number and tracked her here, we are *totally* in the shit," she yelled. "Now, search them."

Roman told Lauren to raise her arms in the air and began turning out her pockets. He got the pepper spray and the small penknife that Lauren kept on her key ring, but he didn't notice the knife strapped to the inside of her thigh when he patted her down.

"Where's this from?" Abby asked Lauren, as she suspiciously pulled the cap off the pepper spray. It wasn't the kind of thing you expected to find in a twelve-year-old's pocket and Lauren knew it was illegal to sell pepper spray in Britain.

"There were a lot of attacks going on near where I used to live, so I bought it off this boy," Lauren lied. "He brought it back from his holiday in America."

Abby raised the can and squirted it at Roman. Cherubs carried an extra-strength brand designed to stop charging bears and Roman yelled out in pain. As he clutched his face, Keith backed up nervously. The tangy vapor in the air was enough to make the girls' eyes water.

"Powerful stuff," Abby grinned, as she threw the canister inside her office. "Now, get these little *bitches* out of my sight and make sure there are no customers around before you drag them into the brothel."

A twenty-meter walk along a balcony overlooking the staircase took Keith, Roman, Anna, and Lauren to an anonymous white door with an intercom mounted at its side. After being buzzed in, they passed into a reception area that smelled like cigarettes. The only phones were mobiles, the furniture was made from chipboard, and the whole place gave the impression that everything could be picked up and shipped out in a matter of hours.

A sign behind the desk reassured customers that *all transactions will appear on your credit card statement as North Lane Pizza & Pasta.* A powerfully built bouncer scowled from a leather armchair, as Lauren tried not to stare at the goods: a half dozen girls in their late teens or very early twenties. They sat on modular sofa units, wearing silk gowns and high heels, with nothing but old magazines and a few half eaten boxes of Chinese food for entertainment.

"You fellas don't look so hot," the elderly receptionist said, as she eyed Keith's bloody nose and Roman's streaming eyes.

"Sweetheart, you haven't looked so hot since nineteen fifty-six," Roman snapped back. "So shut your yap and get me two rooms upstairs, well away from action. Don't buzz any customers in till we're out of sight."

After grasping two chunky keys, Roman led the foursome up a narrow staircase and out into a corridor with five doors on each side. Just like downstairs, everything looked cheap. The rooms were nothing but plywood partitions and the doors had clasps and padlocks on them.

Lauren and Anna got shoved into rooms on opposite sides at the far end of the corridor.

"One for the princess," Keith said, as he locked Anna in her room. "And one for my special friend."

Lauren got shoved into a windowless space three meters square. She was surrounded on all sides by bare sheets of plywood and almost choked from the smell of air freshener. A low energy bulb dangled from the ceiling, and there was a double bed with a disposable sheet stretched over the duvet and pillows.

As Keith fastened the padlock on the outside, Lauren pulled back a thin dividing curtain. Behind it was a bathroom of sorts: a set of clean towels, a shower with mold growing on the curtain, and a heavily stained, seatless, toilet. Most disturbing was a washbasin streaked with dried blood.

Lauren backed off and propped herself on the edge of the paper bedsheet. The room made her skin crawl, as she imagined teenage girls being locked up and forced to have sex with strange men: a quick shower, a squirt of air freshener, and a fresh paper sheet before the next customer came in; and your head smashed open on the wash basin if you gave your boss—or rather your owner—any kind of trouble.

Horror movies had nothing on this, but Lauren knew she couldn't let it get to her. Hopefully, John Jones and a bunch of cops would come storming in before too long, but it might take them a while to plan a complicated raid and Lauren had to consider every eventuality. She and Anna were in danger every second they were locked up, so she was determined to get out as quickly as she could.

Lauren heard steps out in the hallway, followed by the sound of a padlock springing open.

"I've got a score to settle," Keith said, putting on a voice like he was teasing a small child. He still wore the bloody shirt, but not the jacket with the gun tucked inside.

"Here are the rules," he smirked, as he pushed shut the door. "You do everything I say or I pop you in the mouth, like that." He slammed his fist into his palm. "Now, take your kit off."

"What kit?" Lauren said, acting dumb as she reassured herself by feeling the surprise strapped to her leg.

"Strip," Keith ordered, as he unbuttoned his shirt. "Then you can come and sit on my lap."

"I'll scream," Lauren said.

Keith spread his arms out wide and laughed. "Scream all you like, honey. There ain't nobody gonna come running to save you."

"Pervert," Lauren sneered. "You make me sick."

"Sticks and stones . . . ," Keith said. "You'd better start being a bit smarter, Lauren. I'm big, you're small. You're going to do everything I tell you to do. The only question is how much I have to hurt you to make it happen."

"Have you tried this before?" Lauren asked. "I mean, raping a twelve-year-old?"

Keith smiled as he pulled off his Reeboks. "Let's see how smart that mouth of yours is in half an hour's time."

"Your mother must be *really* proud of you, Keith."

That snapped it. Keith lunged at Lauren with one leg still in his pants. He tried grabbing her by the neck, but she ripped her hand out of her leggings, ducked down low, and plunged the knife between his legs.

Keith grabbed Lauren's hair as he screamed in agony. Hot blood ran over her hand as she tried to free the knife, but the handle was slippery and it wouldn't budge. Lauren felt a section of her scalp tear as Keith hitched her off the ground. The pain was excruciating, but Lauren managed to smash her palm against the underside of Keith's jaw. Still holding on to Lauren's hair, he staggered back and collapsed across the bed.

"Let me go," Lauren yelled, kneeing the bloody patch between Keith's legs as she landed on top of him.

Keith was bleeding heavily and she felt his grip weaken. She wriggled free and realized that she was covered in blood as she stumbled back toward the dividing curtain.

Lauren wasn't particularly aggressive, but she hated Keith because of what he'd wanted to do to her and probably *had* done to other girls who'd been less able to defend themselves.

"Pedophile," she snarled, as she watched the blood streaking down Keith's legs. "You're lucky I don't strangle you."

She was sorely tempted, but her training overpowered her thirst for revenge. There were only thin wooden partitions between each room. Someone had probably heard the commotion and it wouldn't be long before they came to find out what had happened.

CHAPTER 29

DOCUMENTS

James *had* to do it. He'd agreed with Kerry once he realized that she wasn't going to help, but only because he knew he'd never get a snog while they were arguing.

James's first idea was to sneak across campus in the early hours of the morning, but that would be highly suspicious. He knew from personal experience that the mission preparation building was usually almost empty by 6 p.m. If he got caught at that time, he'd be able to claim that he'd found the door open and was looking for Ewart; provided he didn't get caught red-handed with his nose in a secret file.

There was a light drizzle in the evening air as he headed toward mission preparation. James nearly backed out a couple of times and even stopped walking before finally committing himself to the section of curved path leading toward the long, banana-shaped building.

CHERUB training teaches you that confidence is the key: It's best to act like you haven't got a care in the world even when you're crapping yourself. Campus was monitored by numerous security systems, but with hundreds of cameras and hundreds of people moving around, the security staff were unlikely to get excited about anything that didn't look too suspicious.

James approached with a swagger, swiped his card, pushed the door when it clicked, and tried not to make it too obvious that he was attempting to see as far ahead as possible as he peered down the curving corridor that led to Ewart's office.

The office wasn't locked. Ewart usually left early to pick his kids up from nursery, but James knocked just in case. When he didn't get an answer, he stepped in and flipped the light switch.

James didn't have keys to the filing cabinets or cupboards, so it was lucky that Ewart was a slob. He began flicking through some of the papers stacked on the desk: invoices, plane tickets, lists of babysitters for the kids, a vet's bill for Meatball, and a lot of stuff related to an upcoming mission in Taiwan.

Frustrated, James tugged at the three locked desk drawers before eyeing a giant stack of papers on the glass coffee table in front of Ewart's sofa. James saw his own photograph on top of the stack. It had been taken on the day he'd joined CHERUB and James was surprised by how much he'd changed. He barely recognized the chubby, innocent face, and could only envy the absence of zits.

JAMES ADAMS: CONFIDENTIAL FILE.

The cardboard folder was ten centimeters thick, bursting with his entire life: school reports from Year One onward, a summary of his performance in basic training written by Mr. Large, mission reports, punishment reports. There were surveillance photographs of Lauren's dad, Ron, a coroner's report on his mother's death—*"massive cardiac failure caused by interaction of alcohol and anti-inflammatory medicine, secondary cause obesity"*—and even details of his mum's safety deposit box. It was a tantalizing chance to know what people had said about him, but it would take hours to plough through it all and James had to focus on Ewart's investigation.

The stack was thirty centimeters high and certainly gave the impression that Ewart was being thorough. As he flipped through, James found reports on Boris and Isla, including pictures of them when they were younger and of their bloody remains in the Aero City morgue. Isla had been shot in the face and James only recognized her by her evening dress and watch.

The other thing that kept coming up was the name of Lord Hilton, chairman of Hilton Aerospace and a major business partner of Denis Obidin. Hilton appeared on the television every so often, and James remembered the face, not because he was interested in the aerospace industry but because Hilton had a single bushy eyebrow that stretched from one side of his head to the other. It was a cartoonist's delight.

The contents of the next folder hit James like a slap: blurry black-and-white images printed on glossy paper. The stills were from Denis Obidin's office and showed him being murdered by Isla and Boris. It was clearly taken from the CIA footage that he'd seen in Aero City.

The following pages showed more stills, some of them annotated with handwritten notes, while others were huge pixelated enlargements of tiny sections of a particular frame. The last page was a fax message:

Ewart,
I've spent hours going through these images. I've checked shadow details, made enlargements, and broken the video down frame by frame looking for glitches. I have also compared facial images and mechanical details such as stride pattern and mannerisms with surveillance videos of Boris and Isla taken inside MI5 headquarters.

The state of modern computer graphics technology makes it impossible to guarantee that any video footage is real, but if this is a fake or has been staged by actors and retouched it has been produced to a higher standard than anything we are capable of.

For the purposes of your investigation, I think you should consider this footage 100% genuine.

Rod Harper
Metropolitan Police, photo and video forensic department.

James looked at the send date and saw that Ewart had received the fax more than a week earlier, but he'd told

James that he was still trying to get hold of the video less than two days ago.

"Two-faced son of a . . . ," James muttered.

He felt sick. CHERUB wasn't just an organization James worked for. It was his home, it was all his friends, it was his school—basically his entire life. Confronted with the reality that Ewart had lied to him, James realized that Kerry had been right: He hadn't truly believed Mr. Pike's conspiracy theory and had just come here to nose around and see what Ewart was up to.

James's hands trembled as he flipped frantically through more papers. There were thousands of sheets, probably hundreds of thousands of words, and he wouldn't be able to read them if he stayed up all night. He figured he could just skim through and read the basics, but then what?

Ewart was married to the chairman, and as much as James liked Zara, he wasn't sure that he could trust her to take his side over her own husband. She might even be in on Ewart's scheme, whatever it turned out to be.

That left the ethics committee, but its members were designed to be independent. They didn't live on campus and they were all outsiders: lawyers, retired policemen, and the like. Even if James approached one, what was to say that Ewart wouldn't talk his way out of it?

James realized that his only realistic option was to calm down, digest as much as he could, photocopy some of the most interesting paperwork, and then bring it to Mr. Pike, or maybe Meryl.

There was a knock at the door.

James jolted with fright and a stack of papers cascaded

out of his lap onto the carpet. This was a disaster. If the person at the door came in, it would be blindingly obvious that he'd been snooping.

He crossed his fingers and willed the person to go away, but the handle turned and the door began sweeping across the carpet.

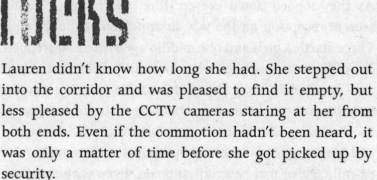

CHAPTER 90

LOCKS

Lauren didn't know how long she had. She stepped out into the corridor and was pleased to find it empty, but less pleased by the CCTV cameras staring at her from both ends. Even if the commotion hadn't been heard, it was only a matter of time before she got picked up by security.

"You okay?" she shouted, as she stared at the hefty bolt and padlock across the door of Anna's room.

"What was that noise?" Anna asked from the other side.

"Stabbed Keith," Lauren explained. "Stand away from the door."

The lock looked sturdy, but any security system is

only as strong as its weakest link and the door itself was flimsy. Lauren grabbed each side of the doorframe of her own room and used it as leverage to launch an explosive, two-footed kick across the corridor.

She had sneakers on, but the force still hurt the balls of her feet as the flimsy wooden walls on both sides of the corridor wobbled. The lock held in place, but a gap had been torn between the door and the chipboard in which it was mounted.

Lauren's second kick knocked the hinged side of the door farther inward. It wasn't a huge gap, but enough for Anna's skinny body to wriggle through. Anna was shocked to see Lauren with blood-smeared clothing and a heavy padlock in her hand.

As they jogged down the corridor, the bouncer they'd seen at reception on the way in appeared at the far end. Three startled girls and one middle-aged man had stepped out of their rooms to see why the walls had been shaking.

Anna looked back for an alternative exit, but Lauren hid the padlock behind her back and strode on toward the bouncer. His scruffy gray suit bulged with muscle and Lauren guessed she was up against someone who was ex-military, or maybe a retired boxer. Even with the some of the best combat training in the world under her belt, Lauren would only get one shot at a surprise attack.

"Where'd you think you're going, missy?" The bouncer grinned as he pointed back along the corridor. "Get back in that room before I clock you one."

Lauren waited until they were less than a meter apart before swinging the heavy padlock. A couple of the girls screamed as metal hit bone, making a sickening thunk and tearing a bloody gash in the bouncer's cheek. As he stumbled forward in a daze, Lauren hit him with a brutal roundhouse kick to the ribs, followed by a knee in the guts and a knockout blow with the padlock.

"We're all getting out of here," Lauren shouted, and set off for the staircase, armed only with the padlock and terrified of finding herself on the wrong end of a gun. Anna kept close as they crept down the stairs, while four slightly older girls trailed nervously.

Lauren peered around the bottom of the staircase into the reception area. The sofas where the girls sat waiting for customers were out of sight, but she could see the receptionist, the bouncer's empty armchair, and Keith's coat hanging tantalizingly from a rack.

"See the coats?" Lauren whispered.

Anna nodded.

"I'll go first. You run across and search the brown jacket. It's Keith's. He had a gun with him earlier."

Lauren raced out into the room, much to the surprise of the receptionist who leapt out of her seat and pointed toward the staircase.

"You'd better get back upstairs before you find yourself in a lot of trouble," the receptionist barked.

The girls on the sofa went quiet and stopped looking bored, but Lauren was furious to see that Anna had panicked and stood limply at the bottom of the staircase.

"For God's sake," Lauren yelled, looking at Anna and pointing at the coatrack.

The receptionist had stepped out from behind her desk and tried to grab Lauren's arm. Lauren snatched the woman's bony wrist, twisted her into an arm lock, and banged her head against the desk before smacking her around the side of the head with the metal face of the padlock.

"Stay down or you'll get another one," Lauren shouted menacingly. Then she turned her fury on Anna. "What's the matter with you? You're bloody useless."

There was now a bunch of younger girls at the bottom of the stairs and the older ones who were on public display were getting off the sofas. As they all started chattering nervously in Russian, bad English, and other languages that Lauren couldn't understand, she made her own way toward the coatrack.

But the main door burst open before she got there. Roman came in first, followed by Abby holding the can of pepper spray.

"Get back to your rooms," Abby ordered, with her thumb clutching the trigger on the canister.

Lauren dropped behind the receptionist's desk. The other girls didn't seem to grasp what was in the canister, so Abby demonstrated with a quick squirt into the face of one of the older girls. She began screaming and a flurry of young legs bolted up the staircase.

"If this doesn't stop now, I'll get Kenneth and a couple of his lads out here," Abby shouted.

Whoever Kenneth was, the mention of his name was enough to have the girls back on the sofa. Anna had disappeared back upstairs, but Lauren had crawled as far as the chromed base of the coatrack and was relieved to see the handle of Keith's gun inside his jacket.

"The revolution is over," Roman smiled. "Get your asses back to work."

"The ringleader's over there," the receptionist said as she staggered up, with her hand covering a small cut where the padlock had struck her temple.

Lauren only had a second to grab the gun. As she shot up from the sticky carpet, Abby swung around and squeezed the cap on the pepper spray. The gooey liquid came through the air like snake venom. Lauren tried hiding her head behind a woman's coat, but it hit the side of her face as her fingers gripped the stock of Keith's revolver.

Lauren felt like her face was on fire, with one eye closed, the other streaming, and the intense odor of pepper spray searing inside her mouth and the back of her throat. Her vision blurred as she aimed the gun toward the ceiling and blasted a warning shot.

"Put the spray down and open the door," Lauren said, trying to sound more assertive than she felt.

She heard some of the other girls, who'd crept back to the bottom of the stairs to investigate the gunshot. The gun felt heavy. Lauren was seeing smears and fighting for breath, but she was less than three meters from Abby and Roman and you don't need good eyesight to shoot someone from that distance.

Abby dropped the pepper spray.

"Now open the door," Lauren said. "And anyone who wants to follow me out is welcome."

Roman stared at Abby for confirmation before stepping backward and opening the door. Lauren searched desperately for Anna, but all she could see were colors and blurry shapes. She realized that there were five or six girls running with her as she felt her way down the hallway toward Abby's office, gun in hand.

"Anna?" Lauren yelled.

"Your friend went back upstairs," a girl not much bigger than Lauren said, in broken English.

"Not going back," Lauren gasped as she pointed inside the office. "Can you see a phone?"

"On the desk."

"Dial for me," Lauren said. Then she realized that the other girls were standing in the doorway awaiting instructions. "Downstairs," she shouted. "There's a room with bottles, run through there, jump over the bar, and run out onto the street."

As six teenaged girls clattered down the metal staircase in mules and cheap dressing gowns, Lauren told her remaining companion to pick up the phone and gave her the digits of John Jones's mobile number.

Lauren screamed into the receiver. "Where are you?"

"We're coming in within five to ten minutes," John said. "But the cops are nervous about storming a building this size without proper reconnaissance or knowing what kind of weapons they're up against."

"Only one gun that I know of and I'm holding it," Lauren said. "There should be girls coming out through the bar at the front any second."

"We'll grab them. Your voice sounds terrible, are you okay?"

"Pepper spray," Lauren explained. "Mostly on one side."

The blurry girl who was helping Lauren spoke anxiously. "Abby and the others are coming."

Lauren yelled into the phone. "John, the rats are leaving the sinking ship. You've got to stop them getting out."

"Are you sure they're not armed?"

"Pretty sure," Lauren said, as she waved her companion toward the staircase.

"Okay, keep safe," John said. "We've got cops on all sides of the building."

"I expect they'll try getting out of the back gates in a car," Lauren said.

John yelled to someone standing close to him: "Get a vehicle parked across the back gates."

Lauren realized that her companion had fled. She clutched the gun as blurry figures passed by in the corridor outside. The big red blur looked like Abby, but whoever it was, they weren't interested in Lauren, just in getting away.

"Girls coming out of the bar now," John shouted. "Cops are on their way in."

"You'd better get some ambulances," Lauren said. "I knocked one guy cold and stabbed another—he might even be dead."

As Lauren said this, she heard the pounding music stop in the bar downstairs. The replacement noises were screams and the sound of boots racing up the metal stairs.

"Put the gun down," a woman shouted.

Lauren rested the gun on the desk and the smeary black figure unbuckled her riot helmet as she stepped toward her. Lauren's eyes still stung like hell, but her vision was improving.

"There are more girls down there through the white door," Lauren said. "I think the staff all ran off."

"You heard her," the cop shouted, as she waved half a dozen colleagues by.

Lauren realized that she still had John on the phone. "Where are you?" she shouted.

"With you in a flash," John replied, before hanging up.

Half a dozen sirens were now squealing in the streets around the warehouse and Lauren heard a huge bang as the cops battered down the white door leading into the brothel.

"You okay?" John asked, as he stepped by the cop.

"Can't see much."

John had grabbed a bottle of mineral water and some paper towels from the bar on the way up. "There's blobs of pepper spray stuck to your top," he said, as he pulled a flick knife out of his pocket. "It might get in your eyes if we pull it off, so I'll cut it; then we can start flushing out the pepper spray."

John sliced a V in the neck hole of Lauren's sweatshirt, before grabbing the two sides and tearing it down. Lauren was relieved to be safe and couldn't resist making a joke.

"You ought to be careful," she grinned. "You should see the state of the last bloke who tried ripping my clothes off."

CHAPTER 19

CAUGHT

James heaved with relief as a chunky female figure came through the door, holding a vacuum and a can of furniture polish.

"*Dana*, thank God it's you."

Dana was a fifteen-year-old cherub who'd been born in Australia. She'd trained with James loads of times and had accompanied him on a mission earlier that year.

"Are you on crack?" Dana gasped, when she saw James rifling through Ewart's papers. "If one of the mission controllers catches you in here, they'll boot your arse out so fast your feet won't touch the ground."

"Desperate measures," James explained. "What are you doing here anyway?"

"What does it look like, brains?" Dana said, as she put the Hoover down and jiggled her can of polish. "This little knob-end cut the queue in the dining room. We got in a row and I ended up whacking him over the head with my tray. Trouble is, two teachers walked in as I was doing it and I copped a month's cleaning duty."

"Injustice," James tutted bitterly. "Campus is crawling with it."

"I heard you went off on some special birthday weekend."

James nodded. "Yeah, the girls did it to cheer me up. It was cool."

Dana raised an eyebrow. "Thanks for the invite, mate."

"Oh, well . . . Umm . . . It was a surprise. Kerry and Lauren set it up and—no offense—but I never thought it was your cup of tea. You're more of a lone wolf."

"Sitting alone in my room, reading *Lord of the Rings* for the seven hundredth time while I boil frogs in my cauldron."

"Something like that," James said. He felt uneasy because Dana was holding all the cards.

"I heard you got suspended after that Aero City thing," Dana said, as she looked at the three-year-old photo of James amid the papers scattered over the floor. "Is this Ewart's investigation?"

James nodded. "I'm here because I've got a nasty feeling that he's trying to stitch me up."

"Why would he do that?"

"I reckon the answer's among this lot somewhere," James said, as he dug out the report on the video surveillance and waggled it in the air. "There's evidence here that puts me totally in the clear. Ewart has had it for more than a week, but when I asked *two days* ago, he told me that he was still trying to get it from the CIA and that there was a realistic chance I could be forced to leave CHERUB."

"He could have just got it before he went off."

"It's dated last week, Dana. And what do you mean, *went off*?"

"Ewart left about an hour ago with an overnight bag. He stopped me and moaned that I wasn't cleaning his office well enough. He said he wants me to do the window ledges properly and make sure that the water doesn't spill over when I water his cactus. I'm sorely tempted to piss in his bloody plant."

"I've never liked him, to be honest," James said. "I had him on my second mission and he was a total pain."

Dana nodded. "It's the cool guy thing that annoys me. You know, Ewart goes around dressed like a surf bum with his tongue stud and ripped jeans, but he's actually thirty whatever years old, with a Vauxhall Astra, two kids, and a mortgage."

"Exactly," James said. "John Jones is an old baldie, but he's actually a million times cooler than Ewart."

"I've worked with most of the mission controllers, and Ewart's definitely my least favorite."

James looked forlornly at his stack of papers, then up at Dana. "I have to know what he's up to, but I can't go through all this on my own. You couldn't give us a hand, could you?"

"This is some serious shit," Dana said, shaking her head uncertainly.

"Please," James said, but immediately regretted it. Dana didn't stand for any kind of nonsense and the plea made him sound pathetic.

"Gimme a second to think," Dana snapped. Then after a pause: "Ewart's not gonna be back until late tomorrow. How about we load all of those papers into a bin liner? We'll have to be careful not to jumble them up. Some of those documents are tagged, so you'd set off the alarm if you went out the front way, but I can stick them on the cleaning cart and put them out with the rubbish. You wait around the back and grab them while I'm putting the real rubbish into the incinerator. We'll go back to your room and start going through them; then I'll put everything back early tomorrow morning."

James broke into a big smile. "You might have just saved my life."

Dana wagged her finger. "And you'd *better* remember it next time there's free go-karting and fancy hotels being bandied about."

Carrying a bin liner across campus might arouse suspicions, so while Dana finished cleaning, James ran off to grab a backpack. Within forty minutes, he was standing in his room with Ewart's paperwork stacked on his bed.

"Gotta do this by the book," Dana said, as she pulled on a set of disposable plastic gloves. "Ewart can't know that we've been through the papers. If anything makes him suspicious, he'll ask for the video footage from the corridor outside his office and we'll be dead ducks."

"Only thing is, they might be a bit fingerprinted and out of order already," James replied. "I dropped some stuff when you came in and surprised me, but I reckon I can put it back more or less as it was."

All cherubs are trained to speed-read and taught proper procedures for going through documents. After removing all the junk from around James's bed, Dana took a digital camera and snapped a couple of photographs so that they'd be able to reassemble the stack precisely after going through it.

"Even speed-reading won't get us through all of this," Dana said. "We'll take half each and try and identify key documents, especially anything written by Ewart that gives us some idea of his thought processes."

James had been on the same espionage courses as Dana and only resisted the urge to make a comment about not being born yesterday because she was doing him a massive favor.

After breaking the stack of papers into evenly sized piles, James took the bottom half and found himself staring at MI5 personnel files for Boris and Isla Kotenkov.

"Snidey," James said, as he held the document up to show Dana. "Here's something else Ewart told me he hadn't been able to get hold of."

He was surprised to learn that as well as being husband and wife, Boris and Isla were also cousins. During the Soviet era they had risked death, or life imprisonment in a brutal labour camp, to pass valuable intelligence on Russian weapons technology to the West.

"Listen to this," James said, as he read a section of the report that Ewart had highlighted. "*The Kotenkovs were financially well rewarded by British and American intelligence services. However, they lost everything trying to set up* a Moscow based dry-cleaning business and offered their services to MI5 once again in 1998. They were able to use long-standing contacts within the Soviet weapons industry to set themselves up as illicit weapons dealers, but have griped constantly about their low wages, low status, and the lack of pension provision."

Dana nodded. "Sounds like the sort of people who'd take a bung to bump off Denis Obidin." Then she burst out laughing.

"What's so funny?"

Dana read an extract written by a health visitor seven years earlier: "James Choke is a bright and thoughtful eight-year-old, although he does have difficulty controlling his temper at times. Unfortunately, James's bed-wetting problem persists and this is not helped by his younger sister, Lauren, who teases him mercilessly and refers to him as Mr. Piddle Pants."

"Hey," James gasped. "Gimme that. You're supposed to be going through Ewart's stuff, not my personal file."

"I've got to be thorough," Dana giggled.

"Dana, I could be kicked out of CHERUB and you're making jokes."

"I know it's serious, piddle pants. It might have escaped your attention, but I'm running as big a risk as you."

Dana couldn't stop laughing as James turned sourly back to his paperwork.

"Is your laptop switched on?" she asked, a couple of minutes later. "I need the Internet."

"Sure. Are you onto something?"

"Maybe; I'll tell you in a minute. What do you know about Hilton Aerospace by the way?"

James shrugged. "Not a huge amount. It's a British company, but it has massive contracts in Aero City, refurbishing Russian airliners and stuff."

"Contracts with Denis Obidin?" Dana asked.

"Absolutely," James nodded. "The Obidin family practically owns the whole town."

"Both dead," Dana said, as she frantically tapped at James's laptop.

"Who's dead?" James asked as he put his paperwork down on the carpet and shuffled over to the computer on his knees.

Dana held up a handwritten list of names. Ewart had scrawled arrows, numbers, and question marks between them. Dana pointed to each name in turn: "Denis Obidin, dead. Boris and Isla, dead. Lord Hilton, still alive but if I'm reading this diagram right, Ewart thinks he used a holding company to pay Boris and Isla fifty thousand dollars. Then there's this guy, Sebastian Hilton; I'm not sure where he links in but I guess he's Lord Hilton's brother, or son, or something."

"Just saw a photocopy of his *Who's Who* entry in my pile," James said. "He's Lord Hilton's son, a Member of Parliament, and the new junior intelligence minister."

"And the plot thickens," Dana grinned, as she tapped another search into Google.

"So what are these four other names?" James asked, as he looked at the bottom of the piece of paper.

"Clare Nazareth," Dana said, reading a local newspaper report from the laptop screen. "*Research scientist Clare Nazareth died tragically from carbon monoxide poisoning in her Hertfordshire home. The fifty-eight-year-old mother of two had worked for Hilton Aerospace for more than thirty years and had published more than eighty scientific papers. Her most notable work was in the field of ceramic jet engine technology."*

"Does it say when she died?" James asked.

"Two weeks yesterday."

"That's just after I got back from Aero City."

Dana had a Google search on another name running in a different tab. "Oh," Dana gasped. "Another one bites the dust."

James looked at an image of an elderly woman on his laptop screen as Dana read aloud: *"Seventy-three-year-old Madeline Cowell was found dead in her Hertfordshire home. Two sons, recently widowed,* blah, blah, blah, *possibly confused over her medication. Police believe there are no suspicious circumstances."*

"Who was she?"

Dana clicked on a couple of different links, but didn't find anything new. "Maybe we'll pick something up in the documents."

"So what about these two other names at the bottom?" James asked. "Jason McLoud and Sarah Thomas."

Dana pointed to a sheet standing in the out tray of James's printer. "Looks like McLoud is a scientific journalist. I did a search for his name and it came up with hundreds of articles, so I narrowed it down by doing *Jason McLoud Hilton Aerospace."*

James pulled the piece of paper out of his printer. The article was from the online edition of *Aerospace World* magazine.

NO SURPRISE AS CERAMIC JET TECHNOLOGY
FACES ANOTHER SETBACK

By Jason McLoud

Since the dawn of the jet age, engineers have tried replacing metal components inside jet engines with ceramics. Theoretically, the thermal properties of a ceramic engine should enable it to spin faster and produce significantly more power than a metal equivalent, but reality has consistently failed to live up to the hype.

The latest blow is the decision by Hilton Aerospace to stop funding its ceramics research facility in Aero City, Russia. This correspondent traveled to Aero City to speak with Denis Obidin.

Obidin remains in typically bullish mood, but many commentators say that the closure is the final nail in Obidin's dream of building a modern Russian aerospace industry to compete with America and the Europeans.

LOG IN TO READ THE FULL ARTICLE

FOR IMMEDIATE ACCESS, PURCHASE AN ONLINE SUBSCRIPTION HERE

"All seems to tie up somehow," James said. "Lord Hilton withdraws funding from Denis Obidin's pet project. They have some kind of falling out and Hilton ends up paying Boris and Isla to kill him."

"I can see that." Dana nodded. "Two businessmen falling out is nothing to write home about, but this is in an entirely different league. What did Obidin have that makes Lord Hilton turn to the dirty deeds department?"

"Something that threatens his life, his career, or his family."

"Obviously," Dana said. "Ahhh, got her. I've found a website for an air show that took place back in 2002. *Members of the press wishing to interview Lord Hilton should in the first instance contact his personal assistant Madeline Cowell.*"

"Blimey," James said. "So that's Lord Hilton's business partner, personal assistant, and one of his top scientists all bumped off in the space of three weeks. You'd think someone would have realized."

"Not necessarily," Dana said. "The secretary was an old lady and Obidin was three thousand kilometers away. The only death likely to raise an eyebrow in this country is the scientist."

"So, apart from Lord Hilton and his son, the journalist Jason McLoud and this Sarah Thomas woman are the only ones on the list who are still alive."

"Exactly," Dana nodded.

James thought for a few seconds. "Anything on who Sarah Thomas is?"

"The name is way too common," Dana said. "I just went into the CHERUB server and accessed the UK electoral roll. There are five thousand three hundred and seventeen people in Britain called Sarah Thomas."

"So what next?"

Dana pointed at the piles of papers.

"Keep shuffling, dude."

CHAPTER 92

ROCK

James and Dana kept going until past midnight. Ewart had apparently conducted a thorough investigation with the help of personal contacts inside MI5 and the CIA. He seemed to have uncovered most of the truth behind the disastrous Aero City mission.

Lord Hilton's son, Sebastian, had run Hilton Aerospace's Russian operations until 1998, when he had left the company to begin a career in politics. During this time, Denis Obidin had gathered some dirt on Sebastian Hilton. When Lord Hilton said he was going to stop funding the ceramic engine research, Obidin had blackmailed him, threatening to ruin his son's budding political career unless . . .

None of the paperwork said what Obidin's hold over Sebastian Hilton was, or what Obidin had asked of Lord Hilton in return for his silence. But it *was* clear that instead of coughing up, recently appointed junior intelligence minister Sebastian Hilton had used a combination of his father's money and his ministerial power to have Obidin killed.

He'd set Boris and Isla up on a legitimate mission in Aero City and then paid them $100,000 to kill Denis. Apparently, a couple of other people who knew or suspected the truth—such as the scientist and Lord Hilton's retired personal assistant—had also been eliminated.

Sebastian Hilton assumed that he'd be able to use his connections inside MI5 to keep a lid on his dodgy dealings. Unfortunately, as the *junior* intelligence minister, he'd never been told about the existence of CHERUB and neither had Boris or Isla.

They received a nasty shock when senior MI5 and CHERUB officials reviewed the slow progress of Boris and Isla's mission and decided to send a CHERUB agent in to help them unearth the truth about Denis Obidin's illegal arms sales.

James's presence was a worry, but not enough to knock Sebastian Hilton or Boris and Isla off their stride. Their plan stayed the same: Boris and Isla would murder Denis Obidin, then escape Aero City and claim that they had killed him in self defense following a violent argument. The fact that James would most likely be captured, tortured, and killed by Vladimir Obidin concerned them so little that they hadn't even bothered to think up an excuse for him to get out of town on the night of the murder.

After the killing, Boris and Isla would have returned to Britain and pocketed Lord Hilton's money. Following a short investigation in which Boris and Isla would have been the only credible witnesses, James's death would be written off as a side effect of a mission that went tragically wrong.

Fortunately for James, Sebastian Hilton had miscalculated. Boris and Isla had been killed, while James had escaped. Worse, nobody within MI5 had known that there was a CIA team working in Aero City, who had not only worked out that Boris, Isla, and James were agents for British intelligence, but obtained clear video evidence showing Denis Obidin being murdered in cold blood.

James was relieved to finally know the truth—at least most of it—but he still had a queasy feeling in his gut. Ewart had known the facts for several days, some for as long as a week; but he'd kept him in the dark and even gone so far as to warn him that his CHERUB career might be over.

James was right at the bottom of his stack when he came to a final batch of Ewart's handwritten notes.

"Appointments," James yelled, with the kind of euphoria that can only come after four brain-numbing hours of speed-reading.

"What's up, doc?" Dana asked.

"The most important piece of paper *would* be right at the bottom, wouldn't it?" James said as he held it out for Dana to see. "Remember the two people on that list who weren't dead? It looks like Ewart has appointments with both of them tomorrow. The first one is at nine thirty, with our journalist friend, Jason McLoud. Then he's going to lunch with the mysterious Sarah Thomas."

"So now we know where he's going," Dana said. "But we still don't know what he's up to. This looks like a pretty thorough investigation for a man staging a cover-up, though."

"I agree," James said. "But I've been getting stick from half the kids on campus, I've been lying awake every night feeling sick to my stomach, and all because Ewart hasn't had the decency to tell me that he knows I'm innocent. There's got to be *something* fishy going on."

"It's certainly freaky," Dana nodded. "But what does Ewart stand to gain?"

"Money, I guess," James shrugged. "The Hiltons are billionaires and Sebastian could end up becoming intelligence minister, maybe even Prime Minister, some day. If Ewart helps the Hiltons out, his lifestyle could become a lot more pleasant."

"And you think Zara's in on it too?"

James wasn't comfortable with that aspect of the situation. Zara had always been one of his favorite people on campus. "Dunno," he said. "Maybe . . . but, for all we know, Ewart's planning to up and run off with a stripper or something."

"On the other hand, maybe he's just being cautious and waiting until he's completely sure about his facts."

"But why lie to me?" James insisted. "The video evidence clears me, one hundred percent. Why make me go through an extra week of torture? I've never liked Ewart and I'm prepared to bet my right nut that he's up to something."

"There's only one way we can really be sure," Dana said.

"What's that?"

"We know where Ewart's going to be at nine thirty tomorrow morning. We can follow him around and see what he's up to and who he's working with."

"That's risky," James said warily.

Dana laughed as she looked around the room at the piles of top-secret documents. "And this isn't . . . ? McLoud's house is only about an hour's drive from here. I'll go and put the papers back in mission preparation now. If anyone stops me, I'll say that I lost a ring when I was cleaning earlier. We'll grab a few hours' sleep, then we'll get up early, sneak down to reception, nab some equipment, and steal the keys to one of the pool cars."

"I can hardly believe you're prepared to go out on a limb for me, Dana," James smiled. "I've got a girlfriend two doors down the hall. I begged her for help and she spent the night watching soaps instead."

"A friend in need," Dana smiled back. "Besides, you're a nice guy, James. And I don't just mean nice; I mean *nice*-nice."

James was suddenly aware that Dana was standing close. She'd spent the whole night helping him, taking a massive risk in return for nothing and now she was saying that she was attracted to him.

The circumstances would have made it hard not to kiss Dana if she'd been a three-eyed monster with pickled onion breath. But she wasn't. James had always been attracted to her, but he'd never acted on it, or even really thought about it. He'd been going out with Kerry since before he'd got to know Dana and besides, Dana was an older girl. Boys on campus usually hit on girls their own age or younger.

"I've always thought you had fantastic eyes," James said, as he stared into them.

Dana was nearly two years older than Kerry. Taller, bulkier, curvier. She had hair that was kind of crazy because she never combed it, but somehow that made it even sexier. Most important, two years older meant that she was much more likely to want to have sex, a prospect that gave James a rush akin to having the Queen's golden jubilee fireworks going off in his boxers.

"Mind the papers," Dana mumbled, as James gave her an experimental kiss on the cheek.

The bed was off-limits, so Dana walked backward, frantically snogging James as she collapsed onto the small sofa by the door.

"I've fancied you for ages," Dana said, coming up for air as James felt her hand slide down the back of his jeans.

"Can I touch your tits?"

Dana laughed. "You're subtle, aren't you?"

Dana rolled off and James thought he'd blown it. But she'd only backed away so that she had room to pull her T-shirt over her head. James took his off too.

"What do I get in return for the bra?" Dana teased.

"Name your price," James grinned.

"No charge."

James couldn't believe his luck. It had taken *months* to get this far with Kerry. He could hardly breathe and practically had drool coming out the corner of his mouth. Then someone knocked at the door.

"Bloody hell," Dana gasped, as she batted James's hand away.

"Door's been locked all night," James whispered. "Just keep quiet for a sec and they'll think I'm out."

Dana smiled as James made a complete hash of undoing her bra.

"Wakey, wakey," Lauren shouted, as she burst through the door. She'd showered at a police station and wore a policewoman's black pullover. "Get your Brighton rock here."

James had finally triumphed over the bra and sprung up with it in his hand as Dana quickly snatched her T-shirt off the carpet.

"You told me it was locked," Dana hissed.

"Didn't you lock it when you came back with the coffees?"

As Dana pulled her T-shirt back on, James realized that he had a big problem.

"You dirty, stinking, *cheating* louse," Lauren snarled, as she brandished the bright pink stick of rock under her brother's nose. "I was gonna give you this, but now I'm tempted to shove it up your arse."

"I can explain," James said weakly.

"Oh, let me guess," Lauren sneered. "You were just sitting there when your T-shirts flew off over your heads and Dana's bra dropped into your hand."

"You're not gonna tell Kerry, are you?"

"Too bloody right I am. I gave you an ultimatum, James. Kerry's my friend too and I'm not gonna sit back and let you treat her like dirt."

James looked uneasily at Dana and decided to play for

time. "We're obviously gonna have to talk this through and I'll be honest with Kerry, I swear to God. But she'll be upset. We've got to break this to her gently."

"How long have you been carrying on with *her* for?" Lauren demanded.

"About five minutes," James said.

"Oh yeah, James, and the other one's got bells on."

James was disturbed by Lauren's face. For some reason she'd started looking more upset than angry.

"James is telling the truth," Dana said calmly. "We've been working on his problem with the investigation. We're both tired and we just got carried away."

"You're such a pig, James," Lauren sniffed.

James could see what he'd done to make Lauren angry, but he was baffled by her crying. "What's the matter?"

"Enjoy your rock," Lauren sobbed, as she held the pink stick out to James.

James took it, but Lauren started crying much harder as she backed out of the room and set off down the corridor.

"What's that all about?" Dana asked. "Lauren never struck me as the jealous type."

"I don't think she is," James said. "There's more to that than me snogging you. I'd better go after her."

Dana nodded, as she took her bra back.

James was annoyed that he hadn't even managed a glimpse of Dana's goodies before Lauren burst in, let alone a feel. But he had too much other stuff on his mind to get wound up over it: Lauren was acting weird, she was planning to tell Kerry, and he still didn't know exactly what Ewart was playing at.

"I'll go put the papers back in Ewart's office," Dana said, as James headed for the door.

James smiled, before giving Dana a quick kiss. "You've been fantastic."

"Fun's only just starting." She grinned.

Lauren had already reached the staircase by the time James began running after her.

"Wait up," he shouted, but not so loud that it woke up the other cherubs sleeping in their rooms.

Lauren didn't try to run when she heard James coming, but she didn't stop either. He eventually cornered her on the landing between the seventh and eighth floors.

"Leave me alone," Lauren sobbed. "I want to go to bed."

"You can talk to me about anything, you know," James said, as he moved in to try giving his sister a hug, but she backed into a corner and adopted a fighting stance.

"You're an animal," Lauren spat. "*Don't* touch me."

"Me and Kerry . . . I mean . . . You know it's never been perfect between us."

"You use girls," Lauren growled. "Sex is like eating chips or taking a dump to you; to all boys. You don't care how it happens, or who gets hurt, just as long as you get plenty of it."

"Come off it. First of all, I'm not getting *any*, and second, the only person in the world I love more than Kerry is you."

Lauren smiled grudgingly, before breaking out in fresh sobs. "I ended up in this room," she sniffed. "It was *so* horrible. They kept the girls locked up and it made me sick thinking about what had happened to them. Then this man came in and told me to get undressed."

"Oh God," James said, completely shocked. "I had no idea. I'm really, really, sorry."

"I don't mean *that*, James. The bloke didn't get his hands on me. But I stabbed him and he's on life support. I hate his perverted guts, but I still don't want him to die."

Lauren finally let James close enough to touch her and he pulled her into a tight cuddle.

"You're safe now," James said soothingly.

"I wanted to speak to you when I arrived back," Lauren sobbed. "But then I saw you with your eyes practically out on stalks and Dana's boobs in your face. It made me want to puke my guts up. Like you were one of *them*."

"I can't help liking girls, Lauren. Sometimes girls are all I can think about, but there's a *massive* difference between getting off with Dana and trying to rape someone."

"It just seemed . . . ," Lauren said, but couldn't finish her thought. "I came to see you because I didn't feel like going to sleep. I thought you'd probably be annoyed if I woke you up, but when I walked in and saw *that* . . ."

"We didn't stop 'cos we thought the door was locked."

"So what's with all those papers in your room?"

"It's to do with Ewart's investigation," James explained. "But don't worry about that now. Do you want me to come up to your room and sit with you for a while? Or you can come back down and sleep in my room."

"Nah, I'll be okay," Lauren shrugged. "By the time I climb into bed, I'll probably be so knackered that I'll just keel over."

"If you're sure," James said, as he gently rubbed Lauren's back. "Good night."

"And you're going to own up to Kerry first thing in the morning, aren't you?"

"Lauren, I can't . . ."

Lauren's tone stiffened as she put her foot on the first step. "If you don't tell Kerry about Dana, I'm telling her about *all* the other girls. It's for your own good, James."

"Please, Lauren," James begged. "She'll kick my arse. How exactly is that *good* for me?"

"You're my brother and that counts for a lot. But that doesn't mean I'm gonna let you go on making a fool of Kerry."

"Whatever," James huffed. "You can bring me grapes in the hospital."

CHAPTER 33

TROUBLES

James set his alarm for 4:30 a.m., but he didn't need it. His head kept churning and sleep remained a remote possibility.

He hoped that Lauren was okay and he was worried about Kerry, but that was nothing compared to going after Ewart. If they were wrong about him, they'd get busted for stealing documents and leaving campus without permission and end up being kicked out of CHERUB.

James looked back into his room as he pulled shut the door, knowing there was a chance that he'd never be back. He knew who lived inside every room, and as he walked down the corridor, he realized that he might never see his friends again either: Bruce, Shak, Mo, Gabrielle, the twins; *Kerry*.

He wasn't looking forward to his next meeting with Kerry, but the thought of never touching her or even hearing her voice again was a million times worse.

James rubbed a tear out of his eye as he waited for the elevator, but he was still determined. The only thing worse than being kicked out of CHERUB was the thought of Ewart framing him. And if Ewart had taken one bribe to cover something up, who was to say that the next one wouldn't lead to the death of a cherub?

"Hey." Dana smiled when James stepped out of the lift on the ground floor. She looked reassuringly calm and tough.

"Thanks for this," James said, as he broke into a massive grin. There was no way he'd have been able to wade through all the paperwork without Dana's help, and he definitely wouldn't have had the stomach to go after Ewart.

"What's in the backpack?" he asked, as they walked toward the ground-floor reception.

"I picked up a few essentials," Dana said. "Pepper spray, stun guns, and listening devices. Plus a few bottles of mineral water and some food in case we get stuck in a car on a long stakeout."

"Good thinking," James nodded.

There was nobody in reception at this time of the morning, so Dana stepped behind the counter to a cabinet filled with car keys. James grabbed a Biro and a clipboard with forms attached to it.

"There's a Mercedes key up there," he grinned.

Dana shook her head as she snatched another key. "Golf GTI. I've driven this one before. It's fairly discreet, but it goes like stink if you need it to."

James quickly filled in the pool car sign-out form. He put their destination as London and wrote *Ewart Asker* in the *member of staff authorizing use of vehicle* box.

The Volkswagen Golf was one of more than a dozen pool cars in the driveway at the front of the main building. It was still dark out and the front and rear screens were covered with frost, which James chipped off while Dana picked a set of magnetic number plates from the collection in the trunk and stuck them on.

Dana took the driver's seat and they both rubbed their hands together to warm up as the heater started running and the lights on the dashboard flickered to life.

"So," James said, as Dana backed out of the space. "What's our plan exactly?"

Jason McLoud lived in a suburban street, with semi-detached houses set behind paved driveways. James and Dana arrived at 8:45, parking up in the curved road and walking the final hundred meters to number fifty-seven.

When they reached it, James put his foot on the front wall and pretended to lace up his sneaker.

"Looks like McLoud's wife has left for work already," Dana said, pointing discreetly toward the dry patches on the brick driveway where a car had clearly stood overnight.

James noticed a figure moving behind frosted glass on the first floor. He turned to Dana and raised an eyebrow.

"I see him," Dana nodded. "Now let's get out of here before curtains start twitching."

They were in a posh neighborhood and two teenagers not in school uniform and staring into a house were likely to arouse suspicion. Instead of turning back toward the car, they carried on past half a dozen more homes before cutting into an alleyway. It led into a sports ground that backed onto the houses.

They squelched around the perimeter of a rugby field, passing by the wooden fences at the end of gardens, stopping when they reached the back of McLoud's house. There were a couple of people walking their dogs on the opposite side of the field, so Dana leaned her back against the fence.

"Make it look like you're kissing me," she said.

James stepped up close to Dana and kissed her on the neck a couple of times before stopping to take a good look through a gap in the wooden slats.

"It's no good," he said. "It's lower on that side, like a three-meter drop into rose bushes or something."

"We'll have to go in by the front way then," Dana said, as James backed away. "Where do you think you're going?"

Dana tugged James's jacket and they exchanged a quick openmouthed kiss. "Later," Dana whispered tantalizingly, as they broke apart.

James thought about Kerry as they carried on toward an exit on the opposite side of the field. Kerry still gave him a buzz every time he was with her but their relationship had gone stale; whereas everything about Dana felt new and exciting.

They emerged into a side road, and two left turns meant that they'd walked in a complete square back to the car.

"Nine o'clock," Dana said, looking at her watch as they clambered in and shut the doors. "We'd better get a move on if we want to find out what Ewart's saying."

James looked down and realized that his muddy sneakers were trashing the carpet in the footwell, but he had more important stuff to worry about. He grabbed a sheet of sticky-backed listening devices from Dana's backpack. The gray pads were smaller than James's little fingernail and looked like something you might use to mount photographs.

"Do you want to do the talking?" James asked.

"If you like," Dana nodded. "You'll need the palmtop to record the signal from the bugs and there's a set of walkie-talkies in there somewhere too."

Once James had everything in his pockets, they got out of the car and walked briskly toward Jason McLoud's house. They kept a cautious eye out, just in case Ewart decided to turn up early.

When they reached number fifty-one, Dana pulled a mobile and called McLoud's home phone number. She'd swiped two unregistered pay-as-you-go phones from a storeroom on campus so that they couldn't be tracked.

"Hello," Dana said brightly. "Is that Mr. Jason McLoud?"

Dana waved James on as soon as she heard the elderly man's voice: If he was on the phone, he'd be unlikely to notice James walking down his driveway.

"Mr. McLoud," Dana continued. "I'm pleased to tell you that Penguin Travel is able to offer you a special four-hundred-pound discount on one of our Caribbean cruises."

As McLoud went into a clearly audible rant, demanding to know how they'd got hold of his number and threatening to complain to the telecoms regulator, James cut down the side of the house and crouched between the wall and McLoud's MG convertible.

"If cruising isn't your thing, how about a Florida vacation? I'm sure your grandchildren would love—"

"Piss off and don't call me back," McLoud shouted, before slamming down his phone.

His voice was so loud that James could hear him through the hallway window. He grabbed his walkie-talkie and whispered: "In position and ready to go."

"Roger that," Dana replied as she pocketed her phone and walkie-talkie. She started walking toward McLoud's front door and rang his bell.

As soon as James heard the bell ringing, he pulled the sheet of tiny listening devices out of his pocket and began creeping into the back garden. The bugs were designed to detect speech through vibrations in glass. His job was to creep around the outside of the house, sticking a bug to each window while Dana kept McLoud busy on the doorstep.

"I'm not buying anything," McLoud said, when he opened the front door. He was clearly still in a mood from the fake sales call.

Dana turned on all of her feminine charm for the slender journalist, who wore carpet slippers and a hearing aid.

"You must be Becky's granddad," Dana said.

McLoud looked confused. "I don't know that name."

While Dana explained that she was here to see her

friend Becky and that she couldn't understand, because she'd definitely been given the address of Becky McLoud at 57 Hillcrest Road, James moved swiftly across the back garden. He stuck bugs to the kitchen window, a small window in the hallway, and the conservatory at the back. Finally, as he heard McLoud tell Dana that his surname *was* McLoud, but that he was one-hundred-percent certain that no one called Becky had ever lived in his house, James crept back to his position alongside the car.

"I'm sorry to have disturbed you," Dana said.

"It's not a problem," McLoud said, though the groan as he closed his front door indicated otherwise.

As James ran back up the driveway toward the road, Dana leaned across and stuck a bug to the long window at the front.

"Needn't have bothered with that one," James said as they walked back toward the Volkswagen. "It'll be in the conservatory at the back. There's cups and biscuits already set out on the table."

"Excellent," Dana said. "We'd have been buggered if he'd taken Ewart upstairs to his study or something. I reckon we ought to move the car out of sight. We don't want Ewart spotting us as he drives by."

CHAPTER 36

SARAH

Dana drove the Volkswagen down the alleyway leading toward the rugby fields, then did a three-point turn so they could pull out quickly. James sat in the passenger seat with the palmtop computer rigged up to record the signals from all six listening devices. He had a power line plugged into the cigarette lighter and another cable going into the iPod socket on the dashboard, so that they could listen through the car stereo instead of the tinny speaker built into the computer.

For twenty minutes, they listened to Jason McLoud as he pottered around his house, listening to Radio Four and humming Bert Kampfert's "Swingin' Safari." Then the doorbell rang.

Dana eyed the clock on the dashboard. "Right on time," she said, as she pressed the engine start button.

"Where are we going?" James asked.

"Now he's inside, we can drive up to the house. We'll get better reception and we can wade in if Ewart tries anything funny."

"Ewart was on campus when the secretary and the scientist were killed," James said. "I don't think he's a murderer."

Dana nodded as she indicated left and pulled out of the turning. "Maybe not, but if he's made a deal with Hilton, tidying up the loose ends might well be part of it."

It was a narrow road, so she pulled up on the curb two doors from McLoud's house, on the opposite side of the street. The road was on a slight hill, and they had a good view down toward the front of number fifty-seven. Ewart had parked a Lexus in the driveway.

"Is that one of the CHERUB pool cars?" James asked.

"Don't think so," Dana said. "At least, I've never seen it if it is."

James shook his head. "So where did the money for that come from, I wonder?"

"Patch the sound through then," Dana said.

James tapped a stylus on the palmtop screen and the background noise from inside the house came through the speakers in the dashboard. James flipped through the different signals until he picked up the sound from the bug stuck to the conservatory window.

"Green fingers," Ewart said, as a cup and saucer chinked.

"My wife," Jason McLoud said. "Gardening not my forte, I'm afraid. Do have a seat."

"So how long have you been retired?"

"Oh, I still dabble with a bit of freelance work. That's the good thing with journalism, you can cut out the nine-to-five grind, but you don't have to give up completely. Now, John Jones told me you worked for a newspaper in Dubai?"

James and Dana were surprised to hear John's name.

"That's right," Ewart lied. "Nice weather, no income tax, but it gets dull reporting on property development and horse racing. So now I'm back here doing some real journalism. Freelance to start with, but I'm looking for a job on a national paper."

"How long have you known John?"

"A few years."

"He's with the firm, you know," McLoud said.

"MI5?" Ewart gasped incredulously. "I never realized. I met John at the Dubai Arms Fair a few years back. He bought me a few beers and told me that he was a security consultant. I bumped into him a few weeks ago and mentioned that I was doing a story on Hilton Aerospace. He told me to contact you because you know more about the Hiltons than anyone."

"I've covered Hilton Aerospace for nigh on thirty years. You've got to tread carefully. The defense industry is very tight-knit and if you step on Lord Hilton's toes, you'll find that an awful lot of people stop answering your phone calls."

"I realize that," Ewart said. "But I want to pursue the story. I mean, if Hilton really was involved with the death of Denis Obidin, the story would be a huge boost for my career."

"True, but you're messing with the big boys if you go up against Hilton. It's not just within the defense industry. He bought his son's way into politics. Son's a junior minister already: good-looking boy, excellent speaker, could be going all the way to the top."

"Prime Minister." Ewart grinned.

"I forget which one, but a Sunday paper did an article about a year back on the ten people under thirty-five who are most likely to become future Prime Ministers. Sebastian Hilton was ranked third."

"So when did this Sarah Thomas first contact you?" Ewart asked.

"The day after Madeline Cowell died. She called me up out of the blue and invited me to Madeline's funeral. I couldn't go because we were flying off to Portugal for a few days at my sister's place.

"When I got home a week later, Sarah Thomas had left me another message and said that she'd like to talk to me about a possible story on Hilton Aerospace. I meant to call her back, but I had a heap of messages on the machine and to be honest, I'm in my seventies and the old brain misfires from time to time. So I didn't think any more about her message until I got the call from John Jones asking if I'd heard anything suspicious about the deaths of Clare Nazareth and Madeline Cowell."

"So Madeline is a person who'd have known what Lord Hilton was up to?"

"Oh God, yes," McLoud said. "She worked alongside him for thirty years. Every appointment, every business trip. He looked after her too. I can remember a shareholders' meeting where someone asked Lord Hilton why his personal assistant earned more than some of the directors. Hilton stood up, pulled on his braces and boomed across the hall: *Because Madeline Cowell is a bloody sight more useful than any of my directors.*

"She was a real tough old bird. You wouldn't believe the number of times I had to call her over the years, groveling for a quote, or an interview with Lord Hilton—or Freddie Hilton as he was known back then. I bought her perfume and chocolates every Christmas, but it never did me any good."

As Ewart laughed, James spotted a large silver Audi pulling up a few doors down the road.

"Anyway," McLoud said, "I've dug out some old notebooks and photocopied some contact details for you. And I understand that you've set up a meeting with this Sarah Thomas?"

"Indeed," Ewart replied. "I've already put together a theory on what Hilton is up to, but I haven't got a smoking gun. To be honest, the evidence I have is pretty feeble."

"You want to get your facts straight," McLoud warned. "Little people like you and me get chewed up and spat out by the Hiltons of this world. They've even been known to disappear clean off the face of the earth."

"Sarah Thomas says she has some documents that Cowell told her to give only to you *if anything happened to her*. She sounded nervous. I told her a little white lie and said that you were retired, but that I'd taken over your old job. Thomas wouldn't let me know where she lives and only gave me her mobile phone number. We're meeting for lunch today and she was at pains to tell me that the restaurant would be packed out and that she didn't have much money so I'd have to pay!"

"Sounds interesting," McLoud said.

"It *could* be interesting," Ewart laughed. "But knowing my luck she'll turn out to be an escaped mental patient."

Back outside, James and Dana watched a redhead emerge from the Audi. She was in her twenties, dressed in jeans and a baggy jumper. There was something about the way she looked around that made her seem suspicious; or at least suspicious to someone who'd undergone espionage training.

Realizing that two people sitting in a car doing nothing might seem odd, Dana unfurled a map as James turned the speaker volume down slightly.

"Dodgy?" James asked.

"Certainly looks it," Dana said, as she tried to look without making it seem like she was looking.

They watched as the young woman stopped at the end of McLoud's driveway. After another furtive glance and a look toward the front of the house, she crouched down by the back end of Ewart's car.

"Holy crap," James mumbled, as the woman took a small black object from beneath the folds of her jumper. She reached under the Lexus and attached the device magnetically inside the wheel arch. After another glance around, she dashed back toward the Audi. The driver pulled away the instant she closed the passenger door.

James and Dana looked away as the big car accelerated past them.

"Do you think it's a bomb?"

James shook his head. "Bomb would be bigger and

you'd put it under the driver's seat, not at the back. It must be a tracking device."

"So someone's after Ewart. Maybe someone else has got wind that he's up to something."

"Maybe," James said. "Or, it could be that Ewart is conducting an honest investigation and Sebastian Hilton has someone keeping an eye on him. In which case we're wrong about Ewart, we've stolen secret documents and a car from CHERUB campus, and we're up to our necks in the smelly brown stuff."

Dana grimaced. "I wish this wasn't so bloody complicated."

"I guess we could drive back to campus," James said. "We'd get busted for nicking the car..."

"No," Dana said definitively, like she'd just thought of something. "If Ewart is honest and someone is following him he could be in danger. If Ewart is dishonest and someone else is onto him then . . ."

"Well, that would be good news, I guess," James shrugged. "I mean, they can hardly chuck us out of CHERUB for suspecting the truth."

"But we've broken every rule in the book."

Back inside the house, Ewart was thanking Jason McLoud for taking the time to meet with him and asked if he could use the toilet before he left.

"This whole thing is doing my head in," James moaned.

"At least we've got each other," Dana said, as she stroked James's hand.

CHAPTER 35

mouse

By the time Ewart left Jason McLoud's house, the morning rush was over and the roads were quiet. Following the Lexus through suburban turnings was tricky: Dana had to keep Ewart's car in view, but couldn't get close in case he suspected that he was being followed.

"Should have brought a tracking device ourselves," James observed.

Dana shook her head. "They work through the control room on campus, so it would have blown our cover."

James wondered if their disappearance from campus had been noticed yet, as Ewart pulled onto a stretch of double highway and squeezed the gas, accelerating past eighty miles an hour. The road was ideal for following, with enough traffic to be inconspicuous but not so much that you risked getting boxed in. Even so, a single car pursuit is never easy and there were a few hairy moments when they thought they'd lost the Lexus.

After a forty-minute cruise, they took a horn blast from a white van as they swerved into the nearside lane and followed Ewart onto a side road. Even worse, the road ended at a set of lights, giving Dana no option but to pull up directly behind Ewart. The Golf's side windows had a slight tint, but the front screen was clear glass. James and Dana spent a full minute staring into their laps, hoping Ewart didn't look back in his mirror and recognize them. It felt like much longer.

They lucked out, but Dana and James knew it was only a matter of time before Ewart caught them. She stayed as far back as she could, while they wound down a country lane with frosty grass and cows with steamy breath on either side of them.

As they approached a small market town, Ewart took a sharp left turn. Dana was being tailgated by a truck and realized that she'd get crunched if she broke sharply and attempted the turn.

"You've lost him," James complained.

"I couldn't brake with that thing up my arse," Dana said, as James looked over his shoulder and saw what she meant.

Dana indicated left and turned into the gravel parking lot of a country pub. She swung around in a full circle and edged the nose of the car out past a hedge, attempting to turn back and catch up with Ewart.

"Get a move on," Dana moaned, as traffic streamed by in both directions.

Half a minute drained away before she jabbed the accelerator, causing an oncoming car to brake sharply as she threw the steering wheel around to avoid a metal gate on the opposite side of the road.

Dana turned off the main road into a curving street more than two minutes after Ewart had done so. There was a riverbank off to one side, with willow trees over-hanging the water and a sign advertising boat trips— SERVICE RESUMES SUMMER 2007. The opposite side had a row of mock-Tudor tourist traps selling antiques, cream teas, and Union Jack souvenirs.

"Can't stand places like this," James said, as he scanned the coachloads of pensioners dawdling along the narrow pavements, hoping to spot Ewart. "Do you reckon he got out around here?"

Dana glanced at the map on the sat-nav screen. "Well it's not on the way to anywhere else, so I guess we'd better park up somewhere and take a look."

"I just hope we see him before he sees us," James said warily. Then he spotted the nose of a large silver Audi, poking out of a narrow lane fifty meters ahead of them. "Hello, old friend." He grinned.

"*Result*," Dana nodded. "We might not know where Ewart is, but they sure do."

The traffic was light, so Dana flashed her headlights and let the big Audi pull out ahead of them. Dana fol-lowed it through a couple of tight turns and quickly realized that the driver was following the blue park-ing arrows. They ended up in a parking lot the size of a couple of soccer fields. There were barriers and ticket booths, but there were less than two dozen cars in the whole space. The gates were locked open and bright yellow signs told them that winter parking was free.

"There's Ewart's Lexus," James said, relieved, as the silver Audi pulled up alongside it.

Dana rolled on for another fifty meters and parked next to an abandoned shopping cart.

"What do you reckon?" James asked. "Sit here and wait for Ewart to come back, or go walkabout?"

"What are we going to find out by sitting here?" Dana asked.

James shrugged. "But we've got no idea where he's gone. If we go, what's to stop him coming back to his car and driving off without us seeing him?"

Dana sucked air through her teeth. "Tell you what," she said after a few seconds' thought. "I'll wait here in the car, you go off looking for Ewart. Zip your jacket and pull the hood over your head. He won't recognize you if you keep your distance."

As James left the car, he noticed that the redheaded young woman was getting out of the Audi, its two occupants having clearly decided on the same strategy.

James walked slowly toward a signpost at the edge of the parking lot. It had arrows pointing toward various attractions: WATERMILL, ST. PETER'S CHAPEL, BOAT TRIPS, PICNIC AREA, LAVATORIES. It was a quarter past twelve, so James guessed that Ewart would probably be heading toward the restaurant for his lunch date with Sarah Thomas.

They'd passed quite a few eateries on the ride through town. James's first thought was to walk back and see if he could spot Ewart inside any of them. But then he realized that the woman from the Audi was moving with a sense of purpose. She'd probably spotted Ewart on the street, and James decided to go after her.

She led him through a couple of winding back streets to a glass-fronted building built on the riverbank. One end had a line of more than a dozen people, huddled against the cold. The front of the line brought elderly customers to a window that served hot drinks and homemade pasties. The opposite side was an Italian restaurant and James felt a shot of adrenalin as he spotted Ewart leaning against a swanky bar, clearly waiting for someone to arrive.

The woman from the Audi passed through the large glass doors and seated herself on a leather stool, two spaces clear of Ewart. James couldn't go inside because Ewart would recognize him if he got close, but he knew that he looked dodgy lurking in the street with his hood up and his hands stuffed inside his jacket.

After crossing the narrow road, James felt in his pocket to make sure that he had some money, before joining the line to buy a pasty. As the pensioners in front of him complained about the weather and the pasties costing more than last year, James peered over their heads, keeping an eye on anyone entering or leaving the restaurant.

"Jumbo traditional and a tea please," James said, when he finally reached the front of the queue.

It was a cold day. The pasties were being sold as fast as they came out of the ovens and James's stomach growled as the woman passed over a paper bag containing a huge, freshly baked crescent of pastry. He sat down at a wooden picnic table as far as he could get from shivering pensioners and tore out a massive bite of shredded vegetables and beef.

It was *unbelievably* hot. James spluttered as steaming potato stuck to the top of his mouth. He ended up spitting a lump of meat onto the pavement, to the obvious distaste of three oldies sitting two tables across.

As he looked up, James saw a solidly built woman walking into the restaurant. She was middle-aged, slightly odd-looking, with a chubby red face and a padded envelope under her arm. Ewart smiled and shook his guest warmly by the hand as the woman from the Audi drained her glass and stepped out into the cold. She grabbed her mobile and dialed. James guessed she was calling her companion back in the car.

He put his pasty down and took his walkie-talkie from inside his jacket. "Dana," he whispered. "Ewart's with Sarah Thomas now. It looks like the girl from the Audi is on the phone to her driver."

"I'm listening to the Audi driver speaking with her," Dana said.

"How have you managed that?" James asked, surprised.

"There's toilets at the back of the parking lot. The driver got out to go for a pee, so I dashed over and put one of our sticky pads on his side window."

"Nice move," James grinned.

"I'll call you back," Dana said. "I'm trying to find out what they're up to."

James tucked his walkie-talkie away and took a more cautious bite out of his pasty. Inside the restaurant, a fit waitress was leading Ewart and Sarah Thomas to a table overlooking the river. James kept a discreet eye on them until his walkie-talkie spoke to him.

"The woman's name is Kate," Dana said hurriedly. "I'm not sure if they're MI5 or private investigators but they're definitely working for the Hiltons. Kate asked if McLoud had made any calls after Ewart left, so they must have his phone bugged."

James ground his palm against his forehead with frustration. "So Ewart's *not* working for Hilton?"

"Certainly doesn't sound like it," Dana said. "They seem to think Ewart is just some freelance journalist trying to stick his nose in. And apparently, Sarah Thomas is Madeline Cowell's former cleaning lady."

"So that's where she fits in," James said. "She's brought Ewart a big envelope. No idea what's inside, but it must be evidence against Hilton."

"Cowell was Lord Hilton's loyal assistant for donkey's years . . ."

James shrugged. "I guess her loyalty wore thin when her boss started bumping people off to protect his son. Cowell must have suspected that he was planning to top her and left a little sting behind."

"So what do you think will happen next?" Dana asked.

"They're following Ewart. They think he's only a journalist, so I reckon they'll try and jump him and steal the evidence before he does anything with it."

"Agreed," Dana said. "It'll either be when he leaves the restaurant or as he gets back in the car."

"I can warn him, but it might freak him out, so I'll have to wait until Sarah Thomas is out of sight."

James had been starving when he first bought the pasty, but the tension had got to him. It now lay on the slatted wooden table in front of him, half eaten and stone cold.

Kate sat at the bar inside the restaurant with a burger, while Ewart and Sarah Thomas were finishing their dessert. Judging from the body language, Ewart was bored, while Sarah Thomas seemed like a lonely soul who was milking her chance of a free meal and a decent conversation.

James had considered calling Ewart on his mobile, but he didn't have the number programmed in to his brand-new phone and the campus hotline staff wouldn't give out that kind of information until they'd received lengthy explanations about what he and Dana were up to.

James watched Ewart get up from the table. He shook Sarah Thomas's hand and gave her a reassuring pat on the shoulder. Sarah gestured toward the ladies' room as James got off the wooden bench. Ewart tapped on his watch, indicating to Sarah that he was in a rush.

As Ewart tucked the envelope under his arm and headed for the exit, Kate wiped her lips on a napkin and settled her bill by placing a twenty-pound note inside her empty tumbler.

"James," Dana said.

"Yep," he replied as he put the walkie-talkie up to his ear.

"The Audi is backing out of its parking space," Dana said.

"Ewart's coming out of the restaurant with Kate on his tail," James said hurriedly. "I wish I'd taken the stun gun out of your bag."

"Too late now," Dana said.

"Okay, I'm on the move," James said. "I'll keep in touch."

Ewart walked briskly, so Kate had to jog to catch up with him. Ewart heard her coming and looked backward, with a curious smile.

James considered shouting a warning, but Ewart's expression changed from *are you flirting with me* to *oh my god* before he got the chance. James couldn't see much from behind, but saw enough to realize that Kate had pulled a gun from inside her jacket.

James's guts somersaulted as Ewart walked obediently into an enclosed courtyard behind the restaurant. For all he knew, Kate was planning to kill Ewart as soon as he was out of sight. The closest thing James had to a weapon was his Swiss army knife. He pulled it from his pocket as the Audi tore down the road and swung sharply into the narrow yard.

James peeked around the corner and saw Ewart looking extremely tense as Kate held a silenced pistol to his chest. She opened the back door of the Audi and gestured for him to get inside as a car horn blasted less than twenty meters away.

James looked up and saw the red Volkswagen. Dana braked sharply before making the tight turn into the courtyard, but made a split-second decision to accelerate hard when she saw Ewart, Kate, the Audi, and the gun. Airbags exploded in Dana's face as the Volkswagen smashed into the back of the Audi, while the Audi ploughed into the courtyard wall.

Both Ewart and Kate instinctively jumped clear as James began sprinting across the courtyard toward them. Ewart had kneed Kate in the chest and was twisting the gun from her hand.

Once he had control of the gun, Ewart knocked Kate to the ground with a powerful kick and turned the pistol on James.

"Don't shoot *me*," James gasped, raising his hands in the air.

Ewart hadn't recognized James with his hood up, but he immediately knew the voice.

"What the hell are you doing here?" Ewart asked incredulously.

"Behind you," James pointed, as he watched the driver jumping out of the car holding another silenced pistol.

Ewart swung around with the gun, so that he and the driver had identical weapons pointing across, with their muzzles less than twenty centimeters apart. James was tempted to turn and run, but then he noticed Kate crawling toward Ewart.

"Watch your leg!" James shouted.

But the warning was too late. Kate plunged a hunting knife through Ewart's shoe and deep into his foot. As Ewart twisted around in pain, the Audi driver grinned. James was certain that Ewart was about to get a bullet through his head and that the driver would probably aim the next round at him.

As James turned to run away, he heard a crackling sound. The driver collapsed to the ground with blue sparks lighting up his face. James realized that Dana had shot him with one of the stun guns. It was a huge relief, but they wouldn't be safe until they had both of the silenced pistols in their hands.

Kate stabbed Ewart for a second time, hitting him in the thigh as she snatched the gun. James raced across the courtyard and dived forward, landing heavily on her chest. Her ribs crunched as he wrestled the gun from her hand.

The front doors of the Audi were both open and James found himself staring at Dana through the plush interior of the car. "Have you got the other gun?"

Dana raised it limply.

"Are you okay?"

"Been better," Dana said. "My ears are ringing from the explosion, but thank God for airbags, eh?"

"Why are you two here?" Ewart groaned, as he looked at the growing patch of blood on his jeans.

"You lied about the security tape," James said, as Kate rolled onto her side and began coughing up blood. "We thought you were working for Hilton."

Dana had grabbed her mobile. "This is agent eleven-sixty-two," she yelled. "I'm here with James and Ewart and we've got a situation. The cops will be here any minute and we need a response team to come and bail us out."

Ewart was in a lot of pain from the two stab wounds but still managed a tiny smile. "Whatever the reason, I reckon you two just saved my butt."

CHAPTER 36

CELLS

The CHERUB control room made immediate contact with the chief inspector in charge of the local police station. After hearing a security password, she agreed to seal the crime scene, take all of the casualties to the local hospital under police guard, and await the arrival of an investigation and cleanup team from CHERUB.

As he was loaded into an ambulance, Ewart told James not to let the padded envelope out of his sight. Kate, who'd suffered several broken ribs when James landed on her, shared the ambulance. The Audi driver had been restrained by Dana after recovering from his fifty-thousand-volt nip. He was arrested and driven to the police station.

After handing the pistols to the cops, James and Dana were given a ride by a tough-looking sergeant, who'd been instructed not to speak to them. When they arrived at the police station, he led them to a deserted corner of the staff canteen and told them that someone was coming to collect them.

As they drank Cokes from the vending machine, James slid out the contents of the envelope. The first page was typed on Madeline Cowell's personal stationery using an old-fashioned manual typewriter:

Dear Jason McLoud,

You and I have a long and combative history, but I have always admired your dedication and integrity as a reporter.

Lord Freddie Hilton and I worked together for more than thirty years and—as I am sure you suspected—we were also lovers. Perhaps it is this that blinded me to the evil nature of the man.

As always, I attended the Hilton summer barbecue this July. Freddie took me aside and made it clear that he was prepared to do whatever it took in order to allow his son Sebastian to reach the highest ranks within British politics. He asked me whether I was likely to have "any kind of problem" with this.

When I said that I didn't like his increasing appetite for power, Freddie began to issue veiled threats. I'd had

310

a few glasses of champagne and soon found myself taking part in a distasteful scene, at the end of which I was escorted from the Hilton estate by a security guard.

Over many years, I have learned much about the Hilton family's business and personal affairs. When I sobered up that evening, I realized that Lord Hilton is not a man who likes anyone to have a hold over him and reached the conclusion that my life might be in some danger. If you are reading this, then I have most likely been proved correct!

I could, of course, have brought this information to you or to the police during my lifetime, but it does not show me in a good light and may even have left me open to a criminal prosecution.

I did not involve my children in this, because I felt that their eyes might be irresistibly drawn toward the contents of this envelope. Instead, I entrusted the documents to my long-term housekeeper, Sarah Thomas, telling her to give them to you in the event of my untimely death. Sarah is a simple, honest soul. My children will be provided for from my estate, but I would ask that you divide any money that you make from this story with Sarah.

The following page contains an index of the cassette recordings and documents in this envelope. Wherever possible, I have also provided additional notes, including extensive details of the Hilton family's overseas bank accounts and details of people who will be able (though not necessarily willing!) to corroborate all of the evidence within.

Yours sincerely,

Madeline Cowell

James flipped to the next page and skimmed over the list of documents. They appeared to detail everything from tax evasion, illegal bank accounts, sales of aircraft components to countries under United Nations embargoes, and favors done for senior politicians to secure Sebastian Hilton's seat in parliament.

"Is there anything about the murder of Obidin?" Dana asked.

James shook his head. "I guess that was after Cowell retired, but with all these details of secret bank accounts, I'd bet that the investigators will find a link."

Dana nodded. "Even if they don't, there's enough evidence here to put Lord Hilton and his son away for a good few years."

James drummed his fingers nervously on the table top. "I guess that's Lord Hilton's fate sorted. I just wish I knew my own."

Zara arrived an hour later. James was relieved to see her smiling as she entered the canteen.

"Have you seen Ewart at the hospital?" Dana asked.

Zara nodded. "I popped in briefly. He seems okay. He's

moaning that they're not giving him enough pain relief, but that's just Ewart. You should see the fuss I have to put up with at home when he puts his back out."

"Cool," James said. "I'm glad it's not serious."

"I have to admit I'm still confused," Zara said. "We realized that you'd both disappeared with the Volkswagen early this morning. Lauren thought you might have run off together, but her theory didn't make any sense because you hadn't packed any clothes or possessions."

James and Dana looked at each other.

"What gave Lauren that idea?" James asked.

"She said that you two were having an affair and that you'd run away because she was planning to tell Kerry all about it. She seemed pretty upset."

"We didn't run away." Dana grinned.

"I figured that much out for myself," Zara said. "I got security to run a check on your movements and they picked you up sneaking in and out of Ewart's office with the documents. What on earth possessed you to do that?"

James looked awkwardly at the tabletop. "I thought he was going to stitch me up in the investigation."

"Pardon me?" Zara spluttered.

James thought about mentioning Mr. Pike's involvement, but couldn't see that it would do anyone any good.

"To be honest, I've never liked Ewart much," he blurted. "I was worried that he was going to make me a scapegoat, like he did with Nicole when we were on the drugs mission a couple of years back."

"Oh, come off it," Zara said. "Nicole consumed a class-A drug. You can't blame Ewart for that."

"I guess . . . ," James said. "I'm just trying to be honest. For *whatever* reason, I didn't trust Ewart so I went to look at all the paperwork in his office."

Zara nodded. "And you discovered that he knew a lot more than he was telling you."

"So *you* knew?" James gasped. "You knew that Ewart had the CIA tape and didn't bother telling me?"

"It was an extremely difficult decision," Zara said. "We wanted to put you out of your misery, but MI5 were pressuring us to send you down to London for more interviews. We couldn't risk even the slightest chance that you'd let something slip out during a long interview."

"I'm trained for that kind of stuff," James said. "You could have trusted me."

"I know you are," Zara smiled. "But MI5 interrogators are trained to wheedle secrets out of intelligence agents with a lot more experience than you. One slip of the tongue, one flippant answer, or even just the fact that you seemed a bit more confident than you had done in previous interviews might have tipped them off that Ewart's investigation was close to uncovering the truth."

"And you were dealing with some powerful people," Dana nodded.

"Exactly," Zara said. "When you're trying to bring down one of the richest men in the country, and his son, who also happens to be junior intelligence minister, you can't take any unnecessary risks."

"We were sure Ewart was taking bribes off Lord Hilton when we saw the new Lexus," James added.

Zara burst out laughing. "It was Ewart's thirtieth birthday present from me. I got a good raise when I was promoted to chairman. We'd never really had a decent car before and I wanted something that was a bit flashy, but also safe and comfortable for the kids."

James decided to cut to the chase. "So are me and Dana getting nailed for going after Ewart, or what?"

Zara shrugged. "I can't condone you going through secret papers in my husband's office, or breaking out of campus in a stolen car. *But*, you've been through a miserable few weeks, what with getting beaten up and then worrying about the investigation, and I can hardly ignore the fact that you saved my husband's life. I guess the two sets of factors just about cancel each other out."

"What about me?" Dana asked.

"How long have you got to carry on cleaning the mission preparation building?"

"Two and bit weeks."

"You can take today off, then get back at it tomorrow, okay?"

James felt like a massive weight had been lifted off. For the first time in weeks he didn't have to worry about the investigation, or the threat of being kicked out of CHERUB.

"What about the envelope?" he asked.

"I spoke to Ewart about it," Zara said. "He reckons that Jason McLoud will want it now that he knows Sarah Thomas isn't a crackpot. McLoud can break the story and save us the awkward task of having to explain where we fit in, but we'll keep the originals of everything just in case."

Dana smiled at James. "Do you realize, we'd have been spared *all* of this if McLoud had bothered returning his voice mail message from Sarah Thomas two weeks ago?"

"Yeah," James moped. "Stupid old codger."

"We'd better get moving," Zara said. "I want to get all of the documents and tapes back to campus ASAP. Once our bods have made duplicates of everything inside the envelope, we'll have someone drive it down to McLoud's house and slip it through his letterbox. If he gets his act together, he should be able to sell an exclusive to one of the Sunday papers."

"We know the Hiltons have McLoud's phone tapped already," James said. "What if they try and bump him off?"

"It's a possibility," Zara nodded. "I'll have someone keep him under close surveillance until the story breaks."

Zara led James and Dana out of the canteen and onto a staircase that led toward the parking lot at the back of the police station.

"You know," Zara said, as they hurried down the steps. "Maybe you snuck out of campus for the wrong reasons, but it took guts to step in when the father of my children had a gun pointed at his head. I reckon you two are gonna look good dressed in black . . ."

CHAPTER 37

FOOD

James got back to campus at three thirty. He ran through the corridors near the science labs and grabbed hold of Lauren as she left her last lesson of the day.

"Black T-shirt." Lauren grinned as Bethany walked out behind her. "Congratulations. Of course, I got mine first, so I'm still senior."

"Whatever," James said anxiously. "What did you tell Kerry?"

Bethany started laughing. "You're ghost-white, James. You're shitting yourself."

"Who's talking to you?" James spat.

"When we saw that you and Dana had gone, I mentioned that I'd caught you snogging," Lauren explained.

"I said that you'd been having an affair and had probably run off together."

"Did Kerry hear about this?" James asked.

"Well . . . ," Lauren said sheepishly.

Bethany butted in. "It's all over campus. It's all everyone's been talking about all day. Kerry was crying. Gabrielle and a couple of the other girls were comforting her."

"She's gonna break my neck."

"I expect she will," Bethany said brightly. "And I *really* hope I'm there to see it."

Meanwhile, Rat had come out of another classroom. "I thought you'd eloped with Dana."

"That was the first time I'd ever kissed her," James yelled.

"Nobody believes that," Bethany sneered.

Rat nodded. "Seriously, James, nobody believes it was the first time. Especially with her boobs out and everything. . . ."

"I didn't even get to see them," James said. "And I don't care whether you believe me or not. It *happens* to be true."

"It doesn't really matter what *we* believe," Rat noted. "If I was you, I'd be more worried about what Kerry believes."

"Where is she now?" Bethany asked.

"She has soccer practice," James said. "It doesn't finish for another twenty minutes. I don't know what to do. I mean, if I confront her she might go nuts. But she might be even madder if I don't have the decency to face her."

"Are you going to try getting back with Kerry, or are

you going to start a thing with Dana?" Rat asked. "I'd definitely pick Dana, there's more of her to grab hold of."

Lauren punched Rat on the arm. "Don't *ever* speak about girls like that. We're not ornaments, you know."

"Rat, I haven't had time to think about that," James said. "Right now I'm just trying to stay alive."

"This is gonna be *so* much fun," Bethany squealed.

Lauren turned angrily toward her best friend. "Will you stop stirring it? I know you two can't stand each other, but he is my brother."

"Fine, I'll leave," Bethany said indignantly. "But don't forget about our biology project. I'll see you in my room later."

James gave Bethany the finger as she walked away.

"I tell you what," Lauren said. "We'll go over to the all-weather pitches together and meet Kerry after practice. She probably won't get so angry if I'm there."

James looked at his watch and shook his head. "It's too soon. I haven't worked out what I'm gonna say to her."

"You can't keep running away," Rat said.

"Maybe not," James admitted. "But right now it's the only strategy I've got."

James wandered back toward his room and popped in to visit Bruce along the way. He was lying on his bed with a cast over the bottom of his leg.

"How's it feel?" James asked.

Bruce broke into a big grin. "You'll find out when Kerry catches up with you."

"I could have done with you as a bodyguard."

"Sorry, old bean. Takes me ten minutes just to hobble

into the bathroom for a piss at the moment. Kevin Sumner came to visit this morning; he seemed pretty chuffed with himself."

"He's a good kid," James nodded. "I hope he gets through basic training."

James's mobile rang. He flipped it open and heard Dana's voice.

"Where are you?"

"Bruce's room."

"I'm outside your door," Dana said. "We need to talk."

James shut his phone and told Bruce that he had to go. He smiled when he saw Dana standing in the corridor in her black CHERUB T-shirt.

"Looks good," James said.

"Yours too," Dana nodded.

James felt awkward as they stepped into his room. He'd have liked time to think everything through, but he didn't have that luxury.

"Is me and you going to be a thing, or what?" Dana asked.

Much to James's surprise, he knew the answer as soon as Dana asked. He'd been going out with Kerry on and off for two years and the whole thing had gone stale. They'd had a lot of good times, but it just wasn't much fun any more.

"You were there for me when it mattered," James told her. "Me and Kerry have been drifting apart almost since we got back together in April. It just took you to make me realize."

Dana smiled. "I'm kind of cranky, you know. I mean, I like being on my own quite a lot of the time and I've had a few boyfriends, but none of them have lasted more than a few weeks . . ."

James shrugged. "We'll see how it goes. No pressure."

"And Kerry?"

"I'll have to face up to her, I guess."

"I've not eaten since breakfast," Dana said. "Do you fancy going down for an early dinner?"

"I could go for that. Then we could come back here and watch a movie or something. I've got . . . ," James stumbled. "You know, I just realized I don't know what kinds of films, or music, or stuff you like."

"I read more than I watch." Dana shrugged. "Two or three books a week."

"I read a book once." James grinned. "It was about this dog called Spot and he was learning all the different colors."

"The disturbing thing is that I don't even think you're lying. I'll lend you one of my copies of *Lord of the Rings*."

James grimaced. "Isn't that about twenty million pages long? And besides, I've seen the movies so I already know what happens."

"Do you like swimming?" Dana asked. "The leisure pool, with all the slides and the water spouts?"

"I could go for that." James nodded. "Kerry hates it because the little kids make so much noise."

"Doesn't hurt to act like a kid once in a while," Dana said. "And if the little dudes get on my nerves I just thump 'em."

The dining room never got busy much before 5 p.m., but there were still enough people in the room for James to feel like everyone was staring as he stood in line with Dana. He stacked up his plate with roast potatoes and veg while the server cut his slices of turkey and beef.

The choice of table was tricky. James didn't know how he and Dana would be received at his usual table, where Kerry and all his mates sat. But on the other hand, if he let Dana lead the way to the small table at the back where she always sat on her own, it would be like sending a signal to his mates that he wasn't part of their gang anymore. On yet another hand, if he sat in the corner he'd be far less likely to encounter Kerry. On the other hand to the other hand, Kerry might be even more annoyed if she thought he was hiding from her. . . .

"Why are you standing there like a lemon?" Dana said, as she led the way toward James's regular table.

"Do you want to sit there?" James asked edgily.

"You always sit here," Dana said, as she pulled out a chair. "You're not ashamed of me, are you?"

"Don't be daft," James said.

But it hardly mattered while none of the others were around. The line for food steadily increased as James and Dana ate their roast. It was mostly little red-shirt kids. They tended to eat earlier because they finished lessons early and didn't get as much homework as the older kids.

Bruce was the first to join James and Dana. He was using two crutches, so one of the kitchen staff carried his tray to the table.

"Seen Kerry yet?" Bruce said, with all the tact of a wrecking ball. "Are you two an item now or what?"

"We're giving it a go," James nodded.

By the time James and Dana had moved on to their

chocolate trifle and brownies, the line was out of the dining room door. Lauren, Bethany, Rat, Andy, and a bunch of Lauren's other mates had settled at two adjacent tables and started chattering among themselves. James tried thinking unscary thoughts when Gabrielle and Kerry came in.

"Fancy another dessert?" Dana asked, as she ran a finger around the inside of her bowl.

James looked over his shoulder and saw that the dessert counter was free. "Go on, you talked me into it," he said, rubbing his belly as Shak came over to the table, accompanied by the identical twins Callum and Connor.

Dana got up to grab the extra desserts as James's three friends sat down.

"One of you sit this side of me," James said anxiously, as he realized that the only two vacant seats were next to him.

"Why would we want to do that?" Callum—or maybe it was Connor—grinned.

"Where have you two scrotes been anyway?" James asked. "You're almost as dark as Shak."

"Down under, mate," the other twin said, in what was easily the worst Australian accent James had ever heard. "Heroin, bent cops, and speedboat chases. All in a day's work for two heroic young studs such as ourselves."

"Any chicks?" James asked.

"Aussie birds are well fit," Bruce said, but the twins kept noticeably quiet.

"I know they are," James said, as Dana came back and put two desserts on the table. "I've got my own Aussie bird right here."

323

"One girlfriend too many if you ask me." Shak cringed as he saw Gabrielle and Kerry coming toward the table.

James realized that everyone at the surrounding tables was watching as Kerry closed in. He thought she might take a swing at him with her tray, but she settled calmly in the seat next to him.

"Hello, James," Kerry said, as she took her fork and used it to stab a roast potato. "Hello, Dana."

Everything went quiet for a moment and James realized that the pressure was on him to speak.

"Kerry, I'm really sorry," he said. "I didn't mean to hurt your feelings. . . ."

"Really." Kerry spoke calmly, but swept her hair off her face like she always did when she was angry. "So how long were you going to carry on with Dana behind my back before you bothered to tell me?"

"It wasn't like that, I swear," James said. "I never laid a finger on Dana until last night."

"At least have the decency to be honest," Kerry said. "I'm sick of you anyway, the bitch is welcome to have you."

A couple of whoops went up from Lauren's table.

"Hey," Dana said indignantly. "For what it's worth, James happens to be telling the truth. And I don't appreciate being called a bitch."

"Well, bitch," Kerry snapped. "I don't care if you like it and to be frank, I don't believe one single word out of your lying *bitch* mouth."

"Why don't you both calm down?" James said.

But Dana jumped to her feet. "The only reason James dumped you is because he begged you for help and you sat on your skinny little *I'm so good* arse and watched *Eastenders* instead."

"I heard what happened." Kerry snorted. "You lucked out, as per usual. It's a miracle that you didn't both get expelled."

"Yeah," Dana shouted. "Looks like we're wearing the black shirts that show how stupid we are."

Kerry's hand squelched into her trifle bowl. "Here's what I think of your precious black shirt."

James watched as a mixture of chocolate custard and cream splattered against Dana's shirt.

"Oh that's real mature, little girl."

"Have some more," Kerry screamed. "Cheating BITCH!"

James tried to muster a smile. "Seriously, girls, I'm not worth fighting over."

"I know you're not," Kerry snarled. "But you both went behind my back and made me look like a fool."

"No we didn't," Dana insisted. "That's just some stupid rumor Lauren started."

"What was I supposed to think?" Lauren shouted from the next table.

"Stay out of this, Lauren," Kerry yelled. "Haven't you caused enough trouble already?"

"Me?" Lauren gasped. "What did I do?"

James looked up at Kerry. "What are you having a go at my sister for? I'm the one you're pissed at."

"Don't give me that smug little look, James." And Kerry threw the last of her trifle in his face.

"Two can play at that game," Dana said, as she lunged toward Kerry with her palm covered in trifle. The palm hit the crown of Kerry's head, but the trifle splattered everywhere and hit James and Gabrielle too.

"For God's sake," Gabrielle shouted, "this stuff never comes out!"

James found himself trapped between Kerry and Dana as they tried grabbing each other around the neck. He fell backward out of his chair, clattering into Bethany and smearing her top with a blob of cream.

"Careful, moron!"

Gabrielle hadn't picked trifle, so she threw her lump of hot jam sponge at Dana. It shattered into about fifteen different pieces, showering Bruce and Shak.

Annoyed about the greasy cream stuck to one of her best tops, Bethany stuck her fingers in her trifle bowl and flicked a lump at James.

"I'm sick of you always having a go at my brother," Lauren shouted, as she threw a gravy-sodden slice of roast beef in Bethany's face. "Your brother's a bigger dick than James and I always put up with him."

"Oi," Jake shouted. "I heard that."

At the same moment, Bruce yelped because he had a blob of Gabrielle's hot jam burning his bare foot and he was in no position to reach down and rub it off. But he got revenge by aiming a spoon laden with mashed-up peas and carrots at Gabrielle's head. Unfortunately, it flew past Gabrielle and hit the neck of a girl sitting two tables across.

A couple of little red-shirts sitting nearby had decided throwing food looked like fun and joined in. As Dana and Kerry continued trying to strangle each other, Dana got hold of the large water jug in the middle of their table and swung it toward Kerry's head. Water sprayed several meters, soaking kids at the surrounding tables.

And then the shout went up. "FOOD FIGHT!"

Less than two minutes had elapsed between Kerry throwing the first lump of trifle and the outbreak of war. By the time James had hauled himself off the floor, there were hundreds of items of food whizzing between tables. But he only got a brief look before Bethany threw an entire roast turkey dinner in his face.

As he frantically wiped the hot gravy off his new black T-shirt, James felt a baked potato hitting him in the back. He leaned down and—realizing that he had no idea where it had come from—lobbed it the entire length of the dining room where it thumped against one of the plasma screens.

As the kitchen staff yelled out for order, a gang of red-shirts took control of the dessert counter. They repeatedly sank their hands into the giant tubs of trifle and hurled it as hard as they could across the canteen.

Girls were screaming, Kerry had Dana pinned to a table, Rat was trying to pull Lauren and Bethany apart, and a bunch of staff were yelling dire threats as they shielded themselves behind wooden trays. Every so often, James ducked when a particularly large piece of food came his way, but mostly he just watched in awe as total mayhem exploded around him.

He was living through a moment that people would talk about at CHERUB for years to come and it had all happened because of two girls fighting over *him*.

This was going to make him a legend.

327

EPILOGUE

James's mission

Following the death of DENIS OBIDIN, VLADIMIR OBIDIN spent three weeks recovering in a private Moscow clinic. Upon his return to Aero City, he moved ruthlessly against members of his security team whom he suspected of betraying his brother. More than a dozen men were tortured and several ended up dead. The CIA were forced to abandon their Aero City mission.

After a brief feud with other family members, Vladimir took over his brother's position at the head of the Obidins' business empire. Denis Obidin's widow was elected mayor of Aero City in early 2007. No other candidate dared to stand against her.

Six-year-old MARK OBIDIN is still reluctantly learning English and is expected to be sent to a British boarding school shortly after his eighth birthday.

The scandal surrounding LORD FREDERICK HILTON and his son SEBASTIAN HILTON M.P. broke three days after the food fight in the CHERUB dining room. Lord Hilton was arrested while trying to flee aboard his private jet. Sebastian Hilton was arrested by his own protection officer on direct orders from the Prime Minister.

Due to the complexity of the evidence against the Hiltons, it is expected that they will not face trial until late 2007. Both men are currently on remand in Belmarsh high-security prison. They are also wanted for questioning by police in the United States, Russia, and several European countries.

As the scandal surrounding the Hiltons unraveled, police arrested more than one hundred of their associates. The affair also led to the resignation of two cabinet ministers and the entire board of directors of Hilton Aerospace.

The man and woman who followed Ewart Asker were revealed to be KATE MULHROON and JOSEPH GOSLING-BELL. The pair were private investigators who had previously been employed by MI5. They were each charged with possession of illegal firearms and received seven-year prison sentences.

JASON McLOUD received three journalism awards for breaking the story of the Hilton scandal. He felt slightly guilty, because he had actually done little except receive an envelope. McLoud followed Madeline Cowell's wishes and donated half of the fees for his stories and subsequent television appearances to SARAH THOMAS.

The CHERUB ethics committee conducted an investigation into the Aero City mission, after which it put in place a number of new rules to ensure the safety of CHERUB agents. The biggest change is that cherubs are no longer allowed to work overseas without the presence of a mission controller.

The report also criticized EWART and ZARA ASKER for keeping James Adams in the dark over the details of his investigation. In a stiffly worded rebuke the report said, *"It is the duty of all CHERUB staff to ensure the welfare of CHERUB agents first and consider intelligence implications second. James Adams went through a traumatic experience in Russia and his well-being should have taken precedence over everything else."*

The report praised JAMES ADAMS'S conduct, although he was reminded that the ethics committee exists to help CHERUB agents who find themselves having difficulty with senior members of staff. He was criticized for stealing a pool car, but the report accepted that he had been under significant mental stress at the time and said that he did not deserve to be punished in any way.

Lauren's mission
After being guaranteed full British citizenship, ANNA revealed that her surname was CHAIKA. JOHN JONES

made some efforts to track down her baby brother, GEORGY CHAIKA, but he was never found.

Anna now lives with adopted parents in Scotland. Her English has improved and she is doing well in school.

Twenty-eight forced sex workers were captured following the police raid on the brothel. Subsequent questioning uncovered details of three similar establishments. In total, more than one hundred girls aged between eleven and twenty-two were freed from sexual abuse and slavery.

Most of the girls returned willingly to families in Russia and other parts of Eastern Europe. Twenty-six claimed to have no family ties and asked to remain in Britain. Despite the fact that the girls had been imprisoned for up to four years under savage conditions, only three underage girls were granted asylum. In line with government policy, the rest were treated as illegal immigrants and sent back to their own countries.

Human rights campaigners expressed concern that these girls are likely to be recaptured and enslaved once again.

KEITH and the bouncer knocked out by Lauren both spent time in hospital, but survived their injuries. They were tried along with ROMAN, ABBY, the receptionist, and eleven other people arrested during subsequent police raids. Charged with kidnapping, human trafficking, and prostitution offenses, they received prison sentences ranging from eight to seventeen years.

Subsequent raids also led to charges being made against more than a dozen other individuals in what senior Customs and Excise officers described as: "*A major breakthrough in the battle against human trafficking.*"

Meanwhile back on campus . . .
After reviewing CCTV footage of the food fight, more than fifty cherubs received punishment laps and the loss of one month's pocket money. Several children suffered minor burns, and in a special assembly, Zara Asker reminded everyone on campus that throwing hot food could have resulted in a serious injury. She added that much more severe punishments would be handed down if the incident was ever repeated.

The Askers' dog, MEATBALL, has recovered fully from his throat operation, but doesn't appear to have learned his lesson. He still eats absolutely anything.

NORMAN LARGE continues to improve following his heart bypass operation. Although a full recovery is possible, it is uncertain whether he will be able to return to his physically demanding role as a CHERUB training instructor.

Norman has said that he wishes to continue working for the organization and Zara Asker has agreed to consider finding him another job on campus, pending the outcome of a disciplinary hearing into his drunkenness on the night of his heart attack.

KEVIN SUMNER has begun basic training and is doing well. His fear of heights is greatly diminished, although he still gets the jitters sometimes.

BRUCE NORRIS suffered a complex leg fracture. He is recovering, but will be unable to train or go on missions for at least two months.

JAMES ADAMS and DANA SMITH are getting along okay. James is currently on page 415 of *The Lord of the Rings* and hasn't had the heart to tell Dana that he thinks it's boring.

Don't miss Mission 8:

MAD DOGS

Before you entered basic training, you probably heard stories from qualified CHERUB agents about the nature of this one-hundred-day course. Although every basic training course is designed to teach the same core abilities of physical fitness and extreme mental endurance, you can expect your training to differ from that of your predecessors in order to retain the element of surprise.

(Excerpt from the CHERUB Basic Training Manual)

Even by aircraft standards the toilet inside a C5 transport plane is cramped. James Adams had a shoulder touching the plastic wall on either side of him as he leaned over the steel bowl, looking at flecks of his lunch in the disinfectant-blue water.

His girlfriend, Dana Smith, yelled from outside. "Are you okay?"

James had pressed the flush and didn't hear her voice over the roaring turboprop engines as his puke got sucked away. He stood up and turned to face himself in the mirror. He'd spent the last eight days camped out in the Malaysian jungle, and despite regular applications of sunblock, his skin was peeling.

"James," Dana repeated, this time banging the door to make sure she got his attention.

"I'll be out in a sec."

There were no paper cups in the dispenser, so James washed the bitter taste from his mouth by dribbling water into the palm of his hand and sucking it dry.

"Did I just hear you throwing up?"

He gargled and spat out the water before answering. "Must have been those nasty hotdogs we had at lunchtime . . ."

But it had nothing to do with lunch and Dana knew it. "You'll do okay, James," she said soothingly.

James dried his hands by wiping them on his camouflage pants and had to duck under the door frame as he stepped out into the cavernous interior of the aircraft. His hands were trembling and he couldn't help thinking he'd be visiting the toilet again soon.

"I never realized you were scared of heights." Dana grinned as she put a grubby hand on the back of his neck and kissed him on the cheek.

"I'm *not*," James said defensively. "Heights I can handle, but jumping out of an airplane is *slightly* different."

"I'm surprised you've been a cherub for so long without doing a jump. I did one in basic training. Come to think of it, I did a couple before then; when I was a redshirt."

"I don't think I can do this," James said warily as they set off on an unsteady walk through the giant cargo bay. The turbulence did his stomach no favors as they clanked across the corrugated metal floor, heading away from the cockpit.

The Hercules C5 is a dual-role aircraft. For cargo operations the interior can be loaded with anything from United Nations food parcels to Challenger tanks. When the Parachute Regiment comes to town, rows of seats are bolted to the floor and the side doors can deploy a company of paratroops in ninety seconds.

This mission wouldn't stretch the aircraft's capacity: only twelve bodies would make the jump. Eight were ten- to twelve-year-olds nearing the end of CHERUB's 100-day basic training course. James and Dana were senior CHERUB agents, and the final jumpers were adult instructors.

Mr. Pike was the head training instructor. He was tough but fair, and James respected him a great deal. He wasn't so sure about Mr. Kazakov, who'd been appointed less than a month earlier. He was a bully who James had gotten to know rather too well after sharing his tent for the past seven nights.

Like all CHERUB instructors, Kazakov was physically imposing. He was Ukrainian by birth with a dusting of cropped gray hair and a facial scar worthy of an action figure. After serving with the Spetznatz—the Russian special forces—and seeing combat during the invasion of Afghanistan, Kazakov had spent ten years training SAS soldiers in guerrilla combat techniques before making the move to CHERUB.

"What are you lovebirds playing at?" Mr. Pike roared, giving James and Dana the evil eye as he pointed at the drop clock. This bright LED display hung over the door at one side of the aircraft and indicated that there were only one hundred and eighty-six seconds until they were over the landing zone.

"He's crapping himself," Dana explained.

Mr. Pike shook his head. "I can't believe you've never made a drop."

"Don't you start . . . ," James said, feeling even more anxious as he realized that trainees half his size already had parachutes on their backs and equipment packs strapped to their chests. Some of them were so small that they could barely see over the bed rolls on top of their packs.

Mr. Kazakov was inspecting each trainee in turn: checking helmets, tightening harnesses, and screaming abuse when they got something wrong. Right now he was dealing with ten-year-old Kevin Sumner. Ironically, James had helped Kevin get over his fear of heights a few months earlier.

"What's this, *Sumner*?" Kazakov spat as he noticed a metal spork bulging through the fabric of the pack strapped to Kevin's chest. Kazakov unbuckled the pack, ripped out the metal object, and wagged it in the boy's face. "I *told* you to wrap sharp items inside something soft. Do you want to land on that? Do you want to find yourself with a spork sticking out of your chest on an island beach an hour's boat ride from the nearest emergency room?"

James hooked his parachute over his back as Kevin said, "No, sir," guiltily.

"No time to repack," Kazakov yelled, before sending the spork clattering across the aircraft and launching a volley of Russian swear words. "You're not getting that back. You'll remember your lesson every time you have to eat with your fingers."

Unlike the trainees, James didn't have equipment to

contend with because the instructors' stuff was being delivered by boat.

"A hundred and twenty seconds," Mr. Pike shouted. "Start hooking up, people."

As Dana whispered something in Mr. Pike's ear, the eight trainees formed a line and began clipping hooks—known as strops—between the back of their parachutes and a taut metal cable above their heads. The youngsters would be making a static line jump, meaning that a pull on the strop would open their chutes automatically once they were clear of the aircraft.

As the countdown dropped below one hundred seconds, Mr. Kazakov and Dana both started walking towards James, who'd strapped on his helmet but was still struggling to fit his parachute harness.

"Come on," Kazakov said, showering James with spit. "You're *useless*; you're supposed to be helping out with the little ones."

Kazakov grabbed the harness of James's parachute and yanked the straps so tightly that James's shoulders squeezed together. His stomach churned as the giant Russian eye-balled him.

"I can't do this," James said weakly. "I've psyched myself out."

Dana interrupted. "Mr. Kazakov, I spoke to Pike about James and he's changed the drop order. I'll jump last and James second to last so that I can give him some encouragement if his nerves get to him."

Kazakov glowered at James. "I don't share my tent with cowards. You make that jump or tonight you sleep outside with the spiders and snakes."

"I'm not a trainee, you know," James said indignantly. "You can't boss me around."

"You're jumping sixth now," Dana said, diplomatically pointing Kazakov towards the trainees by the door. "I'll sort James out. You'd better go hook up."

A warning buzzer sounded as Mr. Pike began opening the aircraft door, flooding the gloomy metal tube with sunlight. The numbers on the clock began to flash as the count dropped below sixty seconds.

"I feel like such a dick," James confessed as he looked across at the trainees. "Some of them are ten years old."

"Focus," Dana said firmly as their gloved fingers interlocked. "You've been trained for this. Now take deep breaths and stay calm."

"Hook up, you two," Mr. Pike shouted from beside the door. "Eighteen seconds."

James fought a spasm in his gut as Dana dragged him towards the trainees lined up against the fuselage. None of them looked happy, but none had worked themselves into as much of a state as James.

"Good luck, kids," Kazakov shouted. "Remember: three elephants, check canopy, and steer gently if you drift close to another jumper."

James and Dana hooked their straps onto the cable as an announcement loud enough to be heard in a war zone blasted out of a speaker beside them.

"This is the copilot speaking. Navigation confirms we are in location. Winds are nine knots northeasterly, giving us a drop-zone window of fifty-eight seconds on my mark."

James looked over the helmets of the trainees as the

countdown clock flashed triple zero. There was an eleven-year-old boy less than twenty centimeters ahead and Dana right behind with a reassuring glove on his shoulder, but he felt isolated.

Part of him wanted to fling the chute off his back and go spew in the toilet, while another was acutely aware of how much abuse he'd get back on campus if he did. And if he could master his nerves, he'd be down in under two minutes.

"Mark," the copilot announced.

The drop clock changed from red to green as Mr. Pike began yelling, "Go, go, go."

To ensure that as many people as possible made the drop smoothly, the most confident trainees—mainly ones who'd jumped when they were red-shirts—were lined up first. As soon as the first trainee was out, the next had to stand with their toes overhanging the door. After waiting in a crouching position for the two seconds it took the previous jumper to clear the aircraft, it was their turn to leap.

The gap of less than four seconds between jumps turned the queue into a slow walk. Every time someone lined up in the doorway, James hoped they'd mess up so that they'd be out of the drop zone before his turn came around. But each trainee had invested ninety-six gruelling days into qualifying as a CHERUB agent. Bruised, hungry, and exhausted, they'd put in too much to let fear get the better of them now.

So James found himself in the doorway, buffeted by freezing air and sunlight with his strop hooked to the cable above his head. With the drop zone closing in twenty-two seconds, he crouched and felt extremely dizzy as he looked down. They were below cloud cover and the orange chute of the previous jumper was unravelling high above seven kilometers of golden sand.

"Move your arse, James," Mr. Pike yelled impatiently. "Seventeen seconds. Go!"

He was locked to the spot. He felt like he was going to shit and puke at the same time and made a lunge for the handle on the side of the door. But before he got a grip, Dana batted his hand away and slammed her palm into the back of his chute, tipping him forward.

"Chicken," she sneered, exchanging smiles with Mr. Pike as she took James's place in the doorway.

James found himself falling face first towards the beach. The reality of this was more than his brain could comprehend. His pants billowed, air tore beneath his helmet, making his chin strap dig into his neck. It was awful and wonderful. Out of every moment of James's life, freefalling five hundred meters above ground was the wildest.

The shock of being pushed meant that he'd forgotten to count three elephants, but the jump training he'd received the previous day kicked in when he felt a tiny jolt as the line connecting him to the aircraft went taut and ripped open his chute before snapping away.

"Check canopy," James shouted.

His first upward glance only earned him a face full of sunlight, but two seconds later the sun was filtered through a billowing mushroom of orange nylon. If it hadn't opened, he would have had less than five seconds to deploy his reserve chute, but it seemed okay so he followed his training and shouted the next order.

"Make space."

The brilliant sunshine turned the beach below into white glare, but he looked down and was reassured to see the previous jumper hundreds of meters away. You couldn't look up through the canopy, so the rule was that you only worried about people below you.

"Check drift," James gasped, before looking down and realizing that the ground was approaching rapidly.

The weather was calm and the landing zone huge, so he didn't have to open his lift webs to correct his path. This was a huge relief, because you can't get a feel for steering a parachute while standing on the ground, and the most common cause of accidents for inexperienced jumpers is steering too violently before touchdown.

The final part of jump training had involved the landing: you're supposed to know which way the wind is blowing and get your feet in a safe position. If you get this wrong, you'll find yourself falling one way while the wind tugs your chute in another. Instead of crumpling, your body gets twisted in all directions.

So James was alarmed when he looked down and saw a crab the size of a dinner plate coming into focus. His mind was blank: he couldn't remember which way the wind was blowing, or even which way he was pointing.

All he could do was crumple and hope for the best.

ABOUT THE AUTHOR

Robert Muchamore was born in London in 1972 and used to work as a private investigator. CHERUB is his first series and is published in more than twenty countries.

SECRETS. REVENGE.
BUT BEST OF ALL, BLOOD.

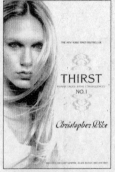

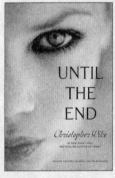

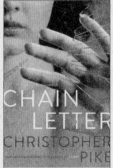

#1 *NEW YORK TIMES* BESTSELLING AUTHOR
CHRISTOPHER PIKE

FROM SIMON PULSE | PUBLISHED BY SIMON & SCHUSTER
TEEN.SIMONANDSCHUSTER.COM

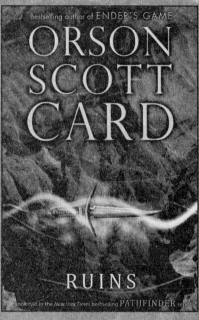

FROM THE BESTSELLING AUTHOR OF *UGLIES*

SCOTT WESTERFELD

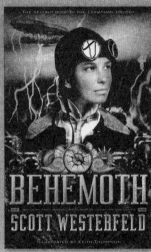

THE *NEW YORK TIMES* BESTSELLING

LEVIATHAN
TRILOGY

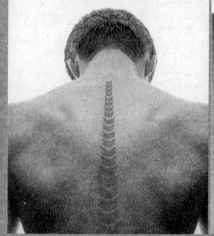
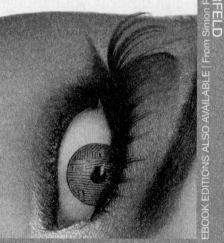

simonTeen

Simon & Schuster's **Simon Teen**
e-newsletter delivers current updates on
the hottest titles, exciting sweepstakes, and
exclusive content from your favorite authors.

Visit **TEEN.SimonandSchuster.com** to
sign up, post your thoughts, and find out what
every avid reader is talking about!